1

Scumbag Rehab

Published by: Fly Pelican Press

Vancouver BC, Canada V6E 1N9

www.flypelicanpress.com

Registration number: 1157856

ISBN E-BOOK: 978-1-9990730-8-4

ISBN PAPERBACK: 978-1-9990730-7-7

First edition

E. S.

Contents

Crack.

The little motherfucker chucked his puny-ass mitt at me like some younger would chuck an ice cream cone at a brick wall.

It was almost cute.

I've eaten a lot of snuffs in my time. Uppercuts. Hooks. Sneaky-ass jabs from bitch-made cowards that come from out of nowhere and leave the same way. Shit. I could tell you almost everything you'd ever want to know about taking fists in the face. I'd taken brass knuckles. Rolls of quarters. Mitts wrapped in barbwire, soaked in plaster, or gauze and glue and glass. Shit. You could say that I'm a connoisseur of getting punched in the fucking mug.

Or a guru.

At least some kind of cat who knows what he's jawing about.

"What were you trying to accomplish here, boy? What the fuck did you think would happen?" croaked a voice from behind.

He sounded older now. His voice was gruffer and huskier. I remembered it, still.

I tried to crane my neck, but being strapped down to a chair doesn't give you much wiggle room.

He didn't wait for an answer.

"Hit him again," the voice said.

CRACK.

The big guy, the other motherfucker... he hit hard. Natural swing. No effort. Brushing crumbs off his lap. Must have been a boxer. I could peep his mug through my swollen orbs. It was all dinged up like an old trip gong. He had some years on him now. Probably used to be chiseled. Fat now. Like them old dicks with hiked up slacks hiding their guts. The sexy-Jesus piece on his chest had some saggy-ass, used-to-hit-the-diesel titty meat to lay on. Swoll arms though, and he could throw them cinderblocks as good as ever. Maybe had a pair of golden gloves looped around the bed-pole at home. Alongside a rosary and a Saint Christopher piece. *Fucking wops and their Catholic-ass bullshit.* Never made sense to an idiot like me. I guess I wasn't smart enough to murder cats and then ask some pedophile to forgive me.

Too dumb... or too lazy. Either way, stupid...

CRACK.

Motherfucker. If he gave me another one of those, he'd be picking my fronts out of his paw as a new hobby. *Everybody needs a hobby! Shit. Did I say that out loud?* The bastard probably wouldn't even thank me for putting him onto it.

"You astound me, February," the voice said again. "I'm perplexed. Truly and utterly *confused.* What did you think your chances were?" He was still behind me. "You've been groping around here for weeks. What, you thought I wouldn't notice? Were you trying to rob me?"

I couldn't see him. *For fuck's sake.* "You want to come around and jaw your little piece from where I can clock you? We can have a real jaw…"

Crack.

Thank *sexy-Jesus-lubed-up-and-tacked-on-the-cross*, it was the little fucker who'd hit me again. It felt like a bump of tequila after a few shots of powder. Ref whistle. Knocked the dust off. I kind of liked it.

I think I got that back…

Crack. Crack.

Dope. That puny bitch could work me over forever and a day with his baby-soft mitts. He must moisturize them little grippers. "One mo' gain!" Might even get me some of my memories back instead of forgetting where I rest at night. *Shit was cute-like.* Slugs like stuffed teddy bears on a little girl's pink-sheeted bed.

You know the ones. The beds with those see-through pink lace curtains that flow from the ceiling like mosquito nets. They're made from the same mesh fabric as broad's lingerie that gets ruined after one good tear up.

Like the kind my daughter had once upon a…

Like the kind my wife wore once upon a…

Ah, shit.

You know what?

I had a concussion.

1

TRAIN ROBBERY

I've got a lot of exes.

Ex-stickup-kid. Ex-soldier. Ex-dealer. Ex-cop. Ex-con. Ex-fiend. Ex-son. Ex-husband. Ex-father. Ex-fella who used to give a shit about himself and those around him. Ex-guy who had a reason to wake up every morning aside from eking out his miserable fucking life for one more day, to do one more job, to get one more ducat for one more beer and one more dick-suck.

Current scumbag, but trying to get better.

The truth is, we've all lived fucked up lives.

I'm not saying mine's any more fucked up than yours or Winston's or Mason's or Preacher's or Marbles'. I only really know that my life has been the victim of some big fuckery because that's what I've been told. If it wasn't for other people, I'd probably think that everyone else had lived through the exact same shit.

All in all, I'm nothing more than some lucky bastard who gets to live out his fucked-up life and try to make sense of it all.

Cats'll lean in when you start jawing about your exes. Usually, they just want you to finish talking so they can jaw about their shit. Cats only listen so you'll listen to their asses back. It's like some contest to see who can talk about their shitty life more. Who's got more tragedy. Who's been dealt the worse hand. Who's baby momma did them the dirtiest. *To what end? Who wins and how? I dunno. I ain't no fucking shrink.* I reckon we're all just obsessed with our own bitch-asses and bitch-ass problems, and most of us are too cheap or poor to pay a cat with a paper on the wall to nod and scribble suns with smiles or cocks-and-balls in a fancy leather notebook. I hate it when cats set to jawing at me about their boring-ass lives: the job, the wife, the kids… *the fuck do I care? I don't remember asking.* Makes me want to mash a dart in their orbs and rip their lickers out.

Still… Everyone, even this scumbag, loves hearing a good break-up story.

Love will fuck you up like nothing else. Every cat's story has it. Taken or lost. Mine's no different. Heartbreak, *sure.* Pain and anguish, *plenty.* Get-backs, *goes with the set.* Moving on, *still working on that.*

I mean, what else do you do when you're sitting in a bar surrounded by cats you don't care about, day in and day out? *Talk and listen. Re-fucking-peat. For-fucking-ever and a motherfucking day.*

"Tell me a bit about yourself, James," Sofia, the bartender, said.

"I don't want that, and neither do you, toots," I said.

She giggled. "Come on, now. You've been sitting here for a while."

"Mans gotta drink somewhere."

She was still smiling. "Of course. But you keep coming back. Listening. Scowling. You look like you have a lot on your mind. I'd love it if you…"

"Ain't got too big a brain, baby. Fills up *quick-fast.*" I winked.

She giggled at my grimy game. "I'd love to hear all about you. How a guy like you ended up in a place like this." She bit her lip. My pesh pushed against my pant leg.

"Where do you want me to start?" I said, knowing that the broad was working me over. "I've lived a life, you know."

"So it seems." Her cat eyes were green flames in the dim light. "Why don't you start at the beginning? Anywhere is fine, but I can get a better idea of who you are if you go back as far as possible."

"Alright." I plugged my drink and tapped the table for another. "I'm going to need a lot more of this then."

Sofia turned to get the bottle. She was wearing a tube skirt that bowed from the waist and tucked back in neatly where her ass met her stems. Broad had a can. I shifted in my seat and almost nutted.

Way before being a regular at The Knowlton Tavern, the crossroads of scumbags, fiends, crimeys, and cheap-fucks on some escapist shit, I'd been a kid.

I hadn't been a *good* kid, but not the worst either. I hadn't lit buildings on fire or clipped the heads off birds and squirrels. Just a kid whose dad had taken off and left his ma to work a few jobs, adding to the generation of seeds who never had to go home, so they didn't.

We lived on the border between the Jewish and Italian parts of the city. A few violent blocks full of what book-learned cats call *diversity* where no one was cool with one another. This was when different whites were still hating on each other for reasons I never understood. It was *just* before different colours came through and started big-hating on each other for the same stupid reasons, but worse. *Stupid as heaven and hell and saving money for your death day.*

It's easy to hate everything when you're poor. And in the hood, everybody was poor.

Ma worked in food spots and hustled on the corner to keep Salvation Army clothes on my back and my belly just swoll enough to not die. I thought seeing your ribs touch through your tummy was normal. She was a good lady. She tried. She liked pills. If it hadn't been for the pills, she might not have had to bang dudes for loot.

Yeah, yeah I know… single mothers need love and affection. Would never say they don't. But this wasn't that. I never wanted to believe that shit, but I was six or seven when I figured out what her *date nights* were with help from the olders on the block. When I saw that cats left after they were done making animal noises and left crumpled up money on the kitchen table, shit got as clear as pre-cum. I didn't know what sex was, but I knew it was her job. Sometimes those cats brought groceries. One even brought me toys. He smelled like barbershops when you could still smoke in them. Nice fella.

You always hear cracker-kids complaining about their stepdads. *Poor them.* None of my ma's johns ever tried to be my dad, and I reckon that was a plus. I was fine with my setup. Truth be told, I didn't know anything else. When the johns didn't bring me sugar cereals or off-brand fruit snacks, I crawled into the room and stole folding from their wallets.

I spent my days doing what any shorty without supervision would do*: I cooled on the stoop and clocked the hood.* When I got bored, I wandered my little ass around the street. I kicked around with the olders on the block who liked me because I'd do dumb shit they could catch charges for.

It was always *simple shit.* Squeezing through barred windows. Getting boosted up fire escapes. Grabbing the coins when the bigger cats went sledgehammering payphones and parking meters. Running up on off-duty pigs and making them run their pockets. Rocking bandanas and robbing corner stores with toy guns. Or real biscuits, depending on who I was rocking with. We *usually* left the money alone because the owners were working stiffs like our folks. Moral code aside, don't open a bodega in the hood.

We'd snip locks and steal bikes, then sell them back to the kids we'd stolen them from. We double-charged the ones who were too pussy to fight and smashed the ones who did. We sold the weed and loose darts and liquor and scratchers that we vicked. Our folks got discounts. We fought and slap-boxed for sport and brawled anyone set tripping. We jumped tourists when they wandered too deep into the hood and college kids when they came to cop drugs.

Like I said, *simple shit.* I Imagined most youngers pulled the same stunts on their block.

Time went on, as it does. The olders went to jail while the youngers took their place before catching their own bids. I needed a plan. To make as much loot as possible before I got my ass booked. A hustle of my own to keep me and ma fed. Something that'd eat up the hours when I wasn't sleeping or supposed to be at school. After a while, I mostly stopped going. I knew I'd never graduate before I even reached junior high.

College? Trade school? Nah. Never that. I needed loot, not learning.

I wanted to help my ma. I rarely saw her, and when I did, she looked older every time. I didn't like watching her lose years quick-fast because of her lifestyle, holding down too many jobs and paying too much rent for a no-frills apartment in the projects. She was all I had, and I didn't even know her big-good. To fix all that, I needed loot.

Jews or wops. That was my choice. I wasn't taking no bus across town.

The Jews wouldn't take me. Those pussies couldn't take no Ls and held onto grudges from when we used to slang their bikes back to them. They used the word *mugging* while we used *fighting*. They weren't built like us. They never chucked mitts for kicks like we did. Truth be told, I don't think it was the brawling or the thieving that *really* heated them. It was paying double for shit that was already theirs and getting their asses beat back home. I don't know if the whoopings they got were for losing the bikes or getting put over barrels. Really, they should've thanked us. I wouldn't be none-surprised if that shit helped them out later in life.

In the end, the choice was made for me. *Italians it was.*

As an outsider, they didn't want to give me much. I got a busboy job at a place called *Pepito's*. I fucking hated it. Always waiting on some *fat-fuck-greaseball-mobsters*. Watching them slap up their young-ass broads for nothing. Spending a grip that would've changed my ma's life on wine and noodles.

It did lead to my big break, though.

One night, a shooter for the Vicenzo family whacked a rival underboss and his bitch as I was topping up their wine. The gunner was sloppy and inexperienced. Probably a rookie mutt. Whoever did it was going to get whacked for get-back, that was for sure. The bottle of *toscana* shattered in my mitt. The bullet, and a few more, hit the underboss. The shooter kept firing and emptied the clip.

I took a step back and clocked the fat-fuck who'd just called me bitch-boy and slapped his woman for looking at me '*like that*' take three in the chest and two in the face. *It was beautiful.* I swear, I'd just been thinking: '*God, I wish someone'd kill this motherfucker.*' Unfortunately, the girl had caught a stray in her eyeball and fallen into her plate of *pasta pomodoro*.

I dropped the bottle and flexed with my arms crossed. I was big-angry that they could try to use the situation as a reason to not pay me for my night's work. I admired the dead man with the kind of upside-down mouth you make when a fine-ass strolls on by. He looked like a sleeping walrus slumped back with its flippers curled in. His fat ass was spilling over his chair with his fork and spoon still in his mitts. Everyone else was running around, scared as hell. The cutlery eventually fell out of his mitts and made a clattering noise that killed my wood.

The shooter had been moving closer and closer to the edge of the table during his frenzy. He'd also been thrusting the biscuit as he shot. Rookie shit, as if it'd make the slugs fly out meaner.

He looked at me and pointed his gat to my dome.

He pulled the trigger once, then a bunch. It clicked, cricket-like. I guess he hadn't realized he was out of ammo. He shrugged and cussed. I nodded. He bolted.

The pigs came. The pigs asked questions. The pigs ate supper. The pigs left without answers.

Still, *I* was the one the Italians were worried about. None of their people would say shit; the code was in effect. But… an outsider? A non-Italian blooded motherfucker? Some godless hoodlum trying to make loot? *Fuhgeddaboudit.*

On my walk home, I got a warning in the form of a biscuit in a brown bag.

Overkill. I wouldn't say shit. I was wrapped tight and I wasn't no fucking rat. The code was in effect with me, too. I kept my branches tucked into my sleeves and stayed quiet as kept when they hauled me in for questioning.

The pigs jacked me up, tried to scare me, put the squeeze on me, and brought up my mama. They got nothing because I had nothing for them. Shit, I'd get fed more and fight less in jail anyways.

I played the part like a fucking champ. I mumbled. I glanced down. I told them I didn't see shit.

On my daughter's soul, I was mostly pissed that I was out of that fuck-shit job. I hated it, but I still needed loot. I'd have to look for a new fuck-shit gig, but now my only nice shirt was covered in red wine and gangster gore.

Luckily, gully motherfuckers always have a need for a closed mouth. A cat like myself can be useful, even if he doesn't have the right blood in his veins.

One day, this youngish block-ruler named Gino D'Antonio rolled up in his *Alfa Romeo* and thanked me for keeping my trap shut personally. He didn't go for the handshake when I held out my mitt, but he did give the green light to make me an errand boy. It wasn't really an offer. I got told. With time, I could become a two-bit jacker. Then, lord willing, a gat-tucking certified goon. Moving work and making hits.

I guess you could call those goals.

The shit was easy. *Light work.* I'd already been doing similar, more or less, for scraps and pocket change.

I had a low-profile status. Mega-low. I was on the part of the totem pole that dipped underground. I wasn't even an associate. Cats saw me, but expected nothing.

They started me off by making deliveries and running numbers, tickets, slips, and kites for bookies, loan sharks, and whoever else didn't want to go outside to use a payphone. Shit, I made deli runs and brought a baptism cake from the baker's to a gangster's rest. Never even got offered a slice. I stuck my finger in it and licked the frosting off, though.

I never asked any questions. Silence was worth my weight in gold bars, and I knew it. A dumb-fuck question like *'What's in the box?'* could leave you inside one yourself. When you keep six, you don't ask why. You just whistle when you see the pigs. Jump over cruiser hoods and boost fences like some crackhead Olympics.

The best shit came when I got to start putting beatdowns on

gamblers and fiends. No one important, no one who'd dream of get-back. Just the pathetic motherfuckers who needed a mash up, quick-fast and heartless. Whenever the goombas didn't want to get any fiend blood on them. It cleared my dome, and, if I do say, I was big-good at it. A natural.

Eventually, I got to help run trucks off the road to hijack them or load the haul into our vans. They sometimes gave me take-home to resell on my block. I'd make a few extra ducats off shit like meats and cheeses like it was commissary in the slam. *Interest always pays more.*

I even started taxing motherfuckers on my block, the shiny ones who acted out of their league, just because I could. I had clout. I was tucking some decent loot. It was *almost* enough for Ma to stop hooking and start breathing. Shit, she could've started dating if she'd wanted to. *Fucking without pay, my dream for my mother.*

I'd never be at no roundtables or know any of the inner work-ings, but I didn't care. I wasn't offended like some of the other non-Italians in the crew. Them cats that wanted the life *so fucking bad. Keep the rep and gimme the loot*, I always thought.

I kept my head down and eyes low and earned for the family. Within a year, I was getting my name out. I got promoted, kind of.

Me and this kid Mario, a Sicilian cat, got put on the same jobs often enough to become homies. We became the go-tos for jack-ing, mashing, and whatever other petty shit came up. I got more important jobs because I was with him: a full-blooded wop. They gave us product to sell at factories and shit: cartons of darts and boxes of booze. We always sold more shit more quickly than anyone else.

At the same time, D'Antonio's set was growing fast. He was wolfish. Young, ambitious, and hungry. He also wasn't against fucking with drugs.

I got on good with Mario. We broke bread. He was a solid older who'd already finished high school. He was also the son of a baker and always brought cannoli on our jobs. His old man wanted him to take over the family business someday, but some kids don't want the life that's been stitched out for them. He never wanted his pop's life. He wanted to be a mobster, to level up in the gang and get made. Didn't matter the hour, the motherfucker would be chucking rocks at my window saying that he got spitted at about a new truck or shipment:

"Hey yo! Let's go! All you need's a good knife and a ski mask!"

He was the dago, so it was always *his* promotion. But we were boys and he liked me and wanted me riding shotgun with him. He wasn't worried about me playing games because he knew I gave no fucks. Me not caring about bolding up in the gang meant that he could trust me. Besides, the better he did, the better I'd do. I was holding onto his cape. Riding the bus with his pass.

Since getting made was all that mattered to Mario, I'd do what I could to get him over. *Why the fuck not?* He was my homie. I had a ceiling, he didn't. *What else was I going to do? Get busted back down to running slips of paper between clubhouses? Stay terrorizing the local cats into my late teens, early twenties? For how long? Then, what? How long could I shit in my own yard before I got pinched or ratted on by the haters?* I had a life that I still cared about and assumed there'd be some kind of a future. *Did I feel fear, respect or none of the above? Was anyone clocking my neck?*

Open mouths always end up with guns in them. Motherfuckers

who claim they're thugs are always whispering out their neck, and small-time goons who piss where they rest get locked up sooner or later. Especially scumbag, mutt-ass, fall guys like me. I had to walk light and carry a big bat.

One day, Mario got a tip. Our first big-boy job was a motherfucking train heist. *Solo.* Well, me and him. On some John Wayne shit. My dick was hard. I mean, cell door and riot shield hard. The job was already all planned out by the cats that mattered. All we had to do was be there, wave some heaters, and hold out some bags. *Light work.* The crew was going to set the diversion by parking an old, busted-ass Ford across the tracks. Me and Mario were supposed to take the conductor hostage and rampage through the motherfucker, vicking all the rich, old crackers for whatever cash and jewels they had.

It was old school. Like one of those Wild West joints. Spaghetti Western, I guess, since it was with a Guinea. Imagine that: Grown-ass kids playing cowboys and bandits. With real heat. *It sounded fucking ill.*

Everything was going according to plan. The Ford got dumped on the tracks. Mario picked me up in a murdered-out van. Both of our gear matched the all-black Econoline. We prowled to the flatlands outside the city and waited for the train to wheeze to a stop. The only thing that had been left to chance was *whether* the train would hit the brakes.

The crew had given us some bammers. Until that night, I'd been a *cabrón* with my mitts and swung an ox just as good. I'd used baseball bats, chains, crowbars, table legs, folding chairs…

sawed-off, sharpened-up, and torn-off everythings. Whatever you could use to stab or swing at a motherfucker, I'd mastered it.

This was the first time I'd been given a heater. No one had near-trusted my ass that much before.

When it got dropped into my mitts, it felt like it had filled a gun-shaped hole that had always been empty. New sock fresh. Comfy as foreskin. It was heavier than it looked, but shit, if my fingers didn't wrap around that handle like it was my own pesh. Even today, when I jerk off, I sometimes feel around for a trigger.

I blasted a cap in the warehouse by accident. Went straight through the tin roof. A goon grabbed the biscuit, slapped the back of my wig, and clicked the safety *off.* "Better to put a hole up there than blow your pecker off," the goon said. "Or mine. Be careful, *maledetto bastardo.*"

We were a perfect fit, like a new couple. It'd be far from the last time I'd hold one. *Come to think of it, mans had a gun in his mitt more often than a broad's hand.*

We had our covers and all-black-everythings on and were ready to fuck the train up. Mario had lost his favourite balaclava, so he'd vicked a stocking from his ma. Mine was one of them joints with a hole where the mouth is. The shit looked spooky. I'd been masked up so many times already that I knew the best ones for different jobs. I'd have preferred a bandana, if only to make everything feel more authentic and old school, but that shit falls off when you start sweating from running for your life.

The train was on schedule. *Time to put in work.*

It seemed like it couldn't have been easier to score if the train had passed and the motherfuckers had thrown their suitcases out the windows for us.

The train ground on its brakes for some time before colliding with the car. It let out some screeching, grinding cries like a cat getting his nails pliered out. Sparks were flying from the wheels like it was New Year's in Chinatown. It crawled for long-minutes and gave the beater a shove. Not much, but enough to move it diagonally some feet down the tracks. I remember asking myself why they didn't just plow through the motherfucker. Another shovel of coal and that pick-up would've been dust.

Anyways, doesn't matter now.

The conductors, two goofy fucks, hopped out to take off their hats and scratch the backs of their melons. They looked at the rusted hooptie like all the hillbillies with all the cans of beer in all the grassed-over driveways in the South do.

They'd taken the bait.

We made our move from behind a growth of waist-high bushes when they came out of the train. One cat went for the e-brake, while the other slid to the back of the car to try and push it off the tracks.

We jogged. We got excited. We ran. We kept low and swift.

Mario went to the driver's side. I hooked wide to take the guy at the trunk from behind. They were struggling to hump the wheels over the rail.

"Hi," Mario said, plain as a church girl as he gun-snuffed the cat on the cheek and put him onto the dry earth with one strong blow.

14

"Hey-yo," I said to the guy at the bumper at the same time. I chopped his throat with an open mitt and slammed his dome onto the trunk. I slammed it down twice for good measure, and because it'd bounced so nicely the first time.

"Put 'em both in the back," Mario said. He fought to get his stocking up, but gave up just below his bottom lip. He popped the trunk. He was breathing hard and his chin was slick with sweat. "My ma'll kill me if I tear this thing," he said.

They were heavy. Full-grown man heavy. We laid them on top of each other in the trunk real gay-like. Not that I find nothing for nothing about being a homosexual. Not at all. I'm a scumbag, not a bitch. *Who gives a fuck?* But at the time, my teenage brain thought the shit was fucking hilarious.

Shit. Still is to grown me, too.

Anyways, we had a problem.

What the fuck did a couple of ghetto boys know about robbing a goddamn train?

They're one-way joints, thank Sexy-Jesus, but neither of us had remembered to bring a motherfucking loot sack. They always had pillowcases or some shit in the movies. Where the fuck were we going to put all our riches?

We went in from where the conductors had come out and emptied their duffle bags outside. Clothes and shit scattered around like garbage in the morning after fiends turn out the trash cans.

It wasn't like one of those grain or fuel joints that takes longer than a honey-dipped blunt to pass by. This motherfucker was short and tight. About 12 cars, and a couple of them were empty.

We came through a door hollering. *No one.* We came through another. Just one cat sleeping, and he didn't even wake up.

We came bursting through the third door and were just as surprised to see the motherfuckers as the motherfuckers were to see us. We waved our pistols after a pause like an awkward *hello.*

"Give up your shit and no one gets shot!" Mario screamed.

I snort-laughed. He shot me a glare like a mad broad and yelled again. I giggled like a bitch because his stocking was giving him a lisp.

"Throw your money in the bag!" I said, trying to keep chill and not trip over my words in my giddy-ass, amped-up state.

"Yea! Cash, ice, gems… Make with all the loot, you sons of bitches!" Once again, those *s* and *th* sounds got me: *'Cath, ith, gemth, make wif all'a loo, you thonth of bitheth!'*

It was mostly wallets, watches, and wedding rings. No big-time scores from what I could see. We went in like a hate-fuck: *hard, fast, and talking mad shit.* Mario duffed a couple of cats on top of their knots with his bammer. *For fun?* Maybe. The cat was excited. We told everyone to keep their heads between their knees unless it was their turn. They did as they were told. *Light work.*

Everything was going smoothly. We looked down here and there to check our haul. It wasn't great, but we'd only gone through one car.

We breezed through the next three cars and added a bit of weight to our duffels. Nothing that I couldn't have stolen on my own, though. On the real, it wasn't much better than sticking up a city bus or subway car. I pistol-whipped a dude's melon almost clean off because I was vexed at him for only having 37 bucks and a *Casio* to his bitch-ass name.

"Chill," Mario said.

According to what he'd heard, the big score would be somewhere in the last three cars. That's where the whales would be.

We blitzed through the dining car. It had a well-stocked bar and some waiting staff that we slapped in the face with a thick load of surprise. Mario told them to empty the register.

I told *him* to leave *them* alone.

"They're just a bunch of working stiffs," I said.

The private sleepers were next. Mario paused at the door. These were the sons of bitches with the gleamy stuff. The elite punks who carried briefcases full of cream and Fabergé eggs and had portraits of themselves beside their trusty hounds and whore wives in their mansions above the fireplace. At least that's what I imagined a rich cat would look like.

We'd split half of everything we collected. Half to the house. And the other half halved between me and Mario. That was the deal.

The thought of pocketing extra riches and keeping it mum from the mob flashed through my head. Less a thought, more a goddamn bolt of lightning inside my skullet. I couldn't say nothing to Mario though. If he caught me stuffing a string o' pearls down my drawers, he might rat. He was in way deeper than me and wanted that made-man stain. Plus, he'd put me on in the first place. If something happened, it'd look bad on him. Then I'd have to get rid of Mario… Didn't seem worth it. I wasn't about to throw my homie in between a rock and a harder rock for nothing more than a month's rent and a two-piece with a biscuit and gravy on the side.

The first sleeper had nothing. The beds were still made. It smelled like a never-used guest room. We shook down a pair of old-ass olders in the next sleeper for some jewelry and traveller's cheques.

I hate robbing old-olders. *Ain't no challenge, ain't no fun.* That's some fuck-shit that gutter-ass fiends do when they're dying for a fix. Lowlife bottom feeder shit. We weren't *that* desperate. Our ribs weren't near touching. We were just worried about getting to the end of the line with small bills, cheap jewelry, and other shit that'd make us look like a couple of mooks.

Turns out, cats that ride trains aren't wealthy. They're just too shook or too cheap to fly.

BLAOW!

Off the rip, I had my dick in my hand. I was stuck-stupid as to why a loud noise had put a hole in the door at the end of the hall.

A second blast put my ass on the ground like it knew where my pops had run off to.

The sound of *old-man-yelling* came from the room at the end of the car. I didn't understand a word, but I knew he was pissed.

"Mario!" I called out. I shimmied onto my gut and crawled to him.

He was on his ass. He'd gotten got and thrown into the wall. He was dazed and sitting up with his drool-covered chin on his chest and his mitts on his gut. I shook his leg. His eyes were cinched closed. I heard a cat dropping shells, reloading, and shouting in what I figured was Italian. He sounded like the same greaseball-fuckheads that used to get lit up at the restaurant and break their throats with cigar-smoke laughter.

Mario lifted his wig and winced. He poked a hole in his stocking to breathe.

"Damn," he groaned. "Mama's gonna kill me for that."

He tore the stocking wide-open. His mug was slick and his bushy eyebrows were soaked with sweat. Mario peeled a squashed bullet from his breast. It burned his feelers. He dropped it and started sucking on his index.

"That's a big bullet."

He pinched up his digits the way that Italians do. The fucker was doing a goddamn *goomba* bit in the middle of a fire fight. *Cheeky fucker.*

".44mm, if I had to guess… Dirty Harry," he said, trying to right himself.

The shit had me fucked up. "…" I said, or didn't say. I stayed low and tight and propped myself against the joining wall.

"They gave me a vest before we left," Mario said, popping his finger through the hole in his shirt.

"I didn't get no motherfucking vest."

"Well…" He was about to say something and stopped. I followed his gaze and saw him looking straight-ahead with eyes like one of those tree-hugging animals in the jungle.

The older cat was mumbling. His eye was peeking through one of the slug-holes in the door. His gun was poking through the other like a cock through a glory hole. Definitely a Magnum.

The fucking cannon had a neck as long as a giraffe's. *Quality life-ender*, if you're asking me with a gun to the head…

I said a four-letter word that I can't for the life of me remember and reached for my blaster.

The older showed his age. He had to manually cock back the hammer before he could let off another chubby round. Mario struggled to his feet. He stayed down and scrambled ahead for the gun he'd dropped when he'd eaten the slug. I was on my knees, getting up, gripping the heater at the back of my waist.

Even with the extra step, the older shot first.

He got two off. Then three. I lost count around twenty.

The first bullet that tore through Mario didn't come from the door. It'd come through the window of the car to our right. It blew through his cheekbone with a quick flash, like pigs do with stop signs. Mario's arms dropped. His mug was painted with confusion. The hole sucked his facial features towards it like a whirlpool. His blood must've suddenly remembered to start pumping and started squirting out of the gaping puncture in his face.

He turned his head towards me. Slowly. He gave me a *'Do you hear that buzzing sound?'* look.

Another bullet went through his neck. His arm. His scalp. Many more missed. A connect-the-dot puzzle appeared on the wall to my left. I was back on the ground again. Gun in hand this time, ready to fire back.

Problem was, *the fucking bullets kept coming.*

They didn't let up for two full minutes. Two minutes is nothing in a football game when the score's even and the teams have spent all their timeouts. In a lead hurricane, the shit lasts longer than a prison-hour during a lockdown.

When the bullets did stop, it felt like the neighbours had finally finished mowing their lawn early on a Sunday morning after a coke-late Saturday night. My ears were ringing. I got up cautious-like. I stepped over Mario; chunks broken off him like cookie pieces. His vest was a storm-battered boat hull.

It looked like they'd even shot his soul as it'd been flying from his body, throwing its guts against the pock-marked wall. The guy at the end of the car? *Dead-as-a-motherfucker.* Along with a broad and two other cats in Valentino suits.

The older looked like he was a made man. Through the gore and broken shit, strewn about and smashed like bottles in the trap-house, I could tell. His build: *round and well-fed.* His suit: *gaudy and big-expensive.* His crew: *Cosa-Nostra-looking-ass-henchmen and a 19-year-old fox in a red cocktail dress.* The dress might've been white or cream before.

I fleeced those fuckers for their shines. *Mans gotta eat.* Through the fuck-shit, my animal brain was working. Each cat had a bankroll the size of an ankle. I snatched their chains and rings. I had to pull some big-ice baguettes out of the lady's ear like grenade pins. No time to get my bison-ass fingers around the hooks and shit. They came off as easily as size tags on counterfeit shirts.

I searched for more treasure but didn't clock anything good. Other than what they had on their person, I didn't see any more big-time loot to take. I heard someone boarding the train. I ducked down and rolled under the bed. The floor was syrupy and sticky, like cut-up the morning after.

"Ah, fuck," a cat said from the other room. "That's Enzo's kid."

"Ah, yeah… little… Mario," a second voice came. "Damn. Good kid. Had some potential."

"I mean," the first voice again, "we *did* give him a vest."

"Yea… Hey, where's that mutt-kid? What's his face… the kid from Pepito's old joint. He just vanished like a ghost?"

"Who? Oh… right. *The busboy!* You're worried about a fucking busboy? Who gives a shit? We hit Ferragamo. That was the play. Stop the train, get the young fucks to make a scene, whack the fat man."

They walked inside the room. Their loafers lifted like smacked gums, then splatted back down.

"Ugh, what a mess."

"Yea, but we got his ass pretty good, huh?"

A foot nudged the dead, fat man's body.

"Sucks about the kid, though. His papa makes a good *cannolo*."

"On the bright side, I'm sure he'll make some for the funeral."

"Making me hungry just thinking about it. Where should we go to eat after this? You want *lasagne*?"

One of them stopped. I saw his knees fold as he bent down. "Looks like the busboy picked through the bones. Disrespectful. *Look!* He tore the earrings out of the little *regazza* right here. *Look!*" He paused. "Yeah, I don't know why, but yeah. I feel like *lasagne*."

The other cat lowered himself to peep her. They were hunched down with their backs to me. One was bent at the waist with his hands on his knees. The other was squatted like a back-catcher, his block heel lifted from the bloody ground.

"Little psychopath. No respect. Clearly not Italian."

I could've plugged them both, right there. I thought about it. But I didn't know if there'd be a team waiting outside or something. My guess was… yeah. In my older age, I would've done it without thinking twice.

"That's what happens when God ain't in the house. Know what I'm saying? Hey… On second thought, I'm having *lasagne* on Sunday at my *onna's* after little Christoforo's baptism. Plus, it's a little heavy, you know? We still gotta do that thing. I don't wanna feel weighed down, know what I'm saying? How about some…"

Either their conversation trailed off, or I stopped listening. I'm not sure whether I was mad or in shock. This was back when I still had those surreal moments when reality got bitch-slapped out of me. That stopped happening a long time ago. *When?* I can't quite remember. Neither the how nor the who gives a fucking shit.

2

THE KNOWLTON

"Wow," Sofia said.

She didn't say it as much it as she breathed it out in a faded whisper. She did that when she wanted you to keep talking. She was a good listener. Always bouncing her head slightly, letting her pouty bottom lip hover just low enough to throw a shadow on her sharp, little chin, hanging like a plum. She made that sincere kind of eye contact, which always made it seem like she was pleading with you to finish your story. It was subtle, but I picked up on it. I'd always been good at reading tells.

She was leaning on her elbows at the opposite side of the bar between the rocks and the Antoinette glasses. We jawed with our heads tilting at each other over the wood. She had the habit, whether she knew it or not, of making the little waist on her long body look almost nonexistent. She had an ass, though. Full as her lips. I knew that she knew what she was doing. *The tight pants and pencil skirts? The low blouses and make up? Especially in a place like this. She knew.*

The skinny ones with the asses, the slim-thicks, the peaches-on-sticks, they *all* know what they got. They're the dime-piece broads who try to sell their God-given *secrets*, acting like it's not 90% genetics. Ass since birth, my heart and pesh goes out to them.

No rattling bones: *I was big-crushing on the bartender, Sofia.* Just like the rest of those losers must've been. Why else come to a shit hole like The Knowlton? The worn-away stools and the out-of-order pissers? I might've been the only cat who was aware that the attention she was giving us was some calculated jazz. She just wanted to sell her booze. Didn't bother me, though. I get capitalism. She knew how to keep a bar full. *Shit, I was there on the daily.*

"Yeah, Dave!" Winston said from his stool. "You tell one cracking story there, Dave."

"Stop calling everyone Dave, you fucking idiot," Marbles raised her voice and herself from her seat. "His name's not fucking Dave! No one's name is fucking Dave. Unless there's actually someone named Dave here. Fucking limey idiot!" Her mitt turned to a fist and lifted like *why I oughta.*

"Oi, my lady, umm, Dave, I… I meant no harm," Winston was holding his palms outwards in a defensive posture.

"My name's not fucking Dave either, you…" Marbles' wild-like orbs flared like her nostrils and burned at Winston.

"Hey, guys, hey," Sofia kept her voice as low as the bar's lights. "There's no reason to fight. We're all friends here."

Marbles' big, googly eyes squeezed back into her head while she lowered her fine wagon back onto her seat.

Winston was shook. He was easily shook. He took a long, shaking sip of ale.

Marbles was a short, well-built, dark-skinned, sometimes Russian, sometimes Slovenian Jew with a pair of massive, unchained peepers that sloshed around her skull aimlessly like an untrained dog without a leash. That is, until she got pissed off, which wasn't what I'd call an uncommon event. Then, those big orbs turned into exploding suns. I'd given her the name Marbles because that's how those seers rolled around the room with her melon attached for the ride. I never remembered her real name, but that had never been an issue. None of us *really* need names.

Unlike Marbles, I'd gotten used to Win's bizarre shtick of calling everyone *Dave*. Some people, like Marbles and her hot Slavic temper, hadn't. I liked Winnie more than the others. He was a harmless fetus of a Mancunian. Frail and polite. As well-mannered and docile as a doused flame.

Beats me why I started going to The Knowlton. *Geography?* My rest was just one floor above the dive-ass motherfucker. The regulars, bar flies or whatever you call them in your hood, were a bunch of fucking weirdos. It was hard to believe that an angel like Sofia worked there. I could've understood it if she was still in school, but she was done. I don't know why she stayed. She could do better than surrounding her pretty-ass ass with goons and savages. I'm including myself in both categories. Anyways, I'm not complaining. *Every hog needs a trough.*

"Don't you see, Mason?" the brief quiet let Preacher's jawing with Mason be heard from their table behind me. "Acid *is* the body of Christ! Think about it… it's the communion wafer! It's the salvation that all so earnestly seek!" Preacher was breathing all excited-like. "It opens the pathways to the heavens, man! Think about it… you place a small, paper-thin disk on your tongue and become one with the universe. The sun and moon and stars all flow together as one guiding light-force. You become aligned with the planets and converse face-to-face with the one true God. And you know what? *She's* stunning! Think about it."

Mason wasn't paying a dime of attention to the former minister. He was scribbling with king-hell speed on a cocktail napkin in a state of deep, unshakable concentration. His tongue was poking through his missing front pearl.

"That's it!" Mason said, throwing up his hands and nearly tipping over his beer. It rocked on its round heel.

I thought about how funny it'd be if his beer had fallen onto the scribbles he'd spent the last couple hours working on.

"Eureka! I have to call the lab!" Mason's lab coat flapped as he rushed to the pay phone. He thrust in a quarter. "Doctor Chandler? Yes, this is Doctor Mason… Yes! I figured out the schematics for the Animaxitron 5690! And there's an adjoining breakthrough concerning the bafflement over Gluck's theorem! By Jove…"

Doctor Mason could jaw all day on that fucking pay phone. If he wasn't at the hospital or the lab, he was either on that phone with a chalice in his mitt or interrupting you to spit facts you didn't care about. You had to threaten the cat to get him off the fucking horn. He'd be there for a while now, talking science shit.

Cancerface was sitting alone, as usual, at the other end of the bar burning dart after dart like it was still legal to smoke indoors. I never knew how that bitch got away with it. Guess no one even wanted to look at her, let alone waste breath on her nasty ass. She was nursing a water and trying to offer hand and mouth fucks to anyone who'd add a little liquor to her cup. You'd reckon no one would want that cut-up, but they did. She was *never-not-miserable*, throwing evil eyes at everyone in the bar.

Hard up. A real dragon of a woman.

And mans was her most hated.

Right then, she was giving me a sour look for having the gall to open my jaws. She wasn't worth my time. All the drugs she'd done made her look barely human. Crags and divots on her mug. The kind of face that read like a sad, shitty story. The pages were made out of the sore scars on her bony legs and arms. Written with jerky movements and scratchings that'd peeled open her scabs. Puss. Blood like snot. She sneered. Dead black dots for eyes and deep lines slicing around her bulbous cheekbones, hacksawed-in from years of smoking rock and shooting China. I knew that bitch from my time on the streets: as a dealer, pig, fiend, and whatever else in between.

In fact, I knew all these cunts from one time or another, one place or another, one life or…

"James," Sofia laid her hand on my resting elbow. My head snapped towards her like shower shoes on penitentiary concrete.

She was the only broad since my wife to call me *James.* No one even called me Jim. Everyone called me Feb, short for February. If they bothered to call me, that is.

I cleared my throat with the low rumble of a cigarette boat in neutral. She took that as a *yes.*

"Do you want to continue with your story?" She let her fingers slide from my elbow to my mitt and back to the wood.

Goddamn. The lady's eyes had the sparkle of flawless diamonds with the kid who picked em's blood scrubbed off.

"Yeah, maybe, sure… After a dart. I want some air."

I pushed myself off the bar and tossed a coaster over my scotch. I wasn't sitting. I rarely ever sit. Always have to be ready in case someone comes in with a job. Or a blade. Or a burner.

Someone always wants something: a broken leg here, a retrieved engagement ring there. Hell, I'd kidnap and return the same motherfucker for two different clients. I'd run a quick shank for fear or offer protection. I'd tail your husband or fuck your wife.

All at a cost, of course.

Nothing ever mattered a teaspoon of Pope cum to me. Everybody needs a job, even scumbags. *Don't be naïve, mans needs loot, just like you.* My work was all business, and business isn't personal.

There was some shit that I *needed* to do, though. Shit that was more than business. Personal shit. I'd been wronged more than a few times and needed to make things right.

I *still* held a grudge. I was *still* a motherfucker. *Still* a scumbag.

I had to be to do what I had to do.

Different hoods had different names for the shit I did. Probably missed a bunch, but mans wasn't no big-traveller unless it was on a stale grey prisoner transfer bus. I'll add, if only for effect and cheap ad space, that I'm always ready to take things as far as they need to go. Extra mile shit. Over and above shit. I do the dirt most other fucks won't even stick with a shovel. I never fancy shit up with nice smelling words to make anyone feel better. Hurt feelings have nothing on a cracked skull and the dead don't have time for the sads. Look… I'm a fucking scumbag and I do scumbag shit to get loot so I can lean on the wood and stare at the bartender and booze until I can forget about remembering for a few hours. Before the grime signal gets floated on top of the charcoal clouds and I have to throw on the Carhartt and ski mask to do it all over again, that is.

I've been getting better. I even have some rules and shit… Well, shit that I try not to do anymore. You have to, living this life. Staying out of the pen, for one. Jail is hell. The worst day in the streets is still better than the best day on the yard, no matter what the lifers will try to sell you. Not dying is the other thing.

Not yet. Not 'til I'm done. Not 'til I…

"Going out?" Juice asked me. I hummed a two-syllable *yes* sound. He pushed the door open for me. I unscrewed a Pall Mall from my pack and twisted the motherfucker between my lips.

"I come with you," he said, following me out.

I'm not a small man. I stand around six feet tall, give or take the kicks. That big fucker towers over me. Today, he was rocking his usual wool, calf-length trench. The joint must've cost the lives of an entire herd. He was also wearing his *little* wool cap. A decent-sized adult sheep had probably been sacrificed to cover that fire hydrant of a dome. And it didn't even cover his ears. You'd swear that Solomon Grundy'd dressed up as a fisherman and decided to work the door at The Knowlton. I don't know who made fucking stompers in his size, but I'd be damned if both dogs of an average cat wouldn't fit into *one* of his boots. No idea how many cows had had to die for those shits.

"Night's a quieter one," he said, scraping a match against the five o'clock stubble of the brick wall outside The Knowlton. "Hoping it stays that way."

I leaned in and borrowed some of his flame for my dart.

I'd known Juice for what felt like forever-and-a-day. My day-one. Me and him went back deeper than any of the pricks inside. He was my closest friend. Or, only friend, if we're splitting hairs.

"You should really think about quitting." He leaned back and put his foot up against the wall. I think the building moved.

"I would, but… I love hacking darts, big homie. Ain't much a scumbag like me gets to love on this fucking planet. Ain't much I'm allowed to…"

"I was not talking about smoking. I was talking about the bull-shit. The scumbag shit."

He'd been on my ass for a while about giving up the scumbag life and doing something else. Anything else. Forgiving and forget-ting. Moving on. Starting over and all that shit.

"Ain't that easy…"

"I'm disagree. It *is* that easy."

"Oh yeah? What I look like? Some bitch-made, dick-in-the-ass-ass pussy? That's out, big homie. They got to pay. All them."

"Then, what?"

"Then…" I thought. After being on my scumbag shit for however many bullets now, I hadn't thought of much more than the get-back. "I don't know. Ain't much a cat like me's fit to do."

"You no need revenge. You need let bygones be themselves. You need career…"

"Career? You saying scumbag ain't no respectable gig?" I laughed.

"No, sir." He didn't.

"What's on my resume? *Disgraced pig? Violent offender?* What's my list of skills, huh? *Disconnects shoulders from sockets? Slams heads into car doors just before the point of passing out so they can still tell me what I need to know?*"

"Neither that. None of it."

"Look, I ain't never been shit… Probably won't ever *be* shit. Yo… At least I ain't a fiend no more."

He stared at me. I knew what he was getting at. He got at it all the time. What I sometimes talked about when I got greasy, stinking, toe-up, pinned.

"Be a private detective," he suggested.

"Fuck you." I laughed.

"Back at you." He didn't.

"Being serious though, brother. You are better than all this. The things you do for money. Bad things for bad people. Is illegal. Is dangerous. I no want to see you dead or in jail. You can do good things. You can help people. You are not your past. You might not thinking it, but I knowing it. Forget the people that wrong you. You need try for something better."

"Wronged *us*," I poked his chest. "Besides… what the hell does a private detective even do these days? Why would a chunk of filth like me be anyone's *shamus* or *dick*?"

"Well, you need better tagline than *'I will be your filthy dick.'*"

"*Bah.*" I was softening to the idea already, which meant that I was definitely getting drunk. "I'll make you a deal, *comrade*… if I get the chance to do something good… A job that helps someone in a positive way, no matter the loot, I'll take it."

I held my hand out. He accepted. His fingers went around my hand twice, the way blacks lap whites in foot races.

"I hold it to you," he said, sincere as steel.

Now, I had to hope that no poor, down-on-his-luck, no-hope-having bastard came through The Knowlton's doors on his knees with nowhere to turn, needing some kind of favour he couldn't take to the cops or his neighbourhood boss.

I flicked my dart and watched it cartwheel onto the street. Juice held the door open and patted me on the back as I entered.

It took the air from my chest and sent me a foot forward.

"Good talk."

I walked into the bank around half past three. Friday afternoon, first of the month.

The busiest possible day and time. It felt like the universe was helping me out. *That bitch owed me.* This was a small start.

Day-rate flunkies, construction workers, olders, single mamas, junkies, slumlord lackeys, and lames on the tit were holding their cheques like hounds pushing food bowls with their snouts. Bills, deposits, cheque cashing, and withdrawals. *The line was longer than a cokehead fiend's when he ain't paying.*

It was busy. I could do my thing and not get the bitch into too much trouble. It was the least I could do, nice guy I am.

Her head was down, stamping cheques in her stall. Some stooge was in front of her, staring down her shirt. I clocked her and waited for her to peep me back.

I wasn't around when you could light up a dart in the bank, but I missed those days. *The line was big-long.*

The stooge said something. Her head lifted. She smiled and nodded polite-like to him. She was wearing a fake smile that only turned real when she saw me. She was young. Young enough to be brazen. Brazen enough to be stupid. Stupid enough want to fuck a bank robber in the vault.

She had that innocent, mousey look that went to hell once you saw the fire in her eyes.

She didn't wave, but locked eyes with me and licked her teeth. She snarled her lip, bit her tongue, and started stamping faster, harder. I was surprised she didn't moan and make the fucking stamper nut.

The line moved the way lines at banks move, like a tooth-pull without novocaine. I was curious to see how she'd make this happen. Cats were being called to teller stations at random like a lottery.

She was green. A young broad with family money. She'd get another job tomorrow if this one went toe up. If not, she could always strip. She had the body for it. And the attitude. Kinky like a gooseneck. Rich girls with daddy issues always went the hardest on stage. Something to prove or someone to spite. Then, the powder would come along. Then, the dope. Then, she'd be less of a dancer and more of a ho. Then, a fiend. Then, dead.

My brains were wandering. I'd moved around the red velvet rope maze without noticing. When I came to, I was only a few places away.

She threw up her *See Next Teller* sign. A liquor-stank, plaid-shirt-wearing oaf in front of me was catching feelings. He went and waited in front of her booth. Smacked his cheque on the table. She said she had some things to do. He was hot and said that he'd wait there. I could smell his breath from a few feet behind him. She told him it'd be faster if he waited in the line. He doubled down by dropping his fists onto the table. Swaying on his heels.

I moved behind him, slow-like. I clicked up my ox and put the edge into the small of his back. Clicked the blade a little higher. I told him *she had things to do*. I broke his skin with my knife. It was enough to send him back into the line. *Light work.*

"Hello, sir. Name?"

"Miss," I tilted my dome, kissing my teeth. "Joseph January."

What a stupid name.

"How may I help you on this fine day, sir?" She didn't blink. Her eyes were like fireballs.

"I'd like to access my safety deposit box, Miss." Neither did I. I had some flickering flames myself.

"Please," she said, squinting like a jungle cat, "meet me over there and… do you have your key?"

I held up the key in the same mitt as my cutthroat. Just seeing the ox in my palm got her wet. Her eyes were wide.

Her heels tapped away. I watched her stroll on in her *too-short-for-a-bank-job* skirt. I clocked the room before following. I saw the drunk cat eyeing me. I held a finger to my lips. *Silence, fella.* The ox in my mitt was at an angle only he could see.

I clocked the security guard by the front door. The fat fuck was asleep on a stool as he'd always been on all my other visits. I admired his consistency. I didn't want to hurt him if I didn't have to. I was afraid my fist would get stuck in that gut. I'd have to buck-90 him just to get it out.

Every banker's little office was full. Meaning, they were all busy. The bank manager was facing away from the door and laughing on the phone. She'd told me that he talked to his mistress every day from 3:30pm-4:30pm and ended it by jerking off. I saw his shoulder moving through the cubby-window. *Sexy-Jesus,* I thought, *what's the fucking deal with these banker types? Did having a boring-ass job make nymphos out of people?* I didn't know, man. I didn't care.

The vault was down a short hallway. Maria hiked up her skirt and spread her ass. *No panties, good girl.*

"The bank offers quick and easy access."

She winked over her shoulder, put two fingers in her cut-up and then in my grill. Her fingers were wetter than my mouth. She pulled her skirt down. My cock tensed like a snakebite. *I might have to nut before finishing the job,* I thought.

The hardbody, solid metal door, equipped with a combination lock, was wide open. A second door, with bars like old jail cells, was shut. She said the cage door was all they used during a normal workday. It made sense. Why open and close that motherfucker 20 or 30 times a day when a steel grate did the trick well enough?

She unlocked the cage and we entered the first room with all the safety deposit boxes.

The inside of the vault wasn't like in the movies. All the first room had was a table, wall-to-wall safety deposit boxes, and another door that led to the actual safe with the loot.

Before I could get the key out, she slammed the cage-door closed and her body weight into me. I wasn't expecting it and smashed against the security boxes. *Fucking stung.* Solid steel with handles jutting out uneven-like. She slid her hand over my pants, liked what was going on, and purred into my ear while biting it.

She was devil-faced. Growling, kissing my neck and chin. She moved to my lips and ripped the bottom one open with a bite. I moved my mitt up her thigh. She fanned her stems out so my big paw could go higher. Her dress rode up and I felt her pussy quiver and melt. I'd barely stroked it. She gasped, released my poor lip, and pushed me away. Already a baby puddle on the floor. I touched my grill, her pussy juice stinging the cut she'd left. I sucked the rest off.

She threw her long stem up on the boxes and balanced on her other high-heeled foot. She leaned in to fuck with my belt. I pulled her hair back, thrust my finger inside her, bit-kissed up her neck, and sent my tongue down her throat. Water rushed down my knuckles and wrist, soaked my sleeve.

I was losing sight of why I'd come there in the first place and must've figured I'd remember after I came.

"I need to get in the box real quick," I said.

"Oh, you will," she said back.

She'd bought in, maybe too hard. I *had* to get into my box before anything else happened.

"For real… or you'll get hurt."

That did nothing but turn her on. It *was* her fantasy. The shit I was saying played right into that.

"I mean it," I said. I cuffed her. There was a wet mark from my mitt on her mug. Her hair stuck to it.

She liked that. Touched the point of impact. I grabbed her throat. She grabbed my branch, trembled, and complied. She slid her key into my box. I told her to turn around. She said *make me*. I gave her another stinger, chucked her across the room, and plugged my key into the other slot while she scrambled on the floor. She stayed down, juicing herself while I hustled some things from my chest pocket into the box. She got up and rushed me. I caught her in mid-air and swung her by her throat against the wall of safes. I squeezed her neck and drove my tongue into her ear while latching the keys to lock it. She coughed, kicked a shoe off, and rubbed my pesh with her foot.

She pushed me back. "Wait… I'm going to close the big door, just in case someone needs in. It'll give us enough time to look right and tuck our shit back in." She pulled her skirt down and unlocked the cage door. She spied around both coasts.

The vault door closed with a grunt. She spun the inside latch like a child fighting a storm at the wheel of a tall ship. Then, she turned around and braced herself. Her skirt lifted and a perfectly manicured landing strip made me forget what I was doing there again.

"Oh no… *Mr. Bank Robber.* You want to tie me up?"

Beats me whether she knew I was there to do some real-dirt or just some good, old-fashioned, rough-up-the-teller roleplay. Might as well play the part.

I considered how a movie bank robber would talk in this situation.

"Don't you go calling the cops, missy. Now, we're gonna make this easy and you're gonna take me to the loot. I don't want no one getting hurt."

She walked over, unbuttoned her blouse, and pinched the nipples still under her bra. "You going to put that *big, fat gun* inside me?" She reached into my pants, whipped my dick out, slid the head in between her lips, held the shaft, and started grinding it while standing. She had me fucked up in one move, like playing chess against a lifer. She asked me if I liked it. Her pussy lips sucked on my head. My orbs went all-white and I breathed hot out my beak. Her stem curled around my back, pulling me close against her, forcing me inside her. She was as wet as Seattle. I hit the back wall and kept on through it like a tank. She screamed into my shoulder. What can you say: *The broad had talent.*

No matter how good the pussy was, I couldn't let her control the situation. I had to get my head straight. The one in my skullet. *Break the trance. Stay steady.*

I picked her up and slammed her around. I bashed her against the door leading to the safe. I had to get her into the room with the loot and see how far she'd let me take this. She clamped onto me, weaving her stems around mine. Spreading her legs was like fighting a crocodile. *How was she so skinny and so strong?* She buried her nails into my wig and slammed her hips into mine. Her lips gripped me fierce-like. I put my foot on the door frame and my cock came out like a prosecco cork. I slapped her. Twice. Normal, then backhand on the return. I twisted her around and threw her into a head lock. She pushed out her ass and grabbed my pesh from behind her back. Jerked it. Brought it to the hole. Stuck it in. Back arched. Heaved. Humped. Small waves danced up her ass cheeks.

"Open the *fucking* door," I whispered, pulling her head back by her neck and wrenching the air out of her windpipe, driving deep towards her lungs.

She choked and clawed at my mitt. I loosened.

"Yes, sir," she said between gasps. I stroked slower. With one shaking paw, she got the key in. I thrusted deeper. She moaned big-loud.

I covered her mouth and pushed even deeper. It felt like I was tearing through nylon inside her guts. She screamed. It vibrated my fingers. She freed the lock. *Nice.* I slowed and pumped steady-like. The nails on the mitt on her knee drew red and bled down her calf. She squeezed her walls around my pesh. I gritted my molars and the fuckers shot sparks. She turned the handle. I stuck my finger in her mouth. She sucked it. My toes curled and my head bloomed fatter. She pushed against the door frame, bent her knees, and thrust back at me. Ass opened. Threw my thumb in. *Shit.* My leg started shaking. I was about to cum. She said: *'Already?'* I fish hooked her. She pushed the door open.

"Hello, busboy," he said, looking up from a meatball sub. "Is this your idea of quiet? This is… quite the sight."

He had a napkin tucked into his collar and was sitting on a wooden chair with a red-blotched paper plate on a fold-out table. A big fuck and a small fuck were leaning in on either side of him with their guns drawn.

"You've done a fine job, Maria."

"Ah fuck," I said.

Fucking bitch bit my finger.

3

A GOON CAN REALLY DO SOME THINKING OUT HERE

Somehow. *Some-fucking-how*, I'd gotten fingered like a middle-schooler for the screwjob fuckery on the train. Dead men tell no tales and Mario wasn't saying a motherfuck. *So, how'd I get the blame?*

Politics, man.

The guy who'd shot at us and ended up whacked was called Giuseppe Ferragamo. He was an old school don, a real big boy, just like I'd thought. The cat who'd had him offed was his younger. A fast-moving boss for a fast-moving world. *New generation steez.* The kind that fucked with the drugs that the olders thought were too risky or cold or crazy.

The younger cat's name was Gino D'Antonio.

D'Antonio, aside from marking me for dirty work, was as thirsty as a motherfucker. He reckoned his corner was too small for his gut. He was stuck on the block and wanted more than his *familia* was willing to offer.

The Mafia has always been on some army shit. Rank, time-served, and all that fuck-shit. The youngers have to put in work for long bids. Even then, it's not all about smarts or skills. Getting-over might mean waiting for your olders to ghost. Or ghosting them.

The Mafia also ran their shit without opps for a long time. Gambling, unions, booze, and darts… the shit they did was on lock. They were lazy, though. Like, *fuck the rear-view so long as the road ahead looks good.* D'Antonio, he was different. He'd seen the other races sharping their spades, eyeballing recklessly, and clocking throats. It was obvious that drugs were on the come up. D'Antonio wanted to carve out that pie for the Italians, flip the old guard, and headlock some of that new cake coming up from Colombia and Ecuador.

His olders didn't want to hear any of that. He got told *nah* when he asked to break off and start his own crew. He was ambitious, but young. *Big-ambitious.* The kind that worried motherfuckers… especially lazy, well-fed, comfy motherfuckers.

D'Antonio didn't want to work against his own, but the push-back forced his mitt. They told him to play the part and put in work. Climb from soldier to capo and so on. He was impatient and knew he was smart. Too smart for the structure and tradition that had always made the less-smart ones fall in line. Too smart to send his tribute up top for a pat on the head. Too smart to get told *nah* while the higher-ups either stole his shine or missed the boat.

Drugs were the future of organized crime. He'd made the contacts. The connects. The plugs. The shit was on greenlight.

But, there were hold outs.

The Ferragamo cat was one of the biggest dogs in the yard. He was *versus-the-Mafia* fucking with the drug trade. He'd gotten fat and moved from the city to the hills. On the day he got murked, he was leaving his stronghold for a summit he'd set up to take care of this gutsy D'Antonio cat and put the puppy in his place: in the foundation of a new strip-mall. Ferragamo shouldn't have taken the train, though. That was his mistake. Slow movement makes for easy prey.

After making sure that the hitters had bounced, I'd gotten off the train with blood and guts sticking to me like cheap rice, as well as both duffels. I noticed that those fucks had taken the van. *No shit they wanted the keys left in the ignition.* I thought they'd just been coaching a couple of fresh goons on how to make a quick exit. *Nah.* They'd taken the van *and* whatever they'd come in.

I ran back and stole the conductors' clothes that we'd dumped. I was planning to camp out in the woods all night and walk my dogs back to the city… or find a town with a motel or something. Didn't really have a plan. Wasn't my best weapon then, and shit, if it probably still isn't.

The city was far. I remembered seeing a shitty town on the way in. One of those towns with one factory that everyone worked at. I'd always thought I'd rather be poor in the city than chained to a one-horse-town. What I'd give to have that life now…

Where'd the pigs be least likely to find me?

The flashlights, the sniffing hounds, the flatfoots, and the gum-shoes. The bugs, the critters, the bats, and the forest-spirits.

I was a city boy. Fuck the woods. Town it was.

I changed into one of the conductor's gear and left my *all-black-ev-erythings* in the forest. The gear smelled like spending too much time too close to a barrel fire under a bridge. I kept my bammer tucked for the *ol' just-in-case*.

I tried to be like Rambo and stalk my way through the forest, taking a way that wasn't visible from the highway. While I could feel my way through a forest nowadays, back then, as a scum-ass street kid, I had no fucking clue what I was doing. My arms were burning at the wrists and elbows from carrying those stupid bags. *Throw a city boy in the forest, they said. It will be fun, they said.* All the switchblades and tough-jaw that work so well on the eels and urchins in the dark alleys of the city get you soft dick and knuckle-cracks in the wilderness. I was out of my element. The sound of twigs breaking under some tiny animal foot was way scarier than gunshot sounds ringing up my fire escape.

I got shit out the backside of the forest after an hour or several. I kept it moving. I arrived at a long, barely-lit road and followed it. I hoped I wasn't going the same way I'd come from. In the city, I could tell you exactly where I was using just my ears and nose. Blindfolded. *Out there?* Fuck, out there. Darkness, crickets, and the occasional gulping noise from an owl or some shit. *Spooky.*

I followed a string of long-spaced streetlights glowing like poor houses at Christmastime. Jagged, no pattern, half of them burnt out. I was tired and thirsty. *A grumbling sound.* It sounded like a busted-ass washing machine a floor down in a cheap apartment. *Someone coming down the road.* Or up the road, I didn't know. *An engine chugged.* I was tempted to steal away into the bushes, but realized that no pig's cruiser would kick up a racket like that.

It was a pick-up that was coughing like a single prop coke-plane closing in. It had a broken headlight, a smashed grill, and no front plate. I held out my mitt. I'd never hitched before, so I threw up my thumb like I'd heard you're supposed to.

"Where ye headed, stranger?" The truck slowed to a stop and a guy leaned through the open side window. Come to think of it, I doubted that the truck even had a side window.

"Uh, the town?" I said. "Looking to find a motel or something."

"*Whooo weee,* don't think Carlson'll even answer the bell at this hour. The lazy bastard usually kills the lamps at eight. If ye ain't back at the inn by then, well, goin' be a chilly night for ye." The guy spat a thick glob of chew between us. "Ain't ye cold, boy?"

I hadn't noticed. Too much adrenaline. "I'm ok."

"Well," he chewed his tobacco, "ye can always stay the night on my farm. It's a mile outta town the other way. Least I can offer ye's a plate when we get there and a place to lay yer head for the night. Ain't much, but it's what I got."

Fuck it. I shrugged. He tossed his head backwards. I chucked the bags in the back and sat against the wheel-well. He stirred the truck and it shook like a cracker in the ghetto. He pulled onto the road and leaned his beak through the window-less back of the truck.

"Sorry about ridin' in the back. Shelby here, she likes to sit with me. We was out at the ravine and she stinks somethin' awful. What's yer name, stranger?"

"Ain't a thing, sir. My name?" *Ah fuck,* I thought. *What kind of answer was that?*

"Yea, what does ye mammy call ye?"

"Just James."

"Just James? An entertainer, are ye, just James?"

"James. James February, sir. James February."

"Like the month?"

"Yes."

"The one with the cold?"

"Yes."

"Well, that's a neat lil' name, ain't it? I'm Stan Masonovich." He turned his shoulder to shake hands, leaving no attention for the road ahead. He had farm mitts: little paws, but hard as hell and wide as gull-wings. He squeezed like a vice. "Pleasure to make yer timely acquaintance, Jim."

He asked me if he could call me Jim. I didn't care. It was fine.

The balmy draft was cool and the smell of wet dog was leaking from the cab. I was moving away from the scene and had a place to stay. *Jim was fine.*

"Honey!" Stan whooped as he kicked open the screen door, half-shredded resulting from either excited dog or time. It squealed. "We got ourselves a visitor!" He held the door open and shooed me in.

The lighting had a weird yellow tinge, like a lighter flame in a lightless whip. Even the carpet was faintly yellow, although really more grayish-brown than anything else. The wallpaper was yellowed with tobacco stains on top of a yellow floral pattern. The cupboards were flaked with chipped yellow paint. The counters, the tablecloths, the plates, the mugs, the soiled doilies, and the jars full of pickle brine… *all yellow.*

The dog scampered ahead of us with filthy paws across the mustard-yellow, linoleum-tiled kitchen floor and left brown splotches. It slid on slick paws towards its dog bowls. It knocked some water and food out of them. It lapped up the food and went in for more when Stan set to refilling it. The dog was a great Dane. Near horse-size, with big paws and long ears.

There was a towheaded kid in his earliest teens sitting at the table with a *Village of the Damned* steez about him. He was pouring over a giant science textbook with a duo-tang full of hieroglyphics. The lady of the house was wearing a yellow apron over an outdated, blowy yellow dress.

"What I tell you about bringing in strays, look at the last… Oh, you a *human* visitor." She wiped her mitts on her apron and held out her hand. "I'm Caroline."

"This here Jimmy." He patted me on the back and thrust me a foot forward. He asked me if Jimmy was ok, *again.* I said I didn't care, *again.*

I hand-locked the woman and was shocked that her mitts were rougher than his. *She was fucking ugly.* A layer of hairs covered her face like a peach. Her bushy eyebrows looked like they were chasing her retreating hairline. However, she was very sweet.

Very kind and pleasant as ugly people have to be, else be banished from society.

Stan stepped forward and gave the little hairs on her cheek a kiss. He was a short guy, bandy-legged and built like a cannon ball. I hadn't noticed how short he was until he stepped past me. Stan and Caroline were like a couple of friendly trolls.

"This here, is uh, little Jacob," Stan said with sadness, shame, or some other emotion I'd never felt. His mitt glided over the kid's smooth-as-glass bowl cut. A long, tired breath left Stan's mouthhole. "Jake… ye wanna say hi to Jimmy here?"

"Sorry puh-pa, I'm recalibrating the microdynamics of the Thebbe's quantum regulator and engaging in the deeper facets of the Lafleur-Chang didactic for quasi-amplitude." He scratched a nubby pencil against a well-eaten page of lead strokes. "Hi." He turned to face me with a pair of wild eyes made ten times bigger by his pair of cracked-ass coke bottles.

I started making a noise that would've more than likely ended up being *hey*, but was interrupted by Stan pulling my elbow and shaking his head.

"I just heard about an awful thing on the radio out near Dunn's pass!" Caroline said. "There was a train robbery, like the olden days!"

Stan laughed. "Ain't been no train robbery since before we was youngins, honey." Stan looked at me to laugh with him.

"Jimmy," Caroline screwed her eyes at me, holding her mitt out, palm up. "What's this?" She sniffed her hand. It looked like she'd grabbed a rusty metal pipe.

"Blood." I said, gazing at the red stains on each of my hands.

"My word boy, are ye hurt?" Stan said. "I didn't even think to ask where ye was coming from."

"It's uh, from the train. I was there."

They gasped.

"I ran out after the shooting started. I was on my way home, and…"

"You poor thing," Caroline said. "Are you ok? Stanley, get him some clothes and warm water. It's on his face, too." She looked at me sympathetically. "I'm sorry, hon! I thought there was something wrong with your face."

"I'm fine, I swear… saw a couple of people eat some bullets, but I made it out. Ran to the forest and ended up on the road."

They surrounded me, except for the kid, who just sat there with his beak buried in his textbook. I deflected all their questions and concerned comments. I said I could use a wash, but that I was alright overall.

"Right," Stan said. He told me to leave my bags and use the first door on the left. Apparently, there were some towels on the shelves and a bar of soap in the tub.

I stripped down and found my entire body covered in shades of raspberry pie filling. The gun banged onto the floor. I'd forgotten I had it. Caroline yelled, asking what that noise was and whether I was ok. *All good,* I yelled back. The shower melted the pure red off into the yellow tub. It'd really been caked on. The soap had thick, black hairs melted into its slivered hide and the towel smelled worse than the dog. *It still felt fucking good.* The water had a funny taste to it, though.

Stan's clothes didn't fit and smelled worse than the towel. I put the conductor's greasy, stanking gear back on. I tucked the gun back into my pants. I figured I should holler at my ma and find out how to get back to the city.

"Honey, when's supper on?" Stan was asking as I emerged from the bathroom.

"Fifteen," she said. "Why don't you show Jimmy here the back and call Calvin in?"

"Want a beer, Jimmy?"

I nodded. I wanted a drink. It'd been a fucking weird night. I hadn't near-processed the shit, but it wasn't about to get any more normal.

We walked out to the back porch. The light above us buzzed and a swarm of insects were attacking the dingy bulb, pinging against it, also buzzing. Stan grabbed a couple of warm beers from a flat and started staring at a small light in the distance of the dark field.

"Ye need a lift back to the city?"

"Don't want to impose, sir."

"Nah, I'm headed there tomorrow anyways. Can drive you so far as mid-town."

"Sounds good."

"Taking young Jacob there to a *special school.*"

I sipped the warm malt liquor. It felt like I was drinking some-one's metal-tasting spit. My sweet dick if it wasn't putrid as all hell. Nerve-steadying. Did the job. I didn't look at Stan or even nod. I stared into the field.

"He's… he's not a farm boy. Not cut out for this life. Like one of those Alfred Einsteins and the like. A science boy, a special boy, ye know? Ye get those in the city, don't ye?"

"Beats me," I slurped. I wanted him to shut up.

"Well… the wife and I… we figured maybe he was just a queer or somethin'. Prayed for him, as is our way. Caught him with Calvin doin' some monkey business that I care not discuss with a fella I barely know."

"Ok."

"Long story short, he needs to go to a special school for his… *special-ness.*"

"In the city?" I asked when he paused and never picked back up. He'd been looking at me, waiting for me to jaw. I was making an effort to be nice. He *was* putting me up and driving me back, even though I would've rather been by myself.

"Correct. We tried the program put on by the church in the mountains, but I reckon it did more harm than good. He came back *more* special."

I kissed my teeth and sipped. "Well, ok then." I sipped my beer again. I didn't give a shit.

"Ye know… our family done came here from the Ukraine a long

time back. My family, Caroline's something else, British or Hungarian or the like. But, we Masonovich's pride ourselves in farmin'. It's strange that this child of mine's so dinky and bad with his hands." He gazed out for a moment longer, then nodded. "Calvin!" he hollered with one hand cupped around his grill.

The distant light clicked off within seconds.

Like a fucking laser beam, a barbarian of a teenager, maybe a year or three younger than I was, shook the earth around us while running towards the house with bare feet and rolled-up overalls.

"Hey, Unc," he said with full breath and not a trace of sweat. He looked like he was pumped with helium. He must've run at least a quarter-mile from that light.

"How the cows milkin', boy?"

"All good. None I can't do. They think they done and *nah*, I squeeze more outta them teets."

"Clean yeself up and get ready to sup, my boy," Stan said with, I guess, pride.

The kid stared at me for a hot second, then ran into the house. That fucker shook the entire joint down to the termites when he hit the floorboards.

"Quite the specimen, huh?" Stan said. He didn't wait for me to answer. "My brother died, his wife died… leaving me with the lil' runt. Not so lil' no more, huh? Only 15. Kid's goin' be a monster."

I drained the rest of my beer. There was nothing I hated worse than parents talking up their seeds. It bored me and they never shut the fuck up about it. I far preferred the shame in his voice when he spoke of that little Aryan-looking-ass bastard in the kitchen.

"Sups on!" Caroline hollered from the kitchen. *Thank fuck.* I was starved.

The supper was fucking hideous.

The meal was a casserole made from things I didn't recognize except Vienna sausages, frozen peas, and some kind of milk? Maybe? The worst part was that Stan kept piling ladle after ladle of the slop onto mine and Calvin's plates. The kid was gripping on a spoon but ate with his fucking beak in the goop like the dog, grunting the whole time, porn-like. Nah, he was eating *more* savagely than the stupid dog. I don't know if the dog would've even touched the shit. It smelled bad and tasted ten times worse. I just wanted to get it out of the way, but every time I did one of my hosts piled on another scoop.

The kid, Jacob, didn't touch his plate, even with some prodding from his folks. I picked up on how bony and frail he was while sitting across from him. His wrists, elbows, and cheekbones swolled-out like he was protesting the gruel in the mess hall.

They were jawing about the train shit. I was only half-listening because I was getting anxious about calling ma. Not *calling my mommy* like some too-scared pussy at his first sleepover, but that she was *possibly* worrying about me. Normally, it was *me* checking in on *her*. I think I wanted her to notice that I was gone, to miss me. Even if she was in the middle of earning ducats, I'd always given the door a few taps. For her sake or my own, I didn't know.

The truth is, I had a bad feeling in my gut. Like some kind of scumbag spidey sense.

"…is that how it was, Jim?" Stan asked me.

"How what was?"

"The train robbery. Just a bunch of guys coming on and shooting off guns?"

"Oh, yeah… They just came on with pillowcases like Hallowe'en and told everyone to give up their loot."

"Cool!" said Calvin.

"Calvin," Caroline said in one syllable, "Jimmy here could've been killed."

"I'd a wrestled the gun away from those goofs and shot them all in the face. Not like you, you gay nerd." The orphaned nephew slapped the cheaters off of Jacob's face. Stan laughed and Caroline dusted them off and put them back on his head, trying to coax him to eat.

The two *men* sat with their hands at their belts, belching and egging each other on after the gay nerd comment. *I fucking hate bullies.* I didn't think Stan was all that bad, just vexed about his son being a Mary. But this Calvin bastard? The kid had *soon-come-sociopath* written all over his little, bent-up, *boozing-in-the-womb* nose.

"Something troublin' ye, Jimmy?" Stan leaned in.

"Of course, Stanley. The poor soul just escaped a massacre! He didn't even get the chance to talk to the police. You know what, we should take him to Sheriff Paterson and…"

"Nah…" *Nope, there'd be none of that.* "I didn't see none." I gutted out the last drop of milk-stained hotdog and put my hand over the plate when Stan swooped in for another round. "I should really check in with my ma. You see, she was expecting me home, and…"

"Oh, your poor mother!" Caroline said. Nice, I'd hit the *poor mother* bone. It was connected to the *can I use your phone* bone. "Calvin, why don't you take Jimmy to the phone?"

"Fine," he snorted like a wolverine. "Let's go, loser." *Charming little cunt.*

"Ya, so, my folks died and I have to live here. It's pretty ok. I get the farm when I come of age. It's over there."

He pointed. I didn't look where he was pointing.

"So, it's gonna make me rich. I'm gonna be rich and I'm gonna get Sasha Claiborne to be my wife and I'm gonna…"

"We close?" I interrupted instead of reaching for the piece in my waistband.

"Yea, it's right there." He pointed to a little box on a single wooden poll.

I picked up the earpiece and fired in my home number.

Ringing.

"Hello? James?"

"Ma, hey. Yea, it's me… I…"

56

"Oh, my baby. The cops are here and telling me that you're thought to be dead."

"Dead? Nah, I just…"

"Wait…" There was some talking on the other end. "The captain wants to speak with you."

Fishy.

Some confident breathing hit the line. Then, a voice.

"Busboy," he croaked.

"Yes."

"You know me?"

I took a deep one. "Have an idea."

"Smart. You talk to any pigs?"

"Aside from you?"

"Don't get smart. I got four men here and we all got something for your mom."

"Nah. Ain't no rat." The actual response was *she could take it* but it wasn't time to play Russian roulette with the only person I cared about.

"Where are you?"

"Some place near the thing."

"Where?"

"Hell if I know."

"They're looking for you, busboy."

"Who?"

"Ferragamo's crew. Delvecchio's crew. Just about every crew in the city to the hills and back. Pigs too. They all have questions."

"No shit. Why?"

"No shit. They think you did it."

"Why in the name of God's great pussy would they think that?"

"Because, you were always going to be a fall guy."

"…yeah… that makes about *all* the sense."

"We can offer you protection."

"Shit. I should hope so."

"You want it?"

"Maybe. What's the cost?"

"That depends. You thinking 'bout running?"

"Not while you got my ma."

"Smart for a street punk."

"Not just a coat rack."

"Hat rack."

"You can put hats on coat racks."

He chuckled.

"Y'all gonna leave my ma alone?" I asked.

"You can take me at my word, busboy."

I didn't trust a fucking word the guinea fuck was saying, but my ma was all I had. "How noble of you," I said.

"We'll keep a tail on her until you're safe and sound."

 "Thanks."

"They call me the Gentle Don."

"Who does?"

"They do. More will."

"Ok."

"Busboy?"

"Yes, D'Antonio?"

"Excuse me?"

"Yes, Gentle Don?"

"Please, do hurry home."

I hung up the phone and threw a two-piece and a biscuit at the post. Didn't even feel it. The kid, Calvin, watched me hit the pole. He looked at the flakes of skin I'd left behind, blew a raspberry, and started punching up the post until his knuckles bled. *Fuck this kid and fuck this farm.* I had to make it through just one night in the yellow-piss-looking-and-smelling-ass-house and get the fuck home ASAP.

Calvin led me back to the house. I was big-worried, and the big-little fucker wouldn't keep his trap shut. I thought about breaking his jaw more than once. Truth be told, I was pretty sure that he'd maul me like those freakshow commies that wrestle bears in Russia. *Fuck him.*

"Yea, my cousin's pretty gay. Unc says he might be queer. The loser. I hate him. I hate gays. My old man told me that only the strongest, manliest men made it here and that the Masonovich's were the strongest back in the motherland. That's what he said. Bet my cousin wouldn't have lasted a day back in the old country. Bet the wolves would've gotten him. Bet I could beat up a wolf. Bet I could beat you up…"

I ignored him. I had my own shit to think about. He just kept spewing bullshit, though. *Jawing and jawing and jawing.*

"You know… I'm actually kinda sad to see my cousin go. It can get kinda boring here and I like to play games with him. Sometimes, I pretend to be the hunter and make him hide. Tell him to run or I'll whoop him. Threaten to tear his stupid word-books up. Then, when I find him, I whoop him anyways. One time, I made him eat his own shit. Another time, I made him eat mine…"

"You know that's fucked up, right?" I said.

"You don't say that! You don't say that! Unc says the f-word is the worst word and makes Russian Jesus mad."

"Cunt," I said.

"What's that?" he asked.

"Find the phone alright?" Stan asked. He was a shadow in the porchlight. Thank fucking Russian or regular sexy-Jesus.

"Yup."

They set me up on the couch. You'd never guess: A stained, yellow joint. All the rooms were taken. The folks and the nephew had the bigger rooms upstairs. The string-limbed, smart one had a smaller room downstairs.

I laid on the couch and tucked my heater into the cushions. My dome and stems spilled over the couch's worn-to-the-frame arms. All I had to sleep with was a coarse yellow quilt and a yellow-sweat-stained pillow. I could feel tomorrow's knots and rashes already.

The couch smelled. The pillow smelled. The blanket smelled. The carpet smelled. They all smelled different, but equally nasty.

My mitts were behind my head. You know what I was thinking? *What the fuck was I going to do with all those shitty watches and rings?*

It was quiet, which made me big-anxious at first. It's true what they say: you can really get a good night's rest out in the countryside. There were some insects chirping and tall-grass rustling, but little else. The sounds were out-of-rhythm and kind of nice.

The couch was a deserted island. Just me, the easygoing swoon of wooden wind chimes, and the sounds of rape in the next room over.

That last sound wasn't so easygoing and woke me up at some hour that ain't got no name.

I stumbled off the couch in a fucking daze. I reached for the bammer I'd tucked into the cushions. I heard struggling, so my hood-senses reckoned that someone had scaled the fire escape for some rape-murder-thieving.

"Put it in your mouth, little bitch," said an aggressive whisper.

"No," a scared groan replied.

I pushed open Jacob's door to find the cousin with his meat out, pressing it into the side of the defenseless little geek's cheek.

"Open your mouth. You know you will. You always do. You like it."

"No. I don't like you."

"Don't make me make you."

Did I mention that I fucking hate bullies?

I prowled over and made sure that my bammer's safety was on. *One-thou*, I had no idea which way the safety was and it's a miracle that I didn't blow the kid's wig out.

"Put *it* in *your* mouth," I said to Calvin, forcing my gun in between his grill.

I snatched a hand full of his moss. He fought until he figured out what his fronts were closing around. I bulged the biscuit into his cheek like good head. I *still* needed a ride home in the morning. I also wasn't no killer. Then.

"If you tell your uncle about this, then I'll tell him about *that*." My eyes darted towards Jacob. "Only pussies rat, tough guy."

He ran upstairs, like a bitch. The crib swayed.

"Thank you," Jacob said from his knees. He was on top of his covers, massaging his mug.

"Word," I said, listening for the cousin. His door slammed.

The Jacob kid woke me up an hour later trying to blow me.

I declined the offer and nearly gun-butted him to Russian hell.

The next day, the cousin didn't say a word. Barely touched his plate. Grilled me like I'd taken his favourite toy. *Fuck him.* If we'd been in prison, I would've put my spork in his eye socket and made him eat it before the COs came with their pepper canisters.

Eventually, we all loaded into the truck. Caroline cried saying goodbye to Jacob. The boy was quiet and weird: *true-to-form.* Stan seemed like-whatever. He gave mad-dogging Calvin a list of things to do. He patted the boy on the head and asked him if he felt alright. I returned his thousand-yard-stare by grabbing the cannon-handle tucked into my waist.

We hit up a gas station on the way for fuel and Styrofoam cups of hot, piss-flavoured coffee. Stan went inside and started jawing with the owner. Jacob, riding bitch and reading a book, said to me without turning:

"You ever wonder if you're a way because of things that happened or if you were born that way? You ever stop and think that maybe the sum of your experiences work, either with or against, some kind of innate characteristics that you inherited or derived from nowhere in particular?"

The kid had a wicked lisp. He jawed in a way that got higher at the last syllable like a wave, like a question he didn't want answered.

"I," he sang, looking at me with a cupid-like mug, "want to be different from my family. I *know* I am. Different from *them*, you know? I love my mommy, but I have to be my own person. I'll never fit in. I need a fresh start to do things my way. Under my own name."

"What's that now?" I was groggy at best.

"From this day forth," the kid sounded like a full-on stage actor now, "I'm not going to be Jacob Masonovich. I'm going to be Jake Mason, the first, most famous, homosexual scientist." He touched my thigh and looked at me. "Thank you, angel-man."

"You boys ready for the drive?" Stan yelled, trotting back with the coffees.

I slapped the kid's hand off my stem.

The future Dr. Mason said: "Affirmative, puh-pa," like it was a show-tune.

I kissed my pearls and nodded.

4

#8880

I hopped out of the truck in mid-town. My feet were back on city streets. My problems and shit hit me like a sober sniff: *I had two duffels full of loot, a heater, and no plan.*

I declined Stan's offer of a ride the rest of the way home. I didn't know how many hitters were clocking my hood, gunning to retire my life for some shit I didn't even do. I had no juice, no stain, and not a soul to trust. I'd circle around, play the wall, and think up something.

I needed a plan.

Where could a scumbag stash loot? Somewhere I could find it later. Somewhere that was right out there in the open. Somewhere no one would give two blind fucks about…

"The lockers at Central Station?" asked Marbles. Her beak was an inch from my cheek, wide-ass orbs taking up half her mug.

It *was* the fucking Central City train station. "Good guess, Marbs."

"Thanks," she said through the straw planted in her vodka soda, "but, I didn't guess. You've said it before. When you…"

"And," I pulled the key on the chain up from under my shirt, "this the key."

That key had been used more than a dope needle in the pen. Mad shit had gone in and out of that locker: #8880 in the South Building. I'd scratched the numbers off when I was in the force. A pig that didn't fly straight had to cover his own ass in case motherfuckers ever came looking for evidence.

Sofia cooed. "What kind of things do you have in there, James?"

"Things."

"Care to elaborate?"

"Stuff."

"Like what?"

"Mementos."

She didn't need to know anything more than that.

I didn't keep the key on a chain back then. Instead, I'd shoved it in that useless little side pocket all jeans have. For change, I think?

I had to lose the conductor's gear and slide into my own. I stood at the locker, door open, clocking the departures. I should've stowed my ass away and bounced. Could've jetted somewhere far away and used the duffels to start over. As far as a train can take you, at least.

In the end, I pussied out. *I couldn't leave my ma to get deaded.* Plus, it'd been a bad 24 hours for me and trains.

"You were close to your mother, weren't you?" Sofia asked.

I acted like I hadn't heard her. Her question reminded me of the part of the story that happened next. The part I *really* didn't feel like sharing. Guess I wasn't into the cups too bad.

She asked me again. I didn't answer. She was looking at me, I think. Marbles too, maybe. I don't know. I didn't look up. I don't like those kinds of looks. That type of eyeballing... makes me nervous. Makes me wonder what the other's thinking. Pity. Sympathy. Like I'm a pussy. Like I'm special.

I ain't special. I ain't shit. And I ain't the one to pity just like I ain't the one to steal on.

It was just like back at the train station that day. I felt eyes on me. Couldn't see 'em, but I knew someone was there. And it wasn't like the eyes these broads were giving me. More like a shark staring up at some pasty ankles in the ocean. Or many sharks.

I had to get the fuck out of there. It was getting me big-antsy.

Looking back, mans should've felt fucking haunted.

I ducked south and hopped on the subway. I didn't have anything on me but the locker key, my house keys, and a Tootsie Roll
of small bills I'd peeled off a stack. I changed trains three times.
Shook. Eyes like throwing knives. I bent corner after corner. Eyes
like bullets. I came out of the underground a few blocks from
mine. I clocked the corners. Eyes everywhere and nowhere. I went
to cross the street.

A murdered-out Caddy rolled up on me.

"Hop in, busboy." Some big-dago popped the back lock on his
all-black-everything Deville.

Ok then.

There were two big-fucks in the front not jawing a whole lot.
Nothing at me. The interior was leather, all-black, oil-sheened,
greasy to the touch, and smelled like the weight pile in the rec
yard. Every window was tinted, even the windshield. The cats were
rocking shades.

We pulled up at a small gap between two buildings. There was
a gate and an Italian-looking guard down the alley. He opened
it. We passed through an underground parking lot and wound
down a ramp to the bottom floor. The cat in the driver's seat
clicked a garage door button on the visor. Another old, rusted-ass
gate whined open like a spoiled bitch. We snaked through some
catacombs-looking shit. The maze was as narrow as my chances
of getting out of the situation alive. The bricks were uneven and
jutting out in spots. The side mirrors spat sparks where the wall

puffed out its chest. Steel doors and swaying lightbulbs appeared at random.

It was dark. I was dizzy. Motherfuckers still had their sunglasses on.

A few more turns.

A clearing.

A big space like an arena basement.

Beat-up hoopties, construction shit, palettes, crates, oil drums. That's all I could see in the side-headlight glare. We rolled up to some action at the farthest end of the room. Floodlights. An elevator surrounded by a chain link fence. Some cats hand-bombing drums with no-little effort onto the tailgate of a pick-up in the same condition as Stan's.

At that moment, I thought the shit was just a bad dream. The heist, Mario, the farm. All of it. *Was I asleep?*

"Get out," the cat riding shotty said.

D'Antonio was standing there smoking a dart. He slid one out of his case at me. I took it. No word exchange. I lit it. I nodded. He nodded, but past me.

The cats got a barrel up onto the tailgate. It sagged the truck. These weren't small cats. They had on leather gloves, beaters, and golden Jesus pieces in Goa-orange gold. Big-loud and big-corny. I knew the shit was real, but it still looked it'd put a green ring around the collar.

I looked back at D'Antonio. He bit his cigarette between his teeth and gestured for me to follow him.

"My father," he started, "was a *damn good* man." He took the dart from his chops. "Not a mobster. Not a gangster. Not a felon, or even a two-bit crook. That surprises my contemporaries."

Quit bragging, I thought.

"A working man. A man of science. His collar was blue *and* white. A brilliant man. He worked for the city as an engineer." His steps were heavy, filled with purpose and confidence. They muffled the sounds of men jawing and barrels shifting. "Not a lot of people know about this part of the city. It was meant to be a great water purification project."

I knew he wasn't done, so I kept quiet.

"It was going to streamline all the city's water needs and help with sustainability. Converting rainwater, treating it, recycling it, maximizing its potential, and avoiding those pesky summer-time droughts. Pretty ambitious, no?"

I didn't know what he wanted from me, so I tugged up my lip and shrugged like *sure, dog*.

"Well, the mob, the ruling families … they had some problems with him being a man from their neighbourhood *and* a righteous city planner. You know that jealousy breeds envy… and envy's an ugly disease."

He puffed his cigarette and walked over to a table. He pulled a dangling cord and a bulb buzzed on. It stung my seers.

Mario's body was on a stainless-steel table, dismembered at every worthwhile joint: knees, elbows, shoulders, and neck.

"They murdered my father when I was a little boy. Didn't want his great project to ruin the family businesses. Would've eliminated the need for shoddy workmanship and maintaining public works that could've been completed competently and without corruption. Short-sightedness at its finest." He blew a chest-full of smoke onto Mario's bodiless head. "Who in their right mind would think that a huge city project would *kill* jobs rather than *create* them? Sure, maintenance workers would suffer, but technicians and highly skilled professionals would be needed. And labourers. And tradesman of all walks."

"Beats me," I said, twisting my mug away from Mario's half-open eyes.

"Sorry," he said, "coming down here always brings up those thoughts for me." He clapped his hands. "Anyways, you're a *dead man*."

"What?"

"If you stay here, that is."

I didn't peep.

"The Ferragamo family, all the families, think that you did *it*. Because we told them you did."

I sensed the presence of the two guys from the Caddy lurking close behind me.

"It's all part of a plan, I can assure you. I couldn't have done it without you and Enzo's poor son here. I'll see that he gets a tasteful and elegant ceremony. It's very unfortunate that he had to sacrifice his life." He shook his head. "However, we need to rid the neighbourhoods of these black-hands that have had a stranglehold on them for so many years. Choking the vitality out of the proud communities and breathing fear and loathing into them."

"How heroic."

"I know you're being sarcastic, busboy. February, is it? But, it is, and I truly believe that. I don't expect a mutt like you to understand."

One of the *enforcers* started dragging a drum over. It skidded with a hollow, gravelly sound.

"Would you mind helping me?" He stepped on his dart and snapped on a pair of black surgical gloves. He picked up one of Mario's legs like a piece of chicken from a bucket and dropped it inside. It sloshed, then echoed, dull-like.

"Your turn," he said.

I hesitated.

He looked at me like *bitch, please.* I sneered and snatched an arm. It felt rubbery at first, then taut. It also leaked all kinds of damp-ness when I lifted it. There was less of an echo when I dropped it. *Shlock.* Meat on meat.

"I know you're not a rat, kid. You've proven that. You're a stand-up mark, and I salute you." He held out his hand and a goon rolled off his gloves, one mitt at a time, and gave him a kerchief. He wiped his paws and handed it back. "I'll even overlook the items you body-snatched from Ferragamo and his peoples. *The disre-spect. Tsk.* Keep them. My gift."

"Gee, thanks," I said.

He waited with his hands behind his back. He looked at the hunks of body meat still on the table. He looked at me. He looked at the drum. He looked back at me. I got the hint, picked up a thigh, and dropped it inside. It was heavy. I grabbed it by the side instead of the centre. Shit spilled out onto the floor with a *slop*.

"As a token of my esteem, I'll get you out of the city and bargain for your safety." He tapped my arm. "*Smile*, that's good news."

He gestured for the kerchief again and wiped his hand again. More thoroughly than before. He put a fresh dart in his mouth. The cat with the kerchief had the match struck and in front of his mug before the dart was even screwed in.

I picked up more body parts, getting the balance of weight just right so I didn't muck Mario's guts all over the table and get more on the conductor's baggy clothes.

"Thank you."

"Thank you, *Gentle Don*," he said.

I repeated.

I picked up Mario's dome. It was the last thing on the gore-greased table. The mouth wagged open when I lifted it up. *Tell my father I'm sorry*, it said. It startled me. I bobbled it, but kept calm. Controlled my breathing, my mug, and my shaking mitts. Blood was falling from the neck and mouth. It felt like a head of lettuce dipped in cement.

"Are you close with your mother?"

I felt my stone-grill melt away and ears prick when he mentioned Ma. He saw it too. I clocked his smirk from the corner of my eye, exaggerated by the shadows on his mug.

"Ain't got no pops." I cleared my throat and steadied my speech.

"Mothers *are* important."

A brolic goon came over with a metal lid and a mini sledge in his mitts. He put the lid on top of the barrel and pounded it flush to the brim. He kicked it onto its side and rolled it with his foot. It had an off-kilter kind of roll, speeding up for half a turn and slowing down for the other half. Two other goons were waiting at the truck. They got Mario up onto the tailgate.

"The two men in the trunk of the stooge car are in the other barrel if you were wondering."

D'Antonio stepped on his cigarette.

Me, D'Antonio, and one of the goons who'd brought me there went into the elevator. The second goon kicked up the whip and tried a Rockford in the murdered-out Cadillac.

"Break Raffi's nose for that," D'Antonio said to the one guy while he pulled down the elevator door. The goon nodded. "And his arm." D'Antonio paused. "And his leg."

Guess the Gentle Don didn't appreciate someone slabbing on his whip.

The elevator took forever-and-a-day. I'd be lying if I said I hadn't been hoping, wishing, and praying that the cable would snap and we'd all come crashing down. It creaked and shook… but kept climbing. *Cocktease.* God never does a scumbag a solid.

Finally, it stopped and opened. We stepped out into the back of a laundromat. I don't know what the hell I'd been expecting, but fabric softener smells weren't it.

"Take the kid to see his mom and get him on the bus," D'Antonio said to the goon.

The goon nodded to the Don. He grabbed my shoulder to lead me out of the joint. I shrugged him off and told him that I wasn't gonna bolt, and if I did, that we'd be meeting back up at the same fucking place, the fucking twat-fuck.

D'Antonio laughed and commended my spirit. Said he wished I was Italian. Said I'd have made a good pitbull.

I thought about spitting at him, giving him the old Mussolini treatment. I also thought about how much I hated bonesaws and being crammed inside of an oil drum, dead. *Probably.*

There was a town car idling out front with a different goon in the driver's seat.

"Get in the back," the goon escorting me said.

"*No please?*" I said with a piece-of-shit grin, pulling open the door. I was feeling myself a bit too much for his liking, seeing the light at the end of the tunnel now. He cuffed me and pushed me into the back seat, slamming the door and just missing my ankle.

The goon went to the driver's side: "I'm driving," he barked.

"But I'm already here," the other goon answered.

"I was with Raffi all morning, sitting," said the first goon. "I drive."

"But I got the seats and mirrors where I like 'em," the driver-goon replied. "It ain't even that far."

I'm driving after then," the first goon said, walking around the front of the car.

"Fine," I heard the driver-goon mutter to himself.

They could've been brothers the way they were squabbling over the radio, the centre arm rest, and the speed. *Fuck me, they were annoying.*

At one point, the driver-goon started eating a meatball sub.

"How you gonna eat a sandwich and drive? You fucking dummy," the passenger-goon said.

"I'm hungry. Ain't had no time to eat."

"You could eat while I drive."

"I like eating and driving."

"It's dangerous."

"Fuck you it is. I can do two things at once. You think I can't do two things at once…" The driver-goon paused. "Fuck, I spilled red sauce on my pants."

"You wouldn't have if I'd been driving. Like I said," the passenger-goon sneered.

"We'd be wrapped around a lamp pole by now if you'd been driving."

"Fuck you."

"Fuck you!"

Fuck both. They were making my headache worse and it was only a ten-minute drive without traffic.

They stretched the fuck out of the drive. Jawing about this, that, and the third. They started going off about sports.

"He's like Bird," the driver said while wiping his face with a napkin, "the kid at Tech. Heard they brought him in from overseas. Russia or something. Apparently, he's overage. A grown man, lying. Just pretending to be a college student. That's the word on the street, according to my bookie."

"How can you say that? Larry's the best player ever. Bet he's half Italian. Comparing him to some immigrant? A dirty Russian at that? You sound crazy."

"You're crazy. You're fucking garbage."

"I'm garbage? You're fucking garbage, you fuck-head fuck."

They went back and forth for some time.

"Guys," I said while rubbing my temples, "Bird ain't even as good as Magic, or Jordan, or…"

"Shut the fuck up!" they both said. "Fucking garbage mutt."

We pulled up to my building. I was on the stoop dicking with my keys before they even killed the engine. Their jawing had almost made me forget about the last 48 hours. Almost.

"Hold up, mutt," the passenger-goon said, getting out of the whip. "I'll go first." *How chivalrous.*

We climbed up to the third-floor walk-up. Shit was normal. Normal as ever. A rummy who'd pissed himself face down on the second landing. Dope needles kicked into the corners. Whores coming and going beside us on the stairs. Some thugs shooting dice. On my floor, the O'Conners were having a yelling match while one of the Santiago broad's dozen kids was screaming its colic-ass hoarse while she screamed back at it. Puerto Rican Donny and his cracker-ho Bianca la Blanca were jawing that the other *wasn't shit* while their Doberman barked. I could almost taste the froth flying off all their purpling lips. After, they'd bang like they were killing each other, jawing that the other *was the shit*. Or finally, actually, kill each other. Either or.

The window at the end of the hall had the same baseball-sized hole from one of the latchkey kids playing catch with the ghost of their abandoned pops, which was letting in the same cold breeze it had been all year. Some fiend kept tearing off the plywood used to plug the hole to burn for heat. Someone always eventually called the fire department, but they never showed up.

I could still see baby me. Sitting against the door. Reading a comic book or one of those detective joints. Mostly just looking at the pictures. Waiting for Ma to be finished with whichever *uncle* she was fucking with so I could go in and get warm. That's how I learned to read. Helped by the hookers who always said *you look like my son* before their pimp put their asses back on the corner.

After I got the boot and vicked some ducats, I'd cop a Spider-Man from the corner store and post up. I'd read about Spidey, thinking that his problems didn't seem so bad. I'd wonder whether Doctor Doom would finally knock the bitch-ass smirk off that punk-bastard Reed Richards' face and take his woman. At some point, I copped some headphones so I could chill in my room with them *all-the-way-turned-up*.

I'd always loved the villains. Not the mustached, *tie-a-bitch-to-the-railroad-tracks* types, but the ones who were pretty much the same as the heroes but had fucked up family lives and good enough reasons to do the dirt they did. They were trying to get over like the good guys in less-than-good ways. That's why I liked them hardboiled joints so much. There *were* scumbags that did good.

I *still* hate the white knights and Dudley Do-Rights of the world. The *teacher's-pet-ass dicksuckers* that get through life without a knife wound or even a stain.

Also, *Fuck Reed Richards.*

I wondered whether Ma'd be home. She'd probably be pulling the first half of her split at the diner. If the goons were shuffling me out of dodge, the most I'd be able to do would be write a note and leave the loot I had on her nightstand.

The rest was quiet-as-kept. Nothing broken. The lock worked and there was no sign of struggle. Always a nice thing to come home to after a few days in the gutter.

"What do I need?" I asked.

"Fuck if I know," one goon said. I heard the other goon call up the stairs like Marco Polo, out of breath and about to tug the railing out the wall. "Why you asking me, kid?"

I broke to my room.

"What a shithole," I heard the driver-goon walk in and say between heavy breaths.

I changed into my own jeans and t-shirt and threw a hoodie over my wig. I took a shoelace from one of my old tennis shoes and slid my locker key onto it. I double-knotted it and looped it around my neck. I hustled some drawers and socks inside a backpack, as well as an extra pair of jeans, a shirt, a flip-knife, and I can't remember what else. Didn't matter, I didn't own a lot anyways.

I came out and one of the goons asked where all the food was. I said we didn't keep more than cans of Campbell's and pasta noodles in the house. They said that Ragu wasn't proper red sauce and fronted on the bleached heels of two Wonder Bread loaves in the freezer.

I went into Ma's room to leave some folding on her dresser and found her taking a nap. *Ain't no one sleeping with all the noise.* For damn sure not in the projects.

"Ma!" I said.

She didn't flinch.

I shook her bare foot. It was as cold as a steering wheel in December.

Her head fell limp to one side. There was something on her pillow. I went to the side of her bed and lifted her dome. Deadweight. Blood soaked. A small hole at the base of her skull. Crispy hair.

"She didn't feel nothing, kiddo," the driver-goon said from the doorway. "Vinnie's aces with an ice pick. That's why we call him Ice Pick Vin."

I balled the loot into my fist and lunged for the cat. Big-reckless. I chucked. He pivoted. I missed. He snuffed me with his nine on top of my wig, hard. I hit the floor like I was being shot at. I rolled onto my backpack and blinked. It was dark and muddy.

"At least you got to say goodbye…" the other goon said, chewing with his mouth open. He put an open can of diced pineapples on the counter and wiped his mitts on his slacks. He came to where I'd landed and lifted his foot over my mug.

"No… please…" was all I got out. I saw his dress-shoed heel crash down between my orbs before the lights popped and shit went black.

"James?" Sofia touched my arm.

"He ain't said nothing for a while," Marbles said. She was peering up at me and sucking the last bits of her highball noisily through a straw.

"Is he ok? Are you ok?" Sofia asked. Marbles rubbed her beak against my shoulder like a worried pet.

"He's a fucking weirdo. Don't even bother listening to him," Cancerface shouted across the bar. "Don't take anything that motherfucker says for real. Fuck him and fuck you for giving him your attention."

I snapped back to where I was at. I shook my dome, blinked, and clocked the bar. I took a big swig of my scotch and followed Sofia's arm up to her eyes. Marbles was touching my other shoulder. I shrugged both of them off and tucked my key back under my shirt.

I cleared my throat. A few times.

"What'd you say, Sof?" I asked.

"I said, or rather commented, that you were close with your mother."

"I love a man who's close with his mother," Marbles said. "Family's so important." Her hand went down my shoulder, my arm, and my gut, landing on my lap.

"I never even had a mother," Cancerface threw in from across the bar, coughing and laughing.

"Shut up, bitch," I said calmly and without anger.

The girls recoiled. Marbles' hand stayed on my pesh.

"Not you guys," I said to Sofia and Marbles.

They threw each other glances.

"I wasn't," I said to Sofia, flicking Marbles' hand off my dick. "But, I loved my ma. Maybe I should've hated her for shitting me out into this place. But... she was all I had."

Marbles made half-moon eyes and put her head on my shoulder. Cancerface called me a piece of shit and asked me to buy her a drink for a dick-suck. I ignored Cancerface and slapped Marbles' hand away, again.

***

I walked into the bank with a mind to case the joint. For this to work, I had to get an exact read on the motherfucker and study it without looking like I was up to something. That's the hard part, not *looking* like you're planning something grimy while *knowing* that you are. My resting face isn't exactly innocent.

There was a fat security guard asleep by the door. I would've been surprised that the bank only had one guard. *If*, that is, it hadn't been a Mafia bank. There were a bunch of tellers all lined up behind their separate counters. Mostly olders and cracker-broads. I didn't have an account, but I did have a fake passport and booze in my blood.

I walked to the receptionist's desk, over to the left between the banker's rooms and the tellers. You ever see someone and the first thought that comes to mind is that they want Christ to put a seed in them? *Yeah.* The receptionist had that hyper-Christian look: sexless shawl and schoolmarm bob.

"Greetings, sir," she said.

I was dressed in a decent enough business casual suit, whatever the fuck that means. I'd forgotten I still had it. It'd been in a plastic sleeve from the dry cleaners for I couldn't tell you how long. I thought I might've vicked it once upon a... But it fit me too good to be a luck theft.

"Hello," I said. Before I had a chance to follow up, she asked me for my account number.

"I don't have one. But I'm thinking that I'd like one."

"Oh, perfect. We have several options when opening a new account..."

She rattled off a bunch of words. Each one had a different offer, but I wasn't really paying attention. I was scanning the room as low-key as a straight man in a gay bar: admiring the vicinity without making my intentions clear, holding back from accidental eye contact. You know, just checking out the fire exits and shit.

Then, I saw *her* staring at me. This cute, bookworm-looking teller broad. Her mug read young and inexperienced. Fresh. Eager. But... hold up... there was something else. A bit of filth. Maybe more than a bit. Just how I like it.

She was dolled and dressed *just* professionally enough to hide the freak beneath her lenses… to most cats. Not me. *Nice try, lady.* I wasn't falling for that wolf-in-lambs, cloak-and-dagger smokescreen. Shit. I can pick out a morbid-ass degenerate from a line-up with my back turned and sniff out the kind of pervert that'd fuck up their life for a nut from a planet away.

Her. That was my mark. Light work.

"…the jet-setter account gives you points redeemable towards future vacations and holiday travel. *And finally,*" the receptionist was still talking, "there's the safe-keepers plan, which gives you a two-year lease on a safety deposit box for free."

I was making some advanced level fuck-eyes at the teller. *She was in.* She kept brushing away hair that wasn't in her face. It was deep brown with lighter brown swirls in the light.

"Sir?" asked the receptionist.

"Uh, yeah. That one." I responded without knowing what I was agreeing to.

"The safe-keepers account?" she repeated back.

"Sure, why not?" I answered.

"Great, I'll take you to an account specialist…"

I looked back at the teller. She was biting her lip and scrunching her eyes. *Yes.*

"So, I hear you want the safe-keepers account!" exclaimed the banker. Motherfucker was too hyped up this early in the workday.

"Sure."

"Have some family jewels you want to keep safe?" His breath stank like sour coffee and chewed-up aspirin.

I didn't respond. I took out the fake passport from my breast pocket and slapped it on the table.

"Ok, Mister… January. Joseph January. Can I call you Joe?"

"Most do." *Stupid. Fucking. Name.*

"Great, Joe. We can get this account set up and… do you have the $100 minimum deposit? It's a requirement for all new accounts.

I took out a BBC bankroll and peeled off a layer like an Eskimo stripper.

"That's a lot of cash you're carrying around. You know…"

"Business," I cut his ass off. "I need to keep the folding loot on me. For business."

Little did he know, the wad was a hundred-dollar-bill wrapped around 30 fives and 20 ones.

"Ah, well… We have many *businessmen* at this bank." He did that fuck-shit finger quote thing I hate.

"What kind of businesses are they in?"

"Well…" He smiled, sniffed, and bobbed his dome, "I'm unable to discuss details regarding our clients, but given the nature of the bank, I think it's easy to guess how they may dabble." He winked.

I bet his canary-ass could be squeezed real easy. Maybe I was choosing the wrong mark with the teller broad. I could kidnap this fool and, shit, he'd give me the keys before I even got the pliers out.

"Who owns the bank?" I asked, innocent-like. Obviously, I already knew or I wouldn't have been there.

"Gino D'Antonio. I'm sure you've heard the name. Multiple *business* owner and investor. Quite the philanthropist and charitable individual as well." He smiled like he wanted an *atta-boy* for lunch.

Beautiful, I thought and said.

He clicked his keyboard and asked questions I made noises at.

"Ok," he finally said, sliding the c-note back to me. "I'll get the box set up. If you want to take your deposit to one of our customer service representatives, I'll meet up with you after and show you to the safety deposit box room."

Perfect, I thought and said.

When I got close enough to read the nametags, I clocked that my mark's name was Maria. I had my quick read on the chick. She was passive-looking, but only looking. I could tell by the way she followed me with her eyes in the line that she was a dammed-up river of daddy issues, ball-gags, and Astroglide.

Sometimes, you get that feeling. And sometimes, that feeling hunts you down and claws your fucking face off. I ain't every broad's type, but let's just say, I attract a certain kind of trainwreck that looks at me and sees violence. And that violence turns them on in a way they should probably avoid, but need to cum.

This kind of girl, Maria… She doesn't want her man to be laid back and ask her what she wants to have for supper and not scream on her for dumb shit. She wants a *take-charge man*. A *looks-like-he-was-locked-up man*. *A walk-up-dick-swinging-take-her-by-the-throat-slam-her-through-a-brick-wall* man. *Light work.*

I was next. A neat-looking cat with his hair weirdly well-coiffed called me up.

"I was told to wait for a Maria," I said to him.

"Oh! That's Maria." He pointed to her.

She looked at me. He called up the cat behind me.

Eventually, the older she was stamping bills for slugged away. I fantasized about dummying the old fuck in the parking lot for wasting my time. *I'm not crazy, just impatient.*

"Welcome," she said, smiling. "Who told you to wait for me?"

"No one," I said in my low-voiced drawl. "I just wanted *you.*"

She smiled bigger, giggled, and took an elastic from around her wrist. She threw her hair into a ponytail like she was about to give head. I felt my pesh nudge the divider and handed her the new account information.

"Safe-keepers account, huh?" She'd yet to break eye contact. Or blink.

I nodded.

"Joseph January," she repeated. "That's a good name."

"I like it more now that I'm hearing you say it, Maria."

"Joe, hey." That skinny-spined banker came waltzing over. "I see you've met Maria. She's very new. Our most recent hire.

Dope, I thought and said.

"Yes, well, can I take you to the box?" he asked.

I gave Maria a half-smirk and nodded. "Box it is."

I got a better idea of what I could get up to when I saw that the boxes were kept behind the vault door. The banker said that I needed to be accompanied into the vault with an employee to turn the second key, but that I could *peruse* my contents in the little closet-sized room to the left.

"What's in there?" I pointed at the door to the right.

"That's the safe room. Employees only."

Of course.

He saw me to the reception area and shook my hand. *Soft mitts.* He had a better handshake than I would've expected. He'd probably hit a line right after our meeting.

Over in a private office, some cat in a sharp-shouldered suit was laughing like he was being tickled with his back turned to a window and the blinds open.

I flicked my dome at Maria and set off.

Once outside, I lit a dart and copped a newspaper from a box beside the parking lot. I sat on a bench in the courtyard nearby, waiting for her to get off.

I posted up on that bench for three afternoons, clocking Maria. The broad had a routine.

She'd leave the bank at 5:15pm and go to a speakeasy at a boutique hotel called The Grosvenor. It was one of those dark-lit ambient joints with its name written in gold-leaf paint on the window. She'd meet a couple of other females. They'd nurse overpriced cocktails until they were met by two cats in stockbroker suits.

Poor Maria. No square-jawed Hercules was coming for her. Her friends would head out with their cats and leave her alone. She'd stick around and order another drink, excuse herself before it was mixed, step out for a dart she'd nick from someone, go back inside, and finish the night off with a shot of Irish. At 8:30pm, she'd hop on the train and stumble to her rest. A nice building in a nice hood. She was single and lived alone.

On Thursday, I went back to the bank and brought an empty briefcase with me. *No line.* I walked right up to her.

"How's the week?" I asked.

"Nothing too crazy. A little boring."

"But you just started here, ain't you?"

"Yeah. The job's fine, but not too exciting. I already feel like I do the same thing every day."

I nodded. "Can you open your box for me?"

The innuendo was intentional.

"Sure," she grinned. "Follow me."

She said that reception could do it if I didn't want to wait in line. I said I wanted *her,* since that had worked so well the first time. She smiled.

She met me around the side. She was built like a crack pipe, in a good way. Skinny-as-fuck. Rope-like. Little calves, little arms, and little tits. A round ass came out of nowhere behind her. It wasn't obvious from the front, though. It creeped from the top of her thighs, then poked out like a knife fight.

She looked back. I made no secret that I was eye-fucking the shit out of her.

"Mr. January, were you checking me out?" She was still grinning.

I sniffed. "Indeed, I was." I shifted my pesh.

"Good," she said. She kept walking and threw some extra wiggle into it.

When we got to the safety deposit boxes, we turned the keys like we were firing a doomsday device.

I used the little room to the left and pretended to transfer the contents of my briefcase into the box. When I came out, Maria was breathing heavily and unevenly through her beak. Her skirt was hiked up and off-centre. The crotch of her black panties was showing.

"Miss Maria, were you touching yourself?" I asked.

"*Indeed, I was,*" she responded, licking her finger.

That evening, I made sure to be in The Grosvenor's cocktail lounge before Maria got off. I grabbed a little two-person table under a rope-hung, exposed lightbulb. You know, one of those retro joints where you can see the zig-zagging wires glowing their orange glow. I knew that Maria's friends usually arrived closer to 5:30pm. That gave me a tight quarter-hour to put in work.

I saw Maria come in. During my surveillance, I'd suspected that she blasted a peasant's cup before her friends came and got their fancy broad drinks. *You know, classy lady shit.* I reckoned that Maria was putting it all on for them. I knew she was gutter. *We can always spot our own.*

She walked up to the bar and ordered a double vodka soda and a shot of Irish. She clanged back the whisky and chucked the vodka soda straw onto the ground, pumping the clear drink into her grill.

"Another," she said.

"Which one?" the bartender asked.

"Both," she replied.

She plugged the second shot, turned her back to the wood, and surveyed the room. I put my head down and swirled my scotch, looking *aloof-as-fuck* if I do say so myself.

"Mister January!" she approached. "I've never seen you here before."

"First time," I said.

"I come here almost every day after my shift."

I dropped my head slightly to say *alright*.

"I can leave you alone…"

"Sit."

She grabbed her drink and sat.

I looked at her without smiling, then made eyes at the bartender. "Two shots of Irish," I said.

"What's in there?" she asked.

"Scotch."

She leaned over to smell it. "So strong!" She wrinkled her nose.

"I like something with some bite to it."

The bartender brought over the shots. Maria thanked me and we said *salud.*

I clowned on the offended mug she made after taking the shot.

"Shut up!" she said. "I just had two!"

"Then you should be used to it by now." I patted her knee. Left my mitt there. Rubbed her thigh, about the size of my wrist. She put her mitt on mine and moved it up.

"I knew it," I said, letting the outside of my knuckles graze her panties, feeling them wet.

"What?" she breathed hot.

"You a freak. Buttoned-down. Lensed-up. Hair in a bun. Freak."

"You don't know the half." She leaned in and bit my ear.

As predicted, her friends arrived. We had a drink with them, then got the fuck up out of there. They were giving Maria a stern but knowing *that's our girl* look. I didn't know if it was or wasn't uncommon for her to leave all-out-the-blue with a fella, but they seemed fine with it. What's that shit people's moms say? *I'm not mad, I'm just disappointed.* It was that kind of look, but it seemed worn down to the bone from repeat behaviour.

I suggested going to her place. She said it wasn't far. I knew that, and I wasn't taking her to mine: the cramped little shithole above The Knowlton. It was clean, but nah. No broad likes *knowing* they're fucking poor scum. Plus, too many eyes. Juice'd be on my ass, even though this whole thing had been his idea.

We were sardined on the train. Her ass was pressed against my cock. She backed it up and gyrated her hips against my pesh. *If I came, would it count as group sex?* I wondered.

"How old are you?" I asked.

"Just turned 21, you?"

"Older."

"Good," she said. She reached her mitt behind her back and grabbed the tonsils of my cock through my jeans. "I like older men."

"Lucky me." I clamped my teeth on her shoulder after a sloppy kiss and felt her quiver. Little drips of wet shook free and slid down to her ankles.

"You do like some bite," she said. "I gotta warn you, I like it rough."

I squeezed her arm hard and felt her fingers go as limp as party streamers. I could've snapped her branch like a chicken wing.

"Yeah," she turned and kissed my chin, "just like that… that's a start."

We arrived at her rest and she clicked on the lights. Red, like blood on fire. And bright. Sexy-Jesus, the shit almost burned the orbs out of my skullet. Everything was infrared. The motherfucker was lit like a Dutch brothel.

It was a tiny, redone walk-up studio with an island separating the kitchen from the sleeping area. The bed took up most of the non-kitchen area with a TV at the foot and a closet behind it. An armchair and a little table took up the rest.

"Stay here." She pushed my chest and sat me down on her bed. "I'll be right back." She kissed me, bit my lip, and walked off while undoing the buttons of her blouse.

I wondered whether she had any normal lights. The shit blended anything red into the background, making it near-invisible. It was hard on the eyes. I couldn't imagine doing anything there but praising Satan or cutting letters out of magazines for death threats. Maybe you get used to it, or maybe this bitch was crazier than I'd originally thought.

There *were* windows, but they were covered with blackout curtains. I was getting a headache. I had to push my palms into my lids and blink to try and make the shit normal. Didn't work.

Finally, the door swung open. Bright, heaven-like bathroom light let my eyes breathe for a second.

Maria stepped out in fishnets, high heels, and a black mesh bodysuit. Her hair was down. She'd put on black lipstick. It was a good look. The red lipstick she'd been wearing before got washed out in the red light and made her look like a burn victim. She unbuttoned the bottom of her body suit, pulled the flap up, and unveiled a pompous tuft of dark hair.

She walked on up to me until her bush was brushing against my beak. It had a perfumed scent to it. Tobacco and vanilla. *Truth be told, I love me a bush.* I love a bald pussy all the same, but there's just something about an ignorant-ass muff. A little manicured cloud floating over a gorgeous fuck hole. And when the lips are smooth on top of all that? Goddamn. The shit gets me like poetry.

Hers was perfect.

Her stems and gut were long and sinewy. Baby abs. Subtle rib definition. Hip bone indents. A v-shaped border that led to her pyramid-shaped bush. There weren't any loose hairs or razor burn in sight, almost like it'd grown that way. A single tear could've fallen from my eye.

She planted one of her stems on the bed and crammed my face into her cut-up. I ate until her sturdy leg buckled and what dripped from my beard started making rhythmic taps on the floor. She was about to fall. I grabbed her hips and threw her onto the bed. She weighed only a little more than the air in her lung sacks. She spread her legs and told me to lick. Her bed was at least queen-sized and the points of her stilettoes went over both sides of the mattress. She pulled my hair and pushed my face in while grinding. I sucked her clit and fingered her hole. One, two, three digits. I flipped her around, spread her cheeks, and ate her ass. She told me after that that had been a classy move, especially from an older cat. I said that I wasn't old and that her young asshole was still as pink as a puppy's paw. *No man'd say nah.*

The red lights were about to make sense.

She rolled onto her back, pulled her lips apart, and squeezed her nipple. I fought my pesh out of my drawers and dove in. The first half was slick. It got big-tight after that. She wrapped her legs around me and pulled me deeper. I forced my way in like a boot through a bathroom door. She screamed. She hammered her heels onto my kidneys, carved up my back, and left some fake nails broke-off in my chest. She bit *through* my shoulder like a starved pit. I pulled her off. She smiled like a psych patient. Pieces of me in her teeth, my red shining on and around her blackish lips.

I backhanded her mug. Smeared the red.

"Again daddy, harder!"

I milked her with a lead-heavy palm. Her pearls loosened and her beak leaked. She touched it, looked at the invisible red at the end of her finger, and tasted it. Lunging at me, she latched her jaws onto my bottom lip big-hard and busted the shit like a frozen pipe. I pinned her branches and long-dicked, punching my pesh towards her heart.

The sheets, the armchair… everything was black for a reason. The broad gushed like a firehose manned by a toddler.

After the first round, I looked like a newborn baby. My moss was slicked back with all of our bodily fluids. Sweat, spit, blood, squirt, cum, and liquor. When I finally gave up the nut, the shit felt like a road trip piss. I fell dead onto the marshy mattress with Maria's long body snaked around me like the chalice on a European pharmacy sign.

We went at it until I was shooting nothing but air. Both of us looking like a thousand little murders, she clicked off the red lights and laid on my chest. We were as sticky as plums in July. It was pitch black, but I could still see the room like I had night vision goggles on. Her sweat was sweet to the taste and like vinegar to my wounds.

"I'm glad you're a pervert," she said in the darkness.

"I'm the pervert?" I responded, surprised-like.

"I was worried you'd be a cunt-tease and it was going to be one of those things where we both acted like we didn't want to fuck the shit out of each other but did. Then, we'd have to go through two or three dates and then..."

I tried to stop my dick from getting hard again, but a beautiful woman who liberally used the word *cunt* was way too sexy for a scumbag like me.

The next morning, Maria wobbled bow-legged to the window and peeled back the blackouts. Her legs, arms, neck, hips, and ass were suddenly glowing in the daylight, banged-up and bruised. Aside from her wagon, she was probably the skinniest broad I'd ever fucked. No fat, no gristle. She also had this weird-looking nub at the small of her back. The red lights had hidden it before. She was still cuter than your average. Nasty. With a freak ass. *A tail was nowhere near a deal-breaker.*

As for me, I looked like I'd spent the night fighting a crew of pitchforks. My right eye was puffed out. The bed was damp and starched dryly in spots. Everything felt stuffy. I was hungover from cumming. I felt like a rolled-up tube of Colgate.

"Meet me at The Grosvenor after work again," she asked.

"Let's skip the drinks," I said. "Just a couple," I added almost immediately after.

I saw her again on Friday and we *did-the-damn-thing* all week-end. I loved the broad. That is, I loved *fucking* the broad. In my line of work, sometimes you gotta fuck. It ain't always pretty. But Maria, I could fall in love fucking her. She had that cupid arrow cut-up.

"I'm not normally like this, I swear," she said, like they all did.

"Sure," I kissed my teeth and nodded.

We were lying in the puddle she called a mattress.

"Seriously," she scratched me, "I'm not this one-note, sex-hungry *broad*, as you say. I'm not some horned-up teller that lives to serve you. I'm a complex and beautiful flower."

"Whoa, easy there, little girl," I chuckled. "Never said you were. Or weren't."

"Good," she smirked. "The bank is just temporary while I figure out what I want to do." Her body relaxed into mine. "I haven't lived long enough to find my passion yet. I'm capable of great things, I just need to figure out what," she said, more to herself. "I don't want you going and talking about me like I'm some cheap lay." Her brows furrowed, then softened. "I *at least* want to be the best cheap lay…" She kissed me. "Want to go again?"

Like I said, if it wasn't business, I would've carried her off in my jaws.

But it *was* business. I had to keep my mind on getting into that safe room. I couldn't out-and-out tell her that I was going to fuck up the joint, but I needed to get in there. I had a bullshit back-story to spit in between fucks, but the trust was in the orgasms. The dick game earned her respect, but I had to hit her with the right words.

"You ever thought about fucking at work?" I asked one evening while we smoked a joint. Again, on the bed, like we'd never left.

"Oh my god," she said. "That's my biggest fantasy."

"Getting banged at your desk?"

"Well," she said, "something different. It's a little dark."

"I think we're past that, you little psychopath. Go on."

"Takes one to know one." She laughed, rolled onto her tummy, and put her head on my gut. She took a big, spliff-crackling pull and passed me the bone. "Ok... I have this wild fantasy about being taken hostage in a bank robbery. You know, a guy comes in with a mask and a gun or something. Like in the movies. He's got big shoulders and wide, calloused hands, just like you, and he demands that someone take him to the vault. I know the combination because I always spy over the manager's shoulder, and he takes me by force. *Oh!* Maybe he has a knife to my throat. Knives are so fucking hot! Anyways, he grabs me by the hair and makes me take him to the safe. He has his knife at my back. I can also feel his cock poking into my ass and cunt. I'm wet, dripping buckets, because of the danger... fear-moisture, you know? He points the gun at my temple or holds the knife to my jugular. I start rubbing my clit and touching his fat cock. He has to have a big one. It's *my* fantasy. He gets me into the room and bends me over the table. With his weapon in one hand, he pulls my panties down with the other and leaves them around my knees, drenched. From there, he just fucks my brains out… really tries to hurt me. He can't. I'm too horny and wet, so he tries harder. He thinks I'm scared that he's taking my pussy by force, but I'm getting off harder than I ever have in my life. I'd hold my ass open and let him fill me up when he was done."

I listened. There was a good chance I really was in love with this woman. I wanted her finger. Not to put a ring on it, but to bite it off and wear it beside the key on my chain.

"See? You think it's weird." She cuddled into my chest and buried her head, pretending to be embarrassed. Her hair smelled like sweat and squirt, but still had a sweetness to it.

"No, not at all," I said. I stroked her crunchy hair, getting my hand caught in the crispy tangles. "That's a lot to remember."

"Well," she rolled her orbs, "it doesn't have to be *exactly* like that. Just fuck me in the vault, please and thank you."

"How's this week sound?" I was about to ask her if *that* was how complex and beautiful flowers found their passion and did great things, but didn't.

She made a high-pitched noise through her pearls and crawled on top of me, kissing me and guiding my pesh into her cut up.

She decided that Friday would be perfect. It was the first of the month, government pay day, and the place would be running at an insane level of busy. No one would be the wiser.

Easy. Friday it was. *Light work.*

5

SARDUCCI AND O'LEARY

"What about your father?" Sofia asked me.

"What about him?" I shot back.

"Well, did you hear much from him after your mother passed away?"

"Never met the cat. Never knew his name or even what he looked like. Ma never jawed about him unless it was to bitch about leaving her with a seed to feed. Ain't kept no pictures. Of him or me. No birth certificates or nothing. I don't think they had one of those, what do you people call them, *relationships?*"

"You were the postman's sprout, oy Dave?" Winston had walked over.

"Not quite."

"I was the postman's sprout, Dave. Well, I mean that my father, he was a letter carrier. My parents were married at any rate." He turned to Sophia. "Oy Dave, can I get a fresh ale? Thanks, Dave."

Marbles had gone to take a piss or another fight would've started right there. I didn't give a fuck what he called me. The kid was alright.

Sofia came back with a tall amber beer for Winston.

"Much appreciated, Dave. I've grown a horrid thirst. It's quite the sauna in here, is it not, Dave?"

"You're welcome, Winston," Sofia said.

"It is a bit warm," I said.

"So… Dave here was telling me about Jesus and what would happen if he was alive now. It's fascinating. Tell them, Dave!"

Preacher moseyed over and asked for a bottle of beer. I wasn't much for listening to his tinfoil theories, but I didn't have any-where else to be. I was a hostage who was too lazy to scream. *What do they call that, Sweden Syndrome?*

"Yeah, so… Think about this," Preacher started. "Jesus, man, he'd be a *real* celebrity. Think about it. Water to wine, walking on lakes, real illusionist stuff… But really real! No wires, no strings, no special effects. No nothing," Preacher tapped the bar with the toe of his bottle. "I mean, they could look for harnesses and trap doors and whatnot, but he was… he'd *actually* be perform-ing those miracles. Imagine the hoopla back when… now think about if he was alive today…"

Sofia nodded like she cared. It sounded stupid as fuck to me.

"No, Dave. The part about the tabloids," Winston said.

"Right, so, imagine… He, Jesus, the son of our Lord and saviour, is out and about town. He'd be famous! Probably make good money for all his miracles… get big name sponsors like Coke or Apple or whatever other corporation wanted to ride his coattails. He'd be a big-time celebrity, like movie star or singer levels of fame. Imagine how much that would test him. Paparazzi would be following him around with tape recorders and cameras, trying to implicate him with all kinds of doctored photographs and rumours about children and trysts. That's some heavy business right there."

Winston's face was fully stretched out with a goofy-ass, mind-blown expression. He was looking at us, waiting on me and Sof to act like we gave a shit.

"Wow," Sofia let her lips widen and shook her whole upper body with her head. "That's a really interesting theory, Richard."

"Right? Dave was telling me this… and I was thinking that Dave *had* to hear about this!"

I didn't give a shit. I'd been hearing Preacher's cracked-out theories for more than a minute, and they weren't getting any less psych. No cap, this one was better than a lot of them. His alien and illuminati ones were fucking retarded.

"James," Sofia touched my arm. I'd have to invite her upstairs if she kept doing that. Break my gentleman act and dig her back out. *Otherwise, what was the point of all this touching?*

I nodded at her.

"So, your mother passed away tragically. You didn't have a father in the picture. What does a boy do in that situation? Did you have any aunts or uncles? Grand or godparents?"

The fluid in my dome was swirling around like a half-full bottle of booze in the backseat of a getaway car. I squeezed my lids shut. I was coming to, whether I wanted to or not. The backs of my closed eyes were getting lighter. Black to gray. I didn't want to open them. The longer I kept them closed, the longer I could fight thinking, remembering, and facing whatever fuck-shit reality was waiting for me in the seeing world. I ignored the thought of being in a barrel or bag or whatever other container the wops could have thrown me into. *Que sera type shit.*

"Get off me." I heard as I got popped under the chin. My wig snapped leftwards. My shoulders swayed over and my dome thudded against a wall. I groaned. I think I passed out. When I came to again, I felt like I was discovering my arms for the first time, like a starfish or some shit. I used them to mash my mitts into my seers. My mug hurt to the touch. I was dizzy. Sitting down. I slit open my eyes and couldn't see shit. Not at first.

"Awake? Here." The guy next to me thrust something into my chest.

"What?" I snuck words out, mumbling and grunting. Still couldn't see shit. Bright. Ears burned. Beak was plugged. Headache something sinister. Stems as stiff as cheap chopsticks.

"The papers. Your papers," the guy said. I heard an accent, but couldn't tell what kind.

We were moving.

I felt the joint he'd shoved at me and blinked until my vision was only double. I was clutching a big yellow envelope. I laid it on my lap. I thumbed my sockets again. Shit got clearer. My other senses were coming back, too.

Rumbling. Forward movement. *Mans was on a bus.*

I was beside some big fucker who I must've been using as an on-and-off pillow. I couldn't tell where we were by looking out the window. Fields and trees and shit. No city smells.

The big guy was staring ahead. He was rocking a beater and shorts. He had some tats on his arm from what I could see: a statue head, some writing, and an AK.

"Where are we?"

"On the road."

"No shit, Lurch."

"What is Lurch?"

"It's you, you big motherfucker."

"I do not fuck on mothers."

I looked at him stupid. He had a hard-looking mug with a woolly beard. Mean, but with something near-innocent underneath it. I think it was his eyes. Something about him seemed young, younger than he looked.

"Ok… where we going?"

"Training."

"For what?"

"Army."

None of that made a fucking dick-lick of sense to me. As much as it's making to you, I bet.

I tried concentrating on *the-fuck* had happened while I scraped blood-grit out of my beak-holes. I worked my way all the way back from the train heist to Ma lying dead on her bed to getting a block-heeled loafer to the grill. I ticked all the boxes, right down to the stinger that must've put me out.

"Army as in the fighting army? The army that goes to war?" I asked after big-silence.

"Yes. War army."

I didn't want to bother the big dog or draw attention to myself, but I needed to find out what the fuck was happening.

"What's your name?" I asked.

"Mi… Micka… Mickey. O'… O'Lee… O'Leary," he said. Now I heard it: Eastern European accent. Way East. It was his Rs.

"Bullshit you're fucking Mickey O-fucking-Leary."

"Yes, I is."

No, he wasn't.

"Pretty common name in Russia?"

"Lithuania… fuck." He breathed hard out his nose and stayed staring ahead looking pissed as hell.

I sat back and crossed my branches. The envelope slipped off my lap, so I bent down to pick it up. The sludge in my skull kept swishing around. I almost puked.

I opened up the envelope and found a stack of official-looking papers and a handwritten note.

I read the note first.

> As promised, we got you out of town. You're taking the place of a family associate's child named Frankie Sarducci who was selected to fight for our nation. We can't let one of our own be conscripted in such a manner. I'm sure you understand. You're now Frankie. Your name is Frankie. Not whatever it was previously. Frankie. I'm certain you can evaluate the likelihood of what'll happen if you blow your cover, Frankie. You'll be rewarded with being allowed to live after you serve your time. Best of luck. Sorry about your mother. It was unavoidable.
>
> Yours,
>
> Gentle Don

Cunt.

I'd gotten got. Bad. Sexy-Jesus fuck, I'd gotten got.

"What name they give you?" Mickey asked me after I let out a groan.

"Frankie fucking Sarducci," I said. "Who the fuck names their kid Frankie? Not even Franklin or Francesco. Fucking Frankie. That's like being a kid for your whole goddamn life."

"Mickey is name for mouse," he said with some twang of insult. "When child, we catch mouse for eat them. Make soup. And hat."

I groaned big-loud.

"Yup," Mickey said, nodding and staring ahead.

A few hours later, they hustled me, Mickey, and a bunch of other poor motherfuckers off the bus. We stood in a line out in front with our bags at our feet and got our asses roll-called one at a time. Mad cats clearly didn't match their names. The most fucked up were a big, black, country-looking son of a bitch named Feng Sung Po and an albino-white honkey named Hide-toshi Nakatomi. Clearly, we were all there because of some kind of fuckery.

The drill sergeant looked pissed, but I figured that they always looked that way. They shaved us down, took us to the barracks, and sent us to the mess hall where they explained that basic training would start at first light. There was a war going on, and we were next up.

Me and Mickey shared a bunk and got cool off the rip. We both looked like youngers compared to the other cats. Mick looked *30 years* younger with his beard razored off, and like he could handle his own business. That was a good thing; I didn't want to partner up with some pussy that needed to be watched out for.

This was even more important than usual because I still didn't know what the fuck was going on. I could've been dreaming. Or in a coma. Or dead.

In the mess, us fucked-overs all sat together. You could hear the thinking and bottled-up confusion through the silence. Some cats looked like they'd come to grips with the shit. Others were still shook.

"This is how they get their kids out of conscription," a green-eyed, Irish-looking kid named Oleg Mironov said. "How the fuck does an *Oleg Mironov* act and talk? My name is Sean Dougherty."

I tapped Mickey and said that they should trade names. Someone overheard.

"You can't," a black dude whose limbs were so long he could've done with an extra set of knees and elbows said. "We're all here cause we, or someone we know, owes someone. Look, my old earth got a gambling debt with the A-rabs, and… Do I look like an Abdul Ibn-al Muhammed Zahadin to you? Nah, son. It's DeMarcus Love, man… but I ain't letting momma dukes go out like that. I do one turn, and we good. Ya heard?"

The country-looking black said that he *could* look like an Abdul Ib-whatever… there were lots of black Muslims. "Do the knowledge, God."

They started jawing back and forth about some five-percenter shit that I couldn't follow. The same way them *righteous* brothers jaw in the slam after they convert and stop eating swine to survive. How a cat's supposed to believe in any kind of god when he's locked up, I don't know. If you ask me: *A gang is a gang is a gang.* Doesn't matter if you pray five times a day when you're slanging dope on the low.

Around the table, cats were telling their tales. Their heads were low and their tones were hushed. Other tables started looking at us. The chatter got to Mickey.

"You all talking too much," he said. He took his empty tray and left the table.

As usual, I wasn't jawing much. I finished my food and walked around the yard. Back at the barracks, Mickey was lying on the bottom bunk, staring up at the springs.

"How you not gonna take the top?" I asked him.

"I like bottom."

"You're taller."

"I first."

"Why're *you* here, Mick?"

He took a few deep breaths. I could've let it go, crawled onto my bunk, and crashed. Instead, I pushed. *I was bored as a motherfucker.* I must've been annoying the big cat, but I reckoned it was worth it. Least an ass-whooping would give me something to do.

"I miss shot."

"Shot of what? At what? You a hitter?" I asked.

"No. I miss shot. I miss chance for go to NBA."

"Wait… do you play for Tech?" A memory of some guinea-goons jawing about some foreign kid hit me.

"Yes."

"Are you here illegally or some shit?"

"No. I come on visa."

"So, what's the problem?"

"My sister here illegal. No papers."

"So?"

"One gang say make shot, another gang say miss shot."

I didn't understand and said so.

"If I make shot, I keep scholarship and she stay and Irish gang make money. But, Russian gang lose money and say they kill her. So… I miss shot. I make Russian gang money and she live. But Irish gang say I owe favour because they lose much money and will kill my sister. And, school say I no keep scholarship and have to go back to my country."

"So… you both have to go back home?"

"Before, I take scholarship for my family. To be basketball man and play for Bull or Laker. To bring my parent and sister to here. We stay, but, Irish gang say I need do *this*, whatever *this* is. If I do, they leave us alone. Russian gang make so we can stay, scholarship or no. I just have work for them after."

Fucking gangsters. Punk motherfuckers. "Damned if you do, huh?" I said.

That made him confused.

"How old are you?"

"20," he said.

He *was* young.

"What is name, Frankie? Real name," he asked.

"James February. People call me Feb."

"Feb. That is simple."

"Yeah. What's yours, Mick?"

"Justas Saliamonavicius."

I tried but couldn't even get through one syllable. I couldn't figure out where one name ended and the next one began.

"People at the school, they call me *Juice*."

That, I could manage.

I crashed quick-fast after the lights went out. The last time I'd had something near a good night's sleep, I'd ended up stopping an incest-rape at a farm in the middle of nowhere. That could've been a day or a lifetime ago. I no longer had any sense of time.

I slept with my socks on and my boots beside my pillow. The olders from the hood that had gotten locked up schooled me on that when they came home from their bids. I know I wasn't in the slam, but it felt like it. I also tucked my flip-blade under my pillow and kept my mitt on it.

During the night, a couple of privates stepped in to haze us. They were trying to make the new recruits hop out of bed and run laps around the field, assed-out. I was trying to sleep through the noise and ignore it. I was that kind of tired where your whole body aches and you give the thought of dying before moving a long, honest look. I didn't have any time or patience for that punk-shit.

When the privates eventually came for me, I flicked my ox and swung at the fuckers. *Instinct.* I caught a cat in the corner of his kisser. Instinct had me aiming for his neck. Juice stopped snoring and chucked one of his cinderblocks at the same cat and thumped him in the gut. *Deadly combo.* The punk motherfucker spent the rest of basic, and life, with a half-Chelsea.

The cat didn't rat, though. Lucky for him.

No one tried to fuck with us again. Or talked to us much after that.

"I hear a knife story?" asked Juice, who'd been making his rounds. He leaned in. "What talking about?"

"How we met," I said. The cats around weren't paying us any mind. "Your English got better. I guess it couldn't have gotten any worse."

"Like you should talk. Simpson and Seinfeld were good teachers."

"Always reading, too."

"I like to keep mind busy."

"Yeah, I ain't have the mind to read. Patience. Want. Time. Smarts. Pick one."

"Pick what?" Sofia said. "What are you…"

"Reading. I keep my ass too goddamn busy to read. I got to. Otherwise, I get in trouble."

"Don't we all," Preacher said. "Idle hands. That's why the richest people in the world, even though they don't have to work, keep a network of underground lairs to perform ritualistic offerings to a Cthulhu-like spirit in the underworld, which allows them to keep their stranglehold on the planet and its resources. Think about it…"

I ignored him and finished my cup.

"You tell pretty lady about Lieutenant Perry."

"No," I said.

"No to what?" Sofia asked. She'd been cracking a roll of quarters into the till like an egg. She looked confused.

"No one," I said.

"Yes one," Juice said.

"No one, what?" she asked, leaning in. "James, are you feeling ok?"

"I'm fine. Juice wants me to tell you about Lieutenant Perry."

"I see… You don't have to talk about anything you don't want to," Sofia said. "You've shared a lot today. More than usual. It might feel good if you kept going, though. I'd love to hear more. Although, James, something's been bothering me about your story."

"Oh?" I kissed my fronts.

"Well, some of the language you've been using is a little dated.

"Like what?"

"We don't use words like *wop* or *dago* anymore. Also, what *is* a guinea?" Sofia filled my glass, her best-used tactic.

I grumbled.

"Lieutenant Perry. Erik Perry… was our commanding officer in the war. He was one of the closest things that I done ever had to a pops."

"Oh…" Preacher said.

I bit at him with an ice-grill. He started counting his laces, head down like he was praying to whatever god he was hollering at that week. I was using all my power to hold back from rocking his snot-box and flying his knot across the bar. *For now.*

6

IT'S ALWAYS SOMEBODY ELSE'S WAR

Fuck me.

Wouldn't ever have guessed it. Wouldn't have believed your ass in a million years if you told me.

I liked basic training.

It was the first time I'd ever been taken to task. I got worked the way a toothbrush becomes a shiv and I didn't come out of pocket once. The more the drill sergeant tried pushing and punishing me, the more blood I tasted and the harder I came back. At the time, it felt like some kind of rebellion. The more he tried to break me, the more I wouldn't let him. Now I can see that I was only playing myself. I'd fallen in line thinking that I was fighting.

I'd been a stray slug up until then. Going through life in a straight line, ripping through or knocking down whatever was in the way.

Those mafia motherfuckers stopped me dead, like those windows in the cheque-cashing spots. I was a lone wolf, more or less. No real crew, no real day-ones. Ma never told me nothing. She'd been fine with letting her baby come up in the streets, or at least never cared enough to stop it. Teachers couldn't tell me nothing either. *School ain't shit when your ribs touch.*

In the army, I was hit with rules and orders and shit to do. *Mans did the shit out of that shit.*

Run there. *Ok.*

Stand there. *Ok.*

Jump over that. *Ok.*

Drop and give me 20. Now 10 more. Now 10 more. *Ok, ok, ok.*

They taught us fighting-moves and strapped us with bammers, blasters, and bazookas… *oh my.* I could already throw hands pretty nice and was mega-slick with a blade, but they tightened me up real good. Practice makes breaking-an-elbow-in-one-motion *perfect.*

Me and Juice were the best students. He was nice with a handgun. And a rifle. And fucking grenades and whatever other tools they gave him. They fast-tracked him up to heavier artillery. Motherfucker could hit a flipped quarter twice: once on the way up and again on the way down. He put me on how to shoot good: *breathing, blinking, drinking a little booze to steady to nerves, using the kick back.* The cat had had a lot of practice. He'd been a solid thug in the old country. Might've become King if he'd stayed.

I'd gotten good. *Big-good, big-fast.* Whenever we weren't running drills, I was at the range. I'd snatch a stick off the rack or the next cat's mitts and dump their clips.

I didn't know who we were fighting. I didn't know what the war was about. I didn't even know that there *was* a war. My whole universe was nothing more than a few blocks. There was no world outside the brick walk-ups with bars in the windows and roaches and rats. I wasn't worried about a goddamn thing but doing me. This was summer camp. Shit felt like one of those retreats crackers did to *find themselves*.

Lieutenant Erik A.S. Perry came up on me and Juice one day when the sun was crashing behind the foothills. He was as stout as a Guinness and half as dark. A mutt with a military background. Motherfucker still holds the honour of being the only cat I've ever met who didn't look half-queer in a beret. It suited his square-ass head and block jaw. He had the outline of a Neanderthal with the opposite steez. He was standing behind us, smoking a rolled cigarette, and clocking us shredding up the targets like backs after good sex or bad behaviour.

"You boys like guns, huh?" he said, blowing out a puff.

"Yes," Juice stated.

"What do they call you?"

"O… Connor?" Juice said.

"Nah, man. Your name's O'Leary," I said. "I'm Sarducci."

"Bullshit." Perry scrunched his mug into a smirk. "You're some of those *lost boys*, ain't you? Here 'cause you fucked up back home with some bad men. Am I wrong?"

We nodded. Well, Juice nodded *yes* and I nodded *no*. His phras-
ing was confusing.

"Great system we got in this fine country of ours…" Perry said
to himself. "What do your pappies think?"

"Just got out prison back in home," Juice shrugged.

"Ain't never had one," I replied.

He dropped his dart and squashed it under his jackboot. "You
boys'll fit in nicely. Welcome to the family."

He walked away. We shrugged at each other, turned back towards
the targets, and kept blasting.

"I grew up with gun," Juice said. "In my country, Soviets bring
many AK-47. Easy to get as liquor. Guns everywhere. My uncle
made pistols from scrap metals."

"You're a goddamn hillbilly," I added, watching Sofia bend to
reach into the glass-washer.

"Baltic hillbillies, very common. Moonshine and Kalashnikovs,"
he said.

I laughed.

"I'm *almost* jealous," I said. "I took to a burner in my mitts like
a fish to water."

"I want to hear more about this family you mentioned, James,"
Sofia said. She was hanging the cups she'd polished on the rack
above the ice well. They swayed and made a tinkling sound. I
forgot what I'd been saying, watching her snowball-tits stay put

as her snakelike body lengthened. Her gut narrowed and rib bones poked out under her shirt. My fingers would've fit perfectly between 'em. Her hip bones jutted out beneath her thin skirt. I imagined what her cut-up looked like. Grill got watery. *I bet it was nice.* My guess, *smooth and tight as a studio drummer.*

"I used to have a really big family," Marbles said. "My mom and dad got divorced. Then, they both got remarried and had more kids. Some of those kids even had kids. I already had brothers and sisters. I got a Christmas *and* a Chanukah. But… I haven't seen my family for a long time. Any of them." Marbles shrugged. "I fucked one of my stepbrothers and then my…"

"I asked James a question, Serena." Sofia set down a pair of wine glasses softly, holding the stems. She wasn't angry. "We'll… talk about that after."

"Okey-dokes," Marbles said, sipping her drink.

"James," Sofia said. "Please, tell me more about this Lieutenant Perry."

"Perry wanted us for his platoon, which he treated *like* a family. Your platoon becomes your crew. You need each other. Only way to survive. War does that shit."

"You bonded, connected, shared with each other?" Sofia pried.

"Sure, I guess… we spent a lot of time together. Just us, far from home and anything else we'd ever known. As a unit, for as long as they needed us. You argue, you fuck with each other, you get on each other's nerves… you mash each other up, then forget about the shit after. Dap it out, like fam. When it comes down to it, you'd put your life down for one of your brothers."

Juice nodded.

"Do you still keep in touch?" Sofia asked. "It sounds like…"

"Nah."

"Why not?" Marbles asked.

"Can't really, with most of them." I swatted her hand from my zipper.

Lieutenant Perry had good standing in the army. A lifer with legacy status, he could hand pick cats from the fort and drag them into his *special* war reserve. The same way motherfuckers vote for a president who they could imagine getting pissed up with, the lieutenant chose his crew.

"I was in the academy as a pup," he told us as we walked to the plane with our duffels over our shoulders. "Hated the shit, but it got me everything I have today: education, good union job, beautiful wife… and this stupid, mesomorphic gorilla frame."

"Man, what you mean?" Love, the third one of us misplaced-fucks that'd been picked for *Perry's Orphans,* asked.

"Well," he squinted his eyes, nodded, and rolled his top lip under his tongue, "I've had a life, brother."

We boarded the plane, hunching forward like we were in the locker room before game seven. We were all clocking each other's mugs like fresh fish in the pen. I only knew Juice and Love from basic. Luckily, we were now using our *real* names, except for on official paperwork and fatigues. Still, most cats were as unimportant as their deaths would ultimately be. Then, there was this preachy cunt. He was some minister from a rural Christian church who'd joined because Christians were getting got overseas.

He thought that he was carrying the faith of millions on his shoulders and warring for freedom. His name was Richard. He wouldn't shut the fuck up about God and Jesus and shit.

"We all have our stories. Our reasons for being, living, striving." Richard was holding a missal, his fingers pinching the tassel, ready to read. "Did you know that the story of Jesus was changed during the Nicene Creed? Think about it… Jesus lived a whole life and dedicated every shred of His holy existence to the betterment of man and mankind as a whole? He spent his days.…"

"Shut the fuck up, Preacher," I said. "The lieutenant was talking." The name stuck, then and there.

"Whoa now, February," the easy-going, *I-ain't-believe-he-was-in-the-army* lieutenant said. "This boy here is our good luck charm. *A man of God?* Hell, I always try to bring one with me. How can you not have that rabbit's foot in your back pocket? The bastard *has to* pray for us. His God *has to* protect us by protecting him!"

"Faith, sir," Preacher said, "is not luck."

"Anyways," Perry ignored him and began, "I was a war baby. Daddy met Momma while he was serving the cause in Honduras punching down rebels, and the two hit it off. He got deployed elsewhere and she was left with a bundle of me inside her. She moved to Roatan to make better money and be with the family. Wasn't until I was a few years older that Daddy tracked Momma down, somehow, and they rekindled their romance. He loved her, it turned out. *Lucky them.* When he finally believed that I *was* in fact his son, he had me shipped off to the academy to get a rigid kind of education fit for boy with his blood. I was about seven. He died a year later, but kept an education fund for me in his will. I'd go back to the island every summer and stayed in touch with some friends. I also had dual citizenship, so I could come and go as I pleased. I loved football." He thumbed the ring on his fuck-you-finger, a clunky joint with a ruby you could brain a cat with. "I played for the academy and was an all-state as a safety. A big task for a guy from a non-state school. Granted, they put a lot of gear in me and stunted my growth. *Bastards.* I grew out and not up. *Wide as he is tall,* they said. I considered my coach my dad and my team my brothers. I craved that shit… *family, structure, brotherhood.* Not sure why… guess some of us need that shit, you know? Anyway, I'm still a little sore about the roids. Kind of fucked up if you ask me… pumping a kid full of junk without him knowing anything about it. *Vitamins,* they called it. Should've read the bottle. If they ever let me get my hands on it… Oh well. I got crazy acne and beat the fuck out of many a wall and freshman. I never broke a bone though, so there's that. After graduating from the academy, I was about done with the military… rule-heavy bullshit factory that it is. Moved back to the island and opened a bar. Won the heart of the prettiest girl from my childhood visits and planned to start a family with her."

Perry paused.

"What happened?" Love asked.

"Ha!" Perry slapped his drumstick, sounded like a thunderclap. "The army's like crack, man. Once you know it, understand it, get paid by it, and can always go back to it… you do. *It's got something, man.* If you like it even the slightest bit, you'll keep going back to the well. After a while, I was bored there. On the island, I mean. I was thirsty for some action. Something more than college kids and recent divorcees. I let them ship me off here, there, and wherever for a few years. Paid more than my fair share of dues. By the time my old lady was getting annoyed with me for always leaving her with the bar, we packed up and said fuck it. Got her a green card, got us an apartment, and got me a job with the force. Seemed like a natural fit. Order and justice and all that bullshit."

"And now?" Juice asked.

"And now," Perry squinted and nodded, "we live happily ever after."

"Then, why are you here? Going to Something-Stan or whatever? To fight? When you ain't gotta?" I asked. "You love your country or something?"

"Fuck no! I'm here for a fucking vacation, buddy," Perry said. His grin lifted his beret halfway off his head. He licked his rolled-under lips and winked one of his squinted seers: "Get some goddamn rest from the old lady."

A narrow landing strip came into view surrounded by greens: jades, emeralds, forests, limes, and mints. *A jungle of greens.*

We landed far off from the heart of the warzone. *Way the fuck off.* So far off that basic might've been closer to the battlegrounds than our new home.

We hopped into a covered truck and drove through the jungle: past some half-built and half-destroyed chunks of building, through a town with busted-ass, Spanish-type *casas*, and finally arriving at a coastline of golden sand and clear crystal water as far as a motherfucker could shoot a look in any and all directions.

"Not too close to the water," Perry hollered with his mitt cupped around his grill while we hauled out our tents and shit. "Don't want to accidentally drown when you're trying to sleep off a…"

"Sir?" Preacher might as well have been tugging on Perry's pant leg, "Why aren't we in Afghanistan? Iraq? Iran? Lebanon? The Middle East at least? I joined the cause to spread the message and gospel of our only true God. I wanted to defend the lives and religious freedoms of my Christian brethren. Why aren't we in one of the hot zones, sir?"

"Listen, man," Perry put his hand on the minister's shoulder and unscrewed the hand-rolled dart from his grill, "because… *fuck that fighting shit.*"

Perry called us to take a knee and listen.

Yes, coach?

"Boys, part of the reason I brought you here, save for the holy man, was because you've all seen some shit. You've all had hard lives. The *no-daddy-having* club ain't a kind one. I for one have known almost nothing but hard work and received less a thank you than a fuck you."

He wasn't wrong.

"We'll be stationed here on one of the 7000 or so remote and beautiful islands located… somewhere in the Philippines. Pana… Patna… Paci… Palawan? I think? Anyways… it's more of a sleepy little town that'll probably become an enclave of resorts before it becomes an enclave of gun-toting extremists, heretics, and communists. Which, wouldn't you know it, is the scenario I painted to the general in vivid colours when I insisted upon its strategic capabilities. *Fancy talk, huh?*" He smirked. "Yes, there *is* a war going on… There are many! Blood-feuds! Heartless, soulless, and destructive battles that are spreading throughout the globe and eating up lives at an increasing rate."

He curled his upper lip inwards and pressed his tongue against it while toying with his ring.

"But, that's way over there," he threw a meaty digit over the ocean, "or is it that way… Beats me. My compass is packed in some trunk. Anyways, listen, men… We're here on *surveillance*, so let's just sit this round out. Enjoy ourselves and get paid for it. My rank and charm are good for something. Feel lucky we're not over… wherever the hell the fighting is."

He wasn't *all-the-way* lying to the general. The war *was* on some global shit. We *were* technically holding it down in the South Pacific in case some shit popped off, though the same could be said for literally anywhere else on the planet. *The difference?* Other than emptying magazines at empty beer bottles and putting machetes through coconuts, we *weren't* about to get our brains fucked out of our domes with sniper bullets.

Save that shit for the motherfuckers who had moms and dads to protect them, but not a Lt. Perry.

We *did* practice army stuff. We ran a couple miles in soft sand a day, except when we were too hungover from the bungalow bars and cases of booze that the lieutenant had replaced some of our army gear with. We gave a daily ear to the ham-radio to see if there were any distress calls. Shocker: *We never heard any, not even one.*

We even let Preacher wander off. He'd bounce for days at a time, trying to convert the islanders to the cross. He was annoying and stir crazy, not being able to do what he'd joined for. So long as he checked in every so often, it was whatever.

Lt. Perry made it clear when he traded his fatigues for cargo shorts and a flowy, never-done-up Hawaiian shirt that we weren't the cats to turn the tide of the war. All that skill drilling had been for nothing more than fun and future investment.

"Clear!" I shouted. Perry winged a freshly slammed beer bottle at Preacher's God's house. I put a slug right through the fucker. The shards of broken brown glass sparkled in the sun and misted into the ocean. The *bang* lost its breath over the water as it sprinted towards the horizon.

"Great shot," he said.

He patted me on the back and burped. "You know, I almost feel bad, son."

"Why?" I said.

"You could've killed a lot of people. I mean... *a lot.* You're a natural. The army could use an asset like you. It's like you were bred for this shit."

"I know," I said, small-disappointed.

"Is that what you wanted?"

"I mean..." I itched my wig with the biscuit nozzle, "I fuck with it. I've always dreamed about it. Shooting someone. Watching them die. I guess I could stab 'em. Choke 'em. Baseball bat 'em...

but, I mean, who wouldn't want to legally put a blast-hole in some cat's smile just to see what it feels like? Sorry if I sound crazy or on one. I ain't. I just want to see if I can, you know? It looks big-easy. I feel like I could. Sometimes… sometimes, you know… I get so… Shit. I could tear a cats wig off and not think twice about it. Whether he deserve it or not. Is that bad? I mean… I just… I just have so much…."

"Anger?"

"I dunno what to call it."

"Ah man, it ain't so bad. What do you have to be angry about? You're young. No daddy, sure, but who needs one?! You haven't even had the time to get to know yourself. Look at that chin, boy. *Soft as an escort's clam.* Ain't even got a dusting! You're strapping, handsome, have a good head on your shoulders, and ain't no dummy. *Get gone boy!*" He squinted and licked the yellow strip of his rollie. "How old're you anyhow?"

"What day is it?"

"The 7th."

"17 years old, as of this morning. Sometime between 12 and 12."

"Seven… Seventeen, man? Jesus Christ! What the hell did you do to piss someone off this bad? You got naked pics of the Virgin Mary in your footlocker, boy?"

"Beats me. Who's that?"

"Ha! Get gone! Fuck 'em all and fuck 'em good. Be glad you ended up with me." He reached into the cooler and cracked open a couple of beers. "Happy birthday, kiddo."

"Thanks."

We tapped bottlenecks. I sat on the cooler, he sat on the sand.

"What did you do?" he asked, after side-eyeing me for a while, tongue pressed against his top lip. "If you don't mind telling."

I filled him in like a donut with some jelly made of cherry-flavoured fuckery.

"Well…" he squinted, rubbing some sweat off his head with his dart hand. "Jesus. Sounds like things got out of hand, fast."

"Yup."

"They killed your poor momma? Just like that?"

"Yup."

"And they just loaded you, knocked out, on a bus."

"You got it, man."

"Jesus…" The lieutenant did a double take. He gulped down some beer, then made a thinking sound. He lowered his bottle, slowly. He stared at the shimmering waves.

"Man… I don't even know what to say…" the lieutenant said.

"Don't gotta say none," I said. "What's done is done."

"Yeah, but… what's a kid to do? That's heavy as it gets. You ain't got the shoulders for that type of burden, son."

"Word. Makes me think I gotta find me a crew when I get home. Some real ruthless…"

"You talking about joining a gang? *Get gone!*"

"Or starting one. I dunno. Why not?" My mug creased like a pair of khakis.

"Kiddo." He whipped his bottle into the air and took out his glock in a single movement. He shattered the joint over the slow-crawling tide. "The fuck you think the army is?"

I didn't answer.

"Let me enlighten you on a little something…" he said, shooing me off the cooler to grab some fresh beers. "Back home, I'm a cop."

I must've made a face.

"I know, I know… we ain't exactly popular with hoodlums like yourself. But, a little advice… If you want to get back at the people who fucked you over… do it smart. Legally. You want to kill an enemy in the war, cool. *Go bananas.* More power to you. We love that. We even give you the guns and ammo to do it!" He shifted to face me. "But… you want to kill someone in the real world? Little trickier, as in… *illegal-as-fuck.* Now, I don't condone bodily harm, but… Well, there are special cases. Cops… they can get away with… Listen, man… There's nothing better than a referral from an officer."

"For what?"

"To get on the force," he responded, throwing his branch around my neck and squeezing. "I won't push it, but I see a lot of young-me in you. Angry, confused… More than anything, a need for structure. Almost a yelp for it." He tightened up his grip when I kissed my fronts and jerked my dome away. "For real. I see it. Kids like you who get to run wild in the streets find it refreshing to be given rules and orders. To be challenged. To have the opportunity to show that they're just as good as anyone else… even though the world wrote them off. The police could use a guy with your pedigree."

I scoffed, pushed him off, and handed him my emptied bottle.

"Pull!"

Perry was a good cat. A first ballot hall-of-famer. Most of the time, I forgot he was a pig. *Mans hated pigs.* Lying-ass, cheating-ass, crooked-ass, bust-you-for-no-reason-ass, swine-ass motherfuckers. He could've been one of those same devils who always shook me and my friends down for nothing. Well, what I used to think was nothing… but I didn't see that in Perry. Not a pig, just a dude. It was weird.

He talked me down from my plan to try and bring back some of my bammers from the army and go all Frank Castle on the mob. Perry thought that with some grooming I could make a decent cop. I knew all the ins and outs. I could even work out of my hood and make sure that no other kids got orphaned like me. No adult had ever taken the time to get to know me before. *Big-inspiring.*

"He was a good role model for you, wasn't he?" Sofia asked.

"Growing up with snakes… nothing but pimps and pushers, the first half-good cat who comes around seems like fucking Superman," I answered.

"And you *did* take his advice, didn't you?"

"Well, Sof… I tried, baby. I tried." I threw oxes over at Preacher who was jawing with Marbles. "If it wasn't for Perry, things might've gone worse, somehow. But, how shit unfolded… I don't know…"

"You can't blame others for what happens in your life."

"If it ain't clear by now, Sof, I ain't never had too good a handle on the things that've happened in my life. This wasn't even my war to fight in the first place."

"No war is ever yours but the one you start," Juice said. "The best thing you can do is try and not die."

7

FUCKING PREACHER

The God-man was acting strange. *Real weirdo shit.* We'd learned to ignore him, so it took some doing for us to notice.

He'd stumbled upon some smoked-out, ex-pat hippy-fucks who'd been camping out with the locals. He started splitting his time between us and them. The more time passed, the less we saw of him.

When he was with us, and we made the mistake of asking him why he was so quiet, he'd spout off like a fire hydrant in ghetto summertime. Spitting and drooling about this, that, and the third. He was there, but not. He'd go from silence to hollering out his neck in a second. He didn't smell good either, like the rancid stub of a hacked limb.

Those washed-out hippies spent their days getting toed-up and basking in the sun, covered in mango guts, baked and sticky. Or, getting as high as the palm trees the locals climbed for young coconuts. He called them his *fellow philosophers.*

The islanders were dark-skinned cats who dressed in ragged cloths. Real bushman types. There were a fair few of them. Enough to be nervous about. A spear wasn't worth shit against a bullet, but 100 spears... Anyways, Preacher called them his *converts.* The savages he'd set to civilize, I guess.

There were also regular folk running the little bars and little shops in the dirty little town. They seemed fine enough. A few spoke half-good English and pronounced *Fs* like *Ps.* I liked that. Perry was always on our asses about messing with the local broads. If we *had* to fuck them, he told us not to fuck *around* with them. *Use the brothel and use rubbers,* he always said. That way, at least they got some loot and no bastard seed to take care of down the road. Must've hit a little too close to home. There might not have been a whorehouse before we got there, now that I think about it.

Preacher kept getting more unglued until one day, he upped and stayed with the others. He'd left with his duffel, jawing up all kinds of shit and saying that his efforts were hitting with the locals. Saying that his mind was opening up. Saying that the hippy-fucks were schooling him about Buddha, Vishnu, Confucius, and whatever else.

We tracked him down after he didn't check in for well over a week. The whole thing had been Perry's idea. We found him grizzled and filthy, sitting cross-legged with a bunch of old-ass crackers with their balls showing and natives doing native shit all around them. We brought him back, only for him to sneak off again. That time, Perry washed his mitts and let him go. We were good with him staying gone. We checked on him to make sure he was alive, but only when Perry caught a pang of guilt. The hippies were too annoying.

"Have you guys ever experienced third-eye vision?" Preacher asked when Perry and I went to clock on his crazy ass. "Check this out." He handed a little dot of paper to the lieutenant.

"Preacher…" Perry tilted his brow, "this is acid. A hallucinogenic drug. Where'd you get this? All the way out here?"

"What you call a drug, the rest of the world calls a meditative component to achieving a higher state of consciousness and nirvana. Laws exist to limit spiritual freedom through beautiful means, such as this. I should know. I've traveled the world looking for consciousness-opening medication." This *probably-not-as-old-as-he-looked*, long-gray-bearded cunt with wire-rimmed glasses and emery board skin was talking just like someone who looked like him would talk. God, I wanted to drop the back of my rifle against the base of his head.

"Lemme guess… at some point, you were a professor of some kind," Perry said, squinting and licking his top lip.

"*Am*. Of Eastern religion at Berkley," the man responded with closed eyes, tilting his chin skyward. "I'm on a sabbatical."

Perry scrunched away the acid in his fingers and sighed. He pinched the bridge of his nose and said: "This is bad voodoo, kiddo. An omen. Fucking rabbit's foot, mother…"

Preacher tried to stand up, but couldn't. His fatigues were filthy, jaggedly sliced into shorts and a t-shirt. "Guys, I'm telling you. I get it. The mandalas are telling me that the one true God is a mirage! Think about it! There's an organic-geometric-omni-dimensional resonance that you can't detect at first glance. You need to drop everything you think you know about the world and lay down. Allow the bliss to penetrate and invade your every pore. Everything is God and has God-spirit flowing within it. This woman…" Preacher pulled the shoulder of a small, dark-skinned, darker-nippled woman close to him, "is Nib. She's my spiritual equal and co-existent in the stew of cosmic fluctuation. Think of her as a carrot, me as an onion, and the world as a broth that we're all…"

We left him droning on. He was broken, but he'd be fine. The islanders and hippies would take care of him, we hoped.

We saw him creep over on the sly to grab food and shit in the latrine. He just couldn't turn his back on toilet paper. He'd vick a set of fatigues and fuck off again. By then, we pretended that we hadn't seen him whenever he stepped. It was easier that way. The motherfucker had gone psych. Let sexy-Jesus punch my plums if I'm lying when I say that he smelled like a project dumpster in the middle of July.

By my born day, he'd already fucked off real good.

"Boys!" Perry shouted as we were walking back with our rifles slung over our shoulders and pistols in our mitts, "It's this young man's 17th birthday. Know what that means?"

No one seemed to know what that meant.

"Vest up, you sad sack of pricks and hammers. We're having a night."

We all cleaned up real nice and stepped into our finests. We hit the town, that is, the strip of bars with tapas, whores, and year-round Christmas lights. We settled into a spot that looked like someone's backyard, complete with a makeshift awning made of scrounged tin and picnic tables with slats missing here and there. Perry had a stack of small-faced ones that'd buy out the entire fucking bar.

"It's not every day someone turns legal in… England, or… Puerto Rico. Or Quebec. Pour up!" he exclaimed while portioning out stiff ounces from one of the Cutty Sark bottles that the owner kept bringing, along with a cup for himself to steal a few drinks with, a bow, and a *plis plis, pill me up, big man*. The girls brought food and the owner, once he got bent, played old rock jams in a sing-songy style on a steel-stringed acoustic guitar.

The cat really nailed *More Den A Peeling*.

Juice slapped a two-litre of cola out of my hand. "Mix drink is for the pussies. You are man now. You can fight like man? You drink like man." He slammed his cup against mine and put a crack down its middle. Then, he put his hand under my cup and tilted it back. Love started pouring the bottle into my tilted cup. I eventually caught an edge and spat out some whisky, making the same noise as a dog's sneeze.

"Ha-ha!" Perry laughed and kicked his boot onto the table, snapping another slat. "We'll find your drink of ch…" The waitress put down a giant, dusty bottle of dark Caribbean rum. "How did that get here?" Perry's face froze: squint, top lip, curled tongue. "Boys," he panted, wrapping his chorizo-fingers around the bottle and covering its label completely, "I been out of rum for a hot second. This might get messy."

The cat loved his rum. I can't stress this enough. I'm talking dopesick fiend-level *love*. You'd swear the bottle was made of Pyrex the way the hairs lifted on the cat's branches. He'd drunk all that he'd brought within our first week and had been depressed about it during the second. It reminded him of home and made him think of retiring.

Too sweet for me.

We got fucking drunk.

Soon, bottles were lying on the ground like shells after a shootout. The smoke from darts and shit-weed were chimneying at a constant. All the hazes were trapped by the sheet metal awning above our heads like some mid-summer LA smog. Two of the cats whose names I can't remember were playing a game of dead-arm until one of them passed out on the table.

We played cards and talked about pussy. They told me that I was a man and that's what men do.

There's drunk. Then there's prison holiday drunk. And above that still, there's army drunk.

"Man, I finna stay here when the shit over," Love said. "Go AWOL and take up a hammock in this quiet-ass town. All peaceful and shit. Fuck the shit out of a different honey every night and drink my ass to sleep while listening to the ocean. Don't that just sound like heaven to y'all?"

"What about your ma?" I asked. "Ain't you here because you're saving her from some goon shit?"

"Who?" he said with a sly grin. "Oh, yeah, that old bat… Well, Mama Dukes might have to take the hit. I been supporting her for years. Feel like I done paid my debt. First time in years I've felt chill."

"You want to stay here?" Perry joked. "Here? A little fleabag shithole in the Pacific?"

"You see a fleabag shithole. Me, I see a place where I'm different from the average cat and it's not a rat race to the bottom, feel me? I see a place where I'm a rock star with the biggest dick in the known-world and feel like a mix of Jimi Hendrix and Big Daddy Kane! I see potential… think about all the crackers that'd come here to lie in the sun and spend money on watered down drinks and private chairs. I could run a resort or some shit. In ten years… I'd be a fuckin' millionaire."

Perry laughed. "I know that's right."

"You'd get bored. No friends. No English," Juice said to Love.

"Ha! I'm more bored doing those damn runs every morning with Lt. Cardio. Besides, why would I wanna go back to where I'm just a normal guy, slaving away for some other motherfucker who's fighting someone else's war? We all getting fucked and not one of us never cumming. Living a dream that ain't ours. No one rich, but most of us ain't poor enough to be allowed to die. What's the point of all that fuck-shit?"

"So, you have no reason to go back?" Perry asked.

"I mean, my old earth… And I got a shorty back home. But, pussy is pussy. Mama Dukes is the only real thing I'd need to fix. *What?* Am I gonna run back home for a broad who probably fucking my cousin Ray-Ray? Shit. I ain't no one-woman man."

"I had woman back in my country. Did not want to leave, but had to leave."

"She a good woman, O'Leary?" Perry joked and tapped the name sewed onto his uniform.

"She beautiful," Juice said. "She was fair maiden. Hair yellow like wheat and skin white like cocaine. She was my love. Ramona. Soft. Elegant. Six-foot tall. Small woman who fit in arms like *konstruktor* blocks."

"Man, what the fuck is *konstruktor blocks?*" Love asked.

I wondered how six feet could be considered little.

"Like blocks that snap together to build squares and long-squares."

"Man, that's Lego."

"Let go?" Juice crinkled his face.

"Le-go. Lego, man! You get little yellow men with hands shaped like Cs and make castles and spaceships. You know, Kremlins and Sputniks."

"In Lithuania, only squares and long-squares."

"Rectangles?" Perry mused.

He shrugged and looked at me.

"I didn't have Lego either, man."

"You ain't never gonna have Lego now, youngin'. You're officially too old for toys." Love turned to me. "How many girls you fucked?"

I dropped my dome. "Uh, none."

"What? But you in high school. I had at least 20, 30 girls by the time I was in senior year. You be getting chin though, right?

"I was getting sucked off once, in an alleyway after school, but a gun went off down the street and the chick almost bit my pesh off. Some thieves in bandanas came booking 'round the corner, jetting from the one-time. The girl got shook and bounced."

"Haha, almost lost his bird," Perry slapped my back. "Well, kiddo, I mean… Listen, man… Obviously, we're getting you laid tonight… if you want, of course. Call it a birthday present."

"You said not to fuck with the locals," I said.

"And you listened?" Perry asked, surprised. "What a good little soldier. The only one. Take notes, you bunch of dirty dogs." He pinched my cheek. "Ah… we'll get you a hooker, kiddo. On me." He fanned out his folding, all ones.

My mug went cherry. It wasn't that I'd never tried to have sex. I was as horny as the next teenage-scumbag, but never went to school or had any time for flipping skirts. Yeah, I bated every night I couldn't hear my ma getting it in before bed, but when I was on the street, I was always trying to make loot. I didn't have any ducats to spend on a broad. I was out there trying to make them.

"That's bullshit, youngin'," Love said, squeaking closer to me on the bench. "There's always time for pussy. I bet the big guy shishkabobs hoes at school, ain't that right?"

Juice nodded, stopped, and said: *"Shishka-huh?"*

Love moved on.

"Ol' captain there's married, so you know he ain't getting none," he joked.

Perry guzzled some rum and tilted his head back to laugh at his own expense. He smacked the table. Some bottles danced to the edge and rolled off. "Fuck you," he wiped a year from his orb.

"So," Love put his palm and long-ass fingers on my head and turned it, "let's get you a ho and get that dick wet."

"Ok then."

"*Alright.*"

His smile was wide like a shark's.

8

SO THIS IS WHAT MEN DO

"I remember my first time…" Marbles began as she transferred her straw to a new drink. "I was 12 and he was around 30. Such a…"

"Pedophile," I said.

"Nuh uh," she said, giving me a stink-face and cuffing my shoulder.

"Yeah," I nodded, "by law, darling. You were a child. He was a loser."

Sofia told me not to judge, but her face wasn't buying what her words were selling.

"He wasn't a loser!" Marbles screeched. "He was a nice, caring, and gentle man. He was my soulmate. Actually, he was my art teacher. We just connected, you know? On a spiritual level. I was mature for my age. And he had a young sense of humour. He was funny. We just got each other."

I knew all Marbles' stories. She always used to tell me shit, back in the day. After we'd fuck. She'd just start telling me random-ass shit about her life. I'd lie there like it was normal, but even *I* found the shit grimy.

"He was funny, huh?" I asked without knowing why.

"Yeah," she responded, her big eyes only half-eclipsed by her eyelids in anger. "He was. He was charming and had something you don't have. *A fucking heart.*"

"How'd he put the moves on you?"

"He didn't put any moves on me, asshole! He said that I was artistic and beautiful, and that he'd love to paint me in the most natural way possible."

"Naked."

"Yes, obviously."

"A twelve-year-old. Naked."

"I really don't like how you're saying that," she said.

"I really don't like saying it," I shot back.

She gave me that *I'm frustrated* look. A hate-filled look. A *fuck-you-but-still-want-to-fuck-you* look.

"Hey, Marbles," I said. "Why don't you tell Sof what happened to, uh…"

"Mr. Foley."

"Sure. First name?"

"Can't remember. Started with a D I think…"

"Spit," I said.

"Ugh." She made the sound of an old fuck trying to get up from a soft mattress. "He went missing."

"Oh my goodness…" Sofia said. I laughed. "You know… you *were* the victim…"

"He was! He got fired! He didn't deserve that… We were in love."

"He seduced you," Sofia said while touching Marble's mitt. "You were too young to…"

Marbles pulled her paw away. "Fuck that and fuck you! He got fired for no reason. They suspected things, but never proved it. He got depressed. He wouldn't let me come over anymore. Then, just like that, he was gone. They never even found him! Never seen again!" She sniffled for a second, then turned to me. She squeezed the neck of my shirt and looked deeply into my eyes. I didn't see rage. "Fuck you." I thought she was going to kiss me. She let go. "I gotta call my husband."

She stormed off, bumped into a chair, and stumbled towards the pay phone. She was corked and about to have a fight. She did like older men. She liked me. And her husband had some years on me, too.

"She's a little sore," I said.

"You two have quite the history, don't you?" Sofia asked.

"Yeah, you could say that."

"Get the fuck off the phone, you fucking quack!" Marbles shouted at Mason. He finished his jawing quick-fast, ducking under the cocked fist that she was brandishing. "You've been on there for over an hour, you son-of-a-bitch!"

I looked over at Juice. He was cooling at the entrance, watching and smirking.

"Anyways, you were telling me about this Lt. Perry, James?" Sofia asked.

"Yeah."

"And about how Richard was there, too?"

"That's right."

She got Preacher's attention and called him over.

"Richard, what do you know about this Lt. Perry?"

"He was a good man," Preacher sniffled. "I was very sorry about what happened to him. If only…"

I bit my licker. I lowered my mitt before it turned into a fist and slammed through the bitch's fronts. The drugs had melted Preacher's brains into tapioca. Mashing him up would be like beating the brakes off a blind puppy.

I'd wanted to murk Preach and leave his body parts hanging from different lampposts for long-years. Less now. Time softens. Anger fades. Some desires drain away the longer you wait. Some. If you let it, time eases the savage.

Or maybe I'll choke him with the dirty-ass collar he wears on Sundays one of these days.

The jury's still out.

"What happened to him?" Sofia asked.

Preacher started sobbing. He did the sign of the cross and mumbled some prayer to himself. Bitch-ass kept crying.

I asked for a glass of dark rum. *How dark, Sof?* Dark as a dead match on a dark, moonless night in the deep, dark guts of the jungle.

The boys took me, and I suppose themselves, to a massage parlour. We were big-faded. The two-minute walk took *a lot* longer. I wasn't sure that my dick would work properly with all that booze and weed.

I remember being led to a greezy whorehouse, propped in between Perry and Love like I was being dragged off the field. Football or mine.

I remember them jawing about whether me fucking a ho would be a good way for me to lose my virginity.

I remember Love jawing about the fact that the first broad he'd tagged had been a crackhead named Rusty Claire.

Everything shows up in choppy flashes after that.

A chorus line of brown-fleshed broads lined up for my choosing.

Love picking for me and following, or leading, me up some stairs to the individual rooms.

The 'doors' being curtains and the 'walls' being deli-sliced panels of cheap wood that warbled in and out when you breathed.

A broad taking me to a room by my mitt and stripping me down.

A dark room with weak light leaking in from the hall, over the door that didn't reach the ceiling or the floor.

Being told to lie on my back.

Getting squirted with oil and rubbed and poked in the taint with a ghetto-long fingernail.

Someone bouncing on my cock.

I don't know whether I even remember that shit or just made up the memories. Both are possibilities.

Coming to with a thin, stain-spotted sheet glued to my gut and inner-stem. Naked.

A window with a threadbare curtain that did nada to keep the morning sun out.

Alone. Quiet as truth.

It took me more than a minute to get myself less than a quarter together. My poor brain was pounding the sides of my skull like the shit had shrunk in the wash. I got my gear, got dressed, and got the fuck out of there.

I'd like to say that I walked out of the door with my dick swinging like a job well done. Nah, I had no idea what had happened and my head was bumping. All I knew was I was greasy, sticky, and my plums smelled like pickle brine.

Guess I'd fucked.

I opened the door with neither my shirt nor pants buttoned. I saw Juice propped up against the wall, snoring. His stems were twice as long as the narrow-ass hallway and bent at the knees like a sleeping giraffe. I jostled him with my foot.

"You done?" he snorted. His voice was alert after a quick, sharp yawn. His eyes kicked open. "That took long time."

"Think so." I answered. "You wait here all night?"

"Make sure no one kill or rob you."

"Only the booze, man… My head's fucking killing me."

"You are hangover?"

"Like a motherfucker. Worst I've ever felt. I don't even remember fucking or getting fucked or none."

"You will live."

I used both branches and barely got him up.

"How're you not feeling rough?" I asked.

"I no feel great. Not worst. Most of it from bad sleep."

"Goddamn. We drank so much. I done drank, but I'm fucking wrecked. I want to die. How're you ok?"

Juice paused. "You ever drink so much and have so bad ache in head you no remember killing a man?"

"…No."

"Pussy," he said.

The streets were empty. It wasn't normal not to see a flurry of little black heads going to the market to pick through fruit and vegetables. It wasn't a Sunday or a holiday or anything. The little town was dead, it seemed, for no reason.

"Spooky," Juice said.

"Ye…" I started, lighting a dart. My hands refused to steady. The flame wiggled. Two flames, as I saw them.

We bent the corner to the main drive.

Something loud crackled from a distance. Something else fast zoomed by, tearing through the air. A sharp crunch came from behind us. Chunks of concrete sprayed against the back of our necks.

Whatever *it* was had knocked the cherry off my dart. Juice collared me and swung me back around the building.

More shots followed, biting divots out of the corner and denting the pavement.

"Fuck's going on?" I asked, puffing on my unlit dart.

"Get gun," Juice said with his glock held like prayer-hands.

Bap. Bap.

He answered with a couple of blasts. I saw two cats scrambling on the roof of a two-story. It looked like he'd hit someone.

"I've got bad feeling," he said.

I answered by vomiting.

A crushing hangover makes most-everything a hundred times harder. Who knows how those suckers in the Nam did it way back… getting toe-up heavy on liquor every night to drown out the nightmares, only to wake up the next morning and do it all again. I guess they did have sweet, delicious heroin to ease their pain. *Lucky fucks.*

We hustled through the old colonial neighbourhood, lunging and legging past low-rent snipers and firing back with the few rounds we had.

I killed my first man that day.

He was a young-looking cat with a machete. He tried at us from behind while we were taking cover behind a corner. I turned and shot. *I didn't even think twice.* His head snapped back. He faltered, then hit the ground. Mug first, sliding to a dead stop. A pool of blood immediately started crawling out from under his dome.

We didn't know what the fuck was going on and took a round-about way back to camp. If they were waiting, we weren't letting them get the drop on us. We agreed that hitting them from the side would be the perfect play. *Fuck did a couple of privates know?*

We were coming from where the hippy-fucks had been squatting. We figured they might've seen something. Unfortunately, all of them were hanging from trees by their necks. Some had their limbs ripped off and hung like shoes from the powerlines in my old hood.

Preacher wasn't there.

The islanders had been given the same treatment. Men, women, and children. Some had their eyes poked out and tongues sliced off. Looked like it'd probably been done before they ghosted the way their mugs were all twisted-up in fright, mid-scream.

Seeing dead kids is depressing. Kids are innocent. Beautiful. Pure. Things we live to protect. I'd never been one for sparing men, or even women for that matter. If you can kill me, I can kill you back. *I've always been an equal rights kind of scumbag.* But kids? You don't fuck with kids.

Still, no Preacher.

The tide had fucked off a while ago. We could see fresh-enough footprints in the wet sand leading towards our camp. Lots of disorganized, barefoot tracks. There were more than a couple of them. We knew we didn't have enough of anything to take on another platoon. We didn't even know who we were up against. On the plus side, my hangover had turned into a headache and an appetite for blueberry pancakes, even though I'd never had them before. And murder. I got a taste. I liked it. *I wanted to kill, real-bad.*

We kept it moving, low and slow. Then, we saw our camp from a distance. It'd been taken.

Later, we learned that it had been seized by rebels and that the Philippines was going through an uprising of some kind. None-to-do with *our* war, or whatever you call it. They had their own shit going on. No idea what it was all about. Word had spread that we were there. They reckoned we'd come to help their government take care of them. Jokes on them, because we didn't know a goddamn thing about their politics. *Yup. Jokes on them.*

Some of the loincloth-wearing motherfuckers that Preacher had been *'converting'* ended up being rebels: in disguise, on the lam. They'd been hiding on the island, posing as bushmen to avoid getting their asses strung up by the army or police.

Preacher, that bitch, had led them to our base and stash. They'd watched, waited for us to leave, raided the pantry, and lynched some hippy-fucks and savages for style points.

I mean, as far as plans go, it wasn't bad. *Credit where it's due.*

I counted 15. Juice counted more. We were outnumbered. Bad.

Our boys were stripped down to their drawers, kneeling, their mitts tied behind them. They had burlap sacks over their domes. I clocked Love from his gangly limbs, folded over each other the way a horse sleeps. I clocked Perry's hemisphere-wide shoulders, lifting and falling with some slow, silverback-like breathing. Even with a bag pulled over his dome, you could tell that he was fucking pissed.

One cat was being led with a blaster pressed into his back. They ripped the burlap sack off his wig and cut the rope from his wrists. He immediately started rubbing them. *Fucking Preacher.* A rebel yelled commands at him. If I had to guess what they were saying, they were asking if there were any more of us. Being us. Being me and Juice. They were probably wondering whether we had any way of getting off the island, which we didn't. We had a motorboat, but that wouldn't get anyone far. We hadn't filled up the tank after our last rip.

They executed a couple of our men. Shot them blindfolded through the backs of their melons. *Fucking Preacher.* I can't remember their names, but they were bodies we could've used in the fight. Each died the same. *Bap.* Then stiff. Then limp. Then lying still forever. Fucking Preacher was waving his arms and pleading with the rebels, holding his crucifix towards them. He ate a few backhands and a pistol-whip for his protests.

"What're we going to do?" I whispered to Juice.

"Wait," he said.

"I was so scared. They killed Rogers and Winfield," Preacher said with his head down. "It was all my fault."

"I'm sure it wasn't your fault, this would…" Sofia began.

"Nah." I shook my head. "It *was* his fault. If he hadn't mangled his little brain with all them psych-drugs and shit with them hippy-fucks, he…"

"Don't blame the LSD," Preacher adjusted himself. "We did lots of drugs. The philosophers brought a lifetime's worth! A veritable cornucopia of mind-altering ambrosia. One of the philosophers was a professor of pharmaceuticals. Another of chemistry. I just… I got too distracted. I lost my way, my shepherd. I thought I was dealing with a naïve bunch of islanders in need of worship. Most were, but there were wolves amidst the sheep. I didn't fully understand what was going on. Neither did the other philosophers. Some of whom had studied the locals and decided that their way of life was better."

"Dope fiends," I said.

"Blaspheme! The drugs are neither here nor there! The rebels slaughtered the islanders. They basically eradicated the remaining indigenous habitants. I thought I was breaking through, but they took my kindness for weakness. If only…"

"*Actually*, LSD doesn't have an *immediate* effect on a person's ability to rationally analyze a situation. It's a very interesting compound. It takes a long time for the drug to permanently affect a user's psyche. However, yes, that is possible after prolonged or even a single use. It really depends on how the chemical interacts with the individual's mind!" Mason threw in.

He'd sidled over with an empty mug after being kicked off the phone.

"I'd *love* another refreshment, but I *must* run to the lab," he said to Sofia. "If I could…" He gestured for the check with a flourish and big-smiled at me. I stared at his missing front. He tongued the hole.

"Yeah. I don't know what to say to that." I shrugged. "Shit happens… you can't let yourself get run down by what could've happened or could've been stopped. It happened. You push it down and keep going. Try to get over it, which you won't, but don't never forget it. Keep it like a roll of quarters in a tight-wrapped fist and spaz…"

"Things do happen, yes. And you can't change the past, true. But you have to address these things, James," Sofia said.

"I'm talking now, ain't I?"

Sofia blinked slow, nodding while she wrote up Mason's check.

"I tried to barter for the release of the prisoners," Preacher said. "I'd never seen a dead person, or someone get killed. It was… horrific. They just wouldn't listen. Oh, it was terrible. The bludgeoning, the chopping, the killing, the blood, the screams, the look in their eyes… They were making demands to no one in particular. It was like they'd gotten to a certain point and didn't know what to do after."

"Not the brightest bunch of fucks," I said. "Sorry for cussing," I said to Sofia.

"It's quite alright James," she said. "Can you tell me what happened next?"

"Preach, you finna tell her?" I smirked like an asshole.

"N-no…" He looked at the bottom of his glass while he sipped his beer.

"And a great night to you all!" Mason sang. He whipped his lab coat around like a cape and dashed off.

After it got dark, we tried to improve our position. A game of inches. *Keep down, keep quiet.* Bit by bit. They'd lit a fire and found what booze we had left. An hour after it went dark, the bastards were soused. Lightweight motherfuckers. Sky high like they'd won the pennant or something. Our boys were still on their knees with sacks over their heads, wincing whenever the rebels popped shots into the air. Screaming gibberish in high-pitched voices. They'd armed themselves to the teeth. They were wearing our fatigues, playing music, and having a gay old time.

One of theirs came towards our direction to take a shit. He was wearing Juice's greens, but three of him couldn't have filled them out. He was stumbling, partially from the booze and partially from the oversized fatigues that made him look like a little boy playing dress up in his daddy's work clothes. He was holding a bottle of vodka and dropped it into the sand while loosening his pants. In one move, Juice jumped up and chin locked him. I couldn't see anything but the flash of metal buckles dancing. Then, I heard a noise like a twig snapping and Juice say: "Just like chicken."

We fleeced his bitch-ass for an assault rifle, handgun, cutter, and to our delight, a motherfucking grenade.

"I have plan now," Juice said, drinking whatever vodka was left in the bottle. He swished the shit in his grill like mouthwash before gulping it back.

"Uh huh," I responded, feeling bile rush to my tonsils imagining the taste of booze.

We decided that Juice would take the rifle and I'd take the handgun. We'd lob the grenade and try to wipe as many of them off the planet as we could. Then, buck them down while they stood-stuck or scattered from the boom. It was simple, sure, but you come up with something better in the time it takes to sneeze.

Can't do it, can you?

"It felt like big championship game," Juice told me when we got home. "When you go for three-pointer at final whistle and after ball leave the fingers. You hear nothing. Can't guess, only hope. No control. No sound. Only hours of practice. Trust that all the free throws and the luck will happen at same time. Your hand stay in position for scared of moving it back down. You just waiting. You just watching. Can't taking eyes off. Like the baby in the woman. Floating in black nothings, just slave to gravity and the ball in the airs."

Quite poetic for his English at the time.

He snugged the tip of his trigger-finger in the ring, ready to lob the grenade like a buzzer-beating bucket. We'd jawed about where to land it: I said at the tent, he said at the fire. We didn't want to blow the limbs off our homies, but there weren't a lot of big-sexy choices, like a small-town bar at closing time. We weren't sure how big the blast would be. *What if the fucker was dead?* Good as a thrown rock.

A bunch of them pricks had posted up in and around the tent. Preacher had shown them how to use the radio. They made him make demands to lord knows who and scanned the channels for their comrades. Then, they told him to get the man in charge. He brought their leader over to grab Perry. *That was our moment.*

"Just make sure you throw it far enough," I said.

He clicked his fronts.

Juice pulled the pin and chucked the grenade. I lost it in the blackness, but Juice knew where it would end up. I followed his gaze.

It wasn't dead. It worked just fine, and his throw had more than enough sauce on it.

It landed at the opening of the tent and boomed. I jumped. If I'd had any liquid in me, I would've pissed myself. The boom was past-decent. Had things gone differently for Juice, that mother-fucker would've definitely made the League.

The sound of the blast was hanging in the air when he took off. I trailed behind him, biscuit on some ready-aim shit.

I can't say how many we got in the end. A clutch of them had twigs and stems blown off their bodies. It was raining goo and gore. It was too dark to tell, but I guessed that the shit pissing and sprinkling down on my mug was red, because I knew it was guts. It enraged the fire some and put flames to both leaders. Cats were running like deer. The rebels screamed and blasted caps with no targets. Couldn't have helped that they'd been big-in-the-cups.

We sieged. We shot. We killed.

I checked on our men while Juice cleaned up the rest of theirs. In the light of the fire, their eyes were big-opened like Marbles'. I picked up a few more kills. The air filled with Juice's gunfire and the shrieks of quickly-deaded enemies. *Fucking gorgeous.*

"I not know if I get all, but I get a lot," Juice said.

We stepped to their leader. He had his branch around Lt. Perry's neck and a gat to his knot. They were both dripping. They'd dived into the ocean to rinse the fire off their gear. Preacher stood stupid and shell-shocked but was still able to translate with his broken *whatever-language-it-was.*

"Tell him to drop Perry," I said.

The cat answered, through Preacher, that he wouldn't. I couldn't understand the shit he was jawing, but I don't need an interpreter to clock a *nah* when I see one. Or a stutter. *They sound the same in any language.*

The blast had murked two more of ours. Only a scared-shitless Love was left, still on his knees, shaking alongside a hostage-collared Perry and a pants-pissed Preacher.

"Preacher," Perry said calmly and gruffly, "tell him I'm the leader and to take this fucking bag off my head. We'll talk. Tell him I'll give him what he wants."

The rebel leader was shook-as-fuck. His orbs, his sweat, and his trembling said it all. He needed an out. Perry was throwing him a bone.

160

The leader took the sack off Perry's dome. Perry blinked, stretched his jaw, turned to the rebel leader, and latched his pearls onto the cat's neck. With his arms still tied, he took down the leader like a rottweiler and came up with a jaw full of something. He dropped his dome onto the cat like a hammer on a stubborn nail. The rebel's head was either missing or buried in the sand.

"Get gone," he said dazedly as he spat the chunk he'd torn out of the cat's neck into the light of the fire. *"Get these fucking ropes gone right fucking now."*

I cut him free and he hugged me, big-palmed with a single pat.

I caught Preacher with the corner of my orb. He was belly-crawling away, crying.

I got Love out of his ropes too. "What the fuck just happened?" he said while tearing the sack from his dome. He looked around, blind and stunned. "Fuck this!" He swung his mitts wild-like at no one in particular. Juice dropped his rifle and bear-hugged him. Love began to sob. "This is bullshit, man. I don't want to fight other people's battles no more. I'm done."

We regrouped and put out the fire. It was old school, passing buckets to each other from the mouth of the ocean. We couldn't get it all. Eventually, we just watched the wood and whatever else burn until it turned into crisp, black dust.

"Where *is* that Preachy motherfucker?" Love asked as he head-counted four of us.

"He's right…" I pointed to where I'd seen him last. He was gone.

We followed two sets of footprints around what looked like a dragged body, leading away from our base. A hurried motor echoed in the distance.

Perry had a pair of binoculars and followed the bubbling trail of our little power boat. It was ripping away under the moon's rippling tongue on the wavy black ocean.

"Fuck him. Bitch. Let him get whatever his ass gets," Love swatted at an invisible fly.

"Nah," Perry said, lowering his binocs. "That bitch is coming home with us."

Perry led us back to what was left of our camp. Gulls squawked as the sky lighted with a reddish tint. We dropped our knots and sighed at the smoldering bones of our tent. The lieutenant kicked an ammo box, blackened like the bottom of a crack-pot.

"We'll wait," he said, rotating his wig in pain, "salvage whatever you can." He paused. "Tell me there's booze left, for Christ's sake…"

***

"What is your plan?" Juice asked as we walked carefully on the soft, wet planks of the docks. They dipped dangerously when we walked beside each other.

"I've got something in the cooker."

"There are million ways to die, Feb. It's harder to live. You better have great plan to do this."

"You doubt mans? Shit. I could think up two million plans, plus… But no… you don't want *no one to die*."

"*Better* if no one dies. But I rather them die than you die."

"That's the sweetest thing you've ever said to me, homie."

"But… for serious, what is your plan?"

I told him what I had so far while trying not to slip on the slick wood under my boot.

"A mob bank? For real? That's your plan. I know that's not your strong suit, but…"

"Yeah, why?"

"All the gangsters I knew used mattresses, offshore accounts… record labels and nail salons."

"It's old school, but so is he. Catholics, homie, they hate change. Plus, I need the head honcho himself to take notice. What else am I gonna do? Steal quarters from his laundromat? Walk out on a bill at one of his restaurants? Nah, I'll go where he *has* to see me. That'll get his attention quick-fast."

"You will do what in the bank? Rob it?"

"It'd look big-nice on my resume. But then… the pigs might come if the goons don't get the call first. Lord knows mans ain't want to deal with them dick-sucker pigs. Shit. I might catch a hole in me before I get to D'Antonio. Nah, I got a better idea."

"Okay…" he said. "We're here… This is it."

We stood in front of a trawler boat tied off at the end of the dock. The slats were slimy, misshapen, and frayed at the ends like meth-fiend hair, wheezing and cracking at certain spots.

The boat looked like a shot up bulletproof vest. Rust was wrestling the hull from the skeleton out, cringing anything that had once stood upright. I fingered a few holes at the side of the bough. They felt like bullet. The whole thing was tilted like a dive bar pool table. The fender tyres were worn away and broken like curb-stomped pearls. The mooring rope was crunchy and brittle, coiling in a blistered, sludgy heap at our feet.

We heaved ourselves aboard, climbing a new-looking metal ladder. As we landed, a cat in all black with a sexy sniper rifle put a red dot on my head.

"Speak," he said. He seemed quite at ease. He knew he was in control.

"I'm here to see Davydov. It's about a passport."

Juice muttered something to the guy in Russian.

The guy kept his eyes on me. He lowered his gun and resumed chewing what must've been a refreshing piece of gum. He breathed out his beak, banged on the door heading to the bottom of the boat twice, and turned the handle. His mug never changed.

We were still for another second, waiting for a definite sign.

"Go, go," he said, tossing his head towards the entrance.

"I have been waiting for you. Mr. February? Yes?" an older's voice with a Russian accent said from behind a thin-paneled closed door at the bottom of the stairs.

"Word," I said. I opened the door. "Feb's fine."

The place was all shadows and had a vinegary locker room must.

The window above the cat's head was blacked out with a piece of cardboard duct-taped around the edges. He was sitting on the edge of a bare twin mattress with a little card table in front of him. There were boxes of ID cards and booklets of forged documents by the hundreds on wall-to-wall shelves. Sheets of cellophane and metal badges were in shoe boxes scattered on the floor. There was a chrome-wire storage shelf with plastic bottles full of skull and crossbones and corrosive symbols, as well as a puddle of dirty rags and gasmasks beside that.

"Good." He gestured for us to come in further. "Close door."

A soft-bulbed lamp with a dark shade barely lit the room and only illuminated the pointed snout and sharp chin of the older's hatchet-faced mug.

"Do you have the money?" he asked. He was so white that he looked green.

"Cash rules," I said.

He counted it in front of me. *I've always been torn by that move.* On the one hand, you want to be sure that the motherfucker's handing off enough loot. They might short you, depending on who you're dealing with. At the same time, there's something ratchet about it.

What, I can't be trusted?

Anyways, you can tell a lot about cats by the way they handle a bag of cash tossed at them. Quick-fast, you can peep their confidence in the relationship you have. If your name's good, they won't count it. If they trust you, they won't count it. If it's too big a bag, they'll have some broad run it through the money counter while you have a drink and jaw business. Nobody wants a hand cramp. But these back-alley types that pull abortions and fake passports? Oh, those fucks will count two nickels in front of you. Twice.

"All here," he said, nodding and rifling through the loot like a deck of blue-back Bicycles.

"I know."

"Here is," he stated. He tossed me the passport.

He counted my loot, so it's only fair that I checked the motherfucker's work.

It looked good. Real good. The birthdate was random. The expiry date was a few years from that day. The picture was the one I'd put in the envelope and handed off to some knife-cheeked anemic behind a deli a couple of days earlier. The name was…

"J… Joseph January?" my voice inflected.

"Yes, is name like yours. Different month. It good. You like."

"A bit on the nose, ain't it, Pavel?" I asked. "Fucking playing me?"

"You no look like a Luba Grigorenko."

"Alright, but… January? Couldn't rock with Jones or Smith or Williams? You corny."

"It good. It work. Trust. You like."

The smell of the room was giving me sinus pain.

"Fine," I said. I saw him reaching under his mattress. As much as I would have loved to, I didn't have time for a gun fight. We turned and walked out.

Juice asked me about my plan again.

166

"I'm gonna case the joint. Get enough face time so that he sees me on the camera. Mans might even catch some old opps hanging around and break a shoulder for attention. Otherwise, I'll sweet talk a cat on the inside. Or, I'll kidnap one of 'em. Or, I'll walk in waving a heater, on some wild shit like: *Where the big boss at?*'"

"Flimsy, no."

"It's a start."

Up the dock, up the jetty, and up to the loose gravel road. We got into the cab. Me in the front, Juice in the back. I'd promised to bring it back to Crooked Mo with a full tank and break him off for the lost business. I'd left the meter running the whole time.

"And then what will you do?" Juice asked. "Once you have old man's attention."

"Then, the second part of the plan comes in."

"Which is?"

"Do my damndest to make sure that no one innocent gets hurt… while I kill the shit out of him."

9

THE GOOD LIEUTENANT

The radio took a lumping from the grenade blast. It wasn't dead, but it wasn't working well enough to tell whether we were sending an SOS to our team or some villager in the water spearfishing for tilapia. We waited for daylight and armed ourselves as best as we could. The rebel-fucks had wasted big-ammo on celebrating their soon-come massacring.

Blood was dried on the sand and made little balls that you could break apart with your fingers. If shells were gold, we'd have been rich. You couldn't lift your boot without kicking some casings with a foot-full of sand. We left the dead rebels to curl up in the sunlight like cooked prawns. They could keep our fatigues. Our time at war could *get gone*, as the lieutenant would say.

We buried our dead. The shallow graves got shallower each time. Perry had some nice words for the murked ones. I don't remember what he said, or their names. *I ain't care, you don't care, no one fucking cares.* I had blood on the brain and murder on the mind.

"Let's get the fucking God-man," Perry said.

Love asked to stay. He'd had enough.

He thought he could fix the radio. I called him a coward. Juice didn't care. Perry said nothing. Just flared his nostrils with every grunting breath, sharpening his blade against a stone with one pissed off stroke after another. Sparks were spitting off. His orbs were staring off over the water. He was real sore, looking like he wanted to gut Preacher himself.

Us privates were rocking our gear from the night before. Perry was in his boxers because his gear had been burned off. He rummaged through the tent and found a half-burned, blowy cabana shirt and singed, beige cargo shorts. We were all filthy as a motherfucker.

"The Filthy Fatherless Fucks," Perry chuckled. "Wish I had me a camera."

The lieutenant grabbed a map that had survived in a fireproof stashbox. He figured there was only one island the rebels could've scrammed to. The boat barely had any gas. The extra tank was, at that moment, in his gorilla-like fingers as he lit a dart.

"They couldn't have gotten far. They're scared shitless. The pathetic little fucks. My guess is this island right here." He pointed. "We'll take the banana boat the locals used and paddle up. Good? Good!"

"Then what?" I asked.

"Easy." He took a big pull that ate up half his cigarette and held it like an idiot does a stupid opinion. "We fucking kill them. Fuck it. All of them. Then, we hope motherfucking DeMarcus

Marconi gets the stupid fucking radio fixed and we get the fuck out of this shithole."

"Yeah," Love said. "I think I can get her up and running."

I didn't know who Marconi was. I pictured a statue of a man made of macaroni. I wasn't even thinking about going home, but I was ready to get the fuck out of there.

We were in agreement: *Fuck it. Kill 'em all. Every last one.*

We took a long outrigger canoe from where the rebels had slaughtered the locals and the hippies. I heard one of those old hippie-fucks, lynched by his neck with a horror-gaped mouth, telling me in a *know-it-all* voice that he rides a unicycle around his university campus because of the health benefits and that it was easy to use because of the balance he got from doing yoga every morning at 5am on the terrace. *God damn.* Even their ghosts were dickheads. I'm not proud of this, but I shot at his corpse, dangling from a tree. It swayed and squeaked the branch. Perry said not to waste ammo. I felt bad. It shut his ghost-ass mouth up though, quick-fast.

Me and Juice paddled as the lieutenant sat at the tapered front of the boat rotating between pinching the bridge of his nose and engaging us in squinting, upper-lip-curled-in jawings.

"Good luck charm, my ass," he said, leaning in. "When I get my hands on that fucking…" He began a few of those kinds of jawings, always ending with him leaning back and whispering *'nah'* or *'get gone'* to himself to dismiss the thought. It was like he didn't know whether he should worry about getting us home or his get back.

We rowed as smoothly as we could. I was struggling to keep up with the big man's long-ass strides. We worked a system out in the early going to make sure that we didn't turn in a circle like some kind of broken-winged duck in a pond.

"This would be my idea of paradise in another time," Perry said, licking the yellow strip of his hand-rolled dart. "This is the kind of peace and solitude you can't really pay for. The sun that only islands get. The wind that you have to be in the middle of nowhere to feel against your face. The peace that only open ocean affords you. The quiet that being away from the wife and phone…" He trailed off and lit his dart. "Too bad it came with having to bury our men and getting sneak-attacked by a pussy-ass militia. This would've been a near-perfect vacation if that shit hadn't happened."

I was too tired to answer. I lifted my wig just to let it fall back down again. The sun was kicking the shit out of me. I hadn't really slept or even drank a damn glass of water in days. I felt twenty pounds lighter, even though my arms and legs felt a hundred pounds heavier. I could smell the cummy ball odour leaking through my pants.

"Boys, what are your plans when you get back home?"

Me and Juice both shrugged and kept rowing.

"Aw, come on boys. Gotta be something you guys got worth living for. Don't tell me you want to do another tour under these aliases."

"No," Juice started. "I want make sure my sister is safe."

Perry nodded. "A good brother you are. Then what?"

"I not know. I take job with gang if they tell. I prove loyalty. They ask me work, I say yes. Get back them when time right." His English always got sloppy when he was tired back in the day.

"I see," Perry said.

"What about you, kiddo? You *still* want to keep on with the Mafia?"

I almost laughed. "Don't really think that's an option, lieutenant."

"That's good, that's good."

"Well, the whole sticking my mom in the back of the head, putting me on a bus, and sending me to war thing was a bit ultra, you know? I'd be surprised if they let me live, more than anything."

"Oh…" His mug dropped. I hoped he wasn't about to say some reassuring shit. "Ok… Assuming they don't park a bullet in your skull, what'll you do?"

"I ain't thought about that. Not much of a future-thinker."

"Can't blame ya. Who thinks about the getting home part while they're on vacation? You poor kids."

The ocean was chill enough to hear the rowing and his dart sizzling as he sucked on it.

"No way they're keeping us here after this. If they even remember we're out here, that is. Shit like this gets you sent home in a hurry. We don't even have tents or clothes. Or booze. And… let's face it. We're not contributing a whole hell-of-a-lot to the cause. All vacations have to end sometime. That is, once again, if they even remember we're fucking out here."

Got to hand it to the guy. His platoon murdered and kidnapped, his base of operations torched, and his clean sheet for cannibalism corrupted… the lieutenant was still in good spirits.

"Either of you boys ever think about joining the military for real? Under your actual names?"

Neither of us responded with any jazz in our trumpets.

"Sure, it's a lifestyle, a commitment… After this, especially… I don't blame you." He flicked at the water outside the boat. "Feb, given any more thought to police work?"

"I don't wanna be no pig. I mean, cop," I said.

"Why not?" he asked.

"I told you. Where I come from, we don't like pigs. I mean cops. We don't respect them. We hate them even more than our rival sets."

"That's fair. But you like me, and I'm a cop."

"Well," I rolled my head, "I guess there are some good ones out there. Maybe."

"For sure. I mean, there are lots of assholes. You get assholes every-where. Asshole cashiers, asshole doctors. But there are also some of the best men I've ever met in my life. You just gotta know, you know? Get a feel for who's good and who's not. You get a pension and can legally shoot people… if you have to… as a last resort. I'm not condoning that behaviour. Unless you have to."

"You ever capped anyone at work?" I asked

"I've never shot a soul in my blues. I don't go and jack someone up for jaywalking or throw the cuffs on them for a roach in their pocket. I'm not one of those disgraceful worms that earns the name *pig*. I fight *real* crime and make the city safer. *That's making a difference.* I can see it in your eyes, kiddo. You want revenge. You think someone like me can't sniff out your desire to get at the guys who got at you like steak to a bloodhound? I can see it. I can taste it in my teeth. That shit will only end up leaving you dead, though. If not on the streets, then in the slam. Those mobsters, they can make it look like an accident. They have connections... It's sad to say, but the system ain't perfect. Life's not always fair."

I didn't answer him. I had the feeling he had more to say.

"You get yourself a badge, shit… You can do the opposite. Do all you can to put *them* on blast and serve *them* notice. I'm not saying the force is built to exact revenge on the people who've fucked with you, far from it. But, if you see injustice and wrongdoing in the world, it's a better way to confront it than going vigilante on every-body's ass. Help the world, not be a victim of it."

"Maybe."

"I got a maybe out of you," he said, clapping his mitts. "Juice-man? You want…"

"Not chance," the big guy said.

"It's alright. Feb, if you ever want, it's a lot easier than you'd think. I can get you an in. Shit, you know how many cops big cities need? Every second man is a criminal in some places. You don't gotta be the purest, noblest motherfucker. These days, ain't no one a saint. Get gone. Hell, some of the cops I know are as bad as the perps. Or worse."

For some strange reason, my ears lifted when he said that.

"Ain't nothing better than going home after a long day, knowing you made a real difference."

He was losing me again.

"Young man, you ever need a place when all this is said and done… you can come stay with me and my woman. Get out of the hood. Join the academy and live out of our basement suite. The wife ain't a bad little cook. And I'm sure we can find you a nice young lady. That's the play! That's the smart move."

"Maybe."

I didn't have anywhere to go. I didn't have a dime on a dimebag or change for a nickel. I wasn't doing a job, I was paying a debt. It wasn't like they'd throw me keys to a crib and a shoe box full of loot for a job well-done afterwards. I'd be going home to less than what I'd had before. Which, if that was even possible, sure as fuck wasn't saying much.

What was I going to do? I had a few ducats in the locker, but then what? I couldn't go back to my old hood and smile at the scumbags who'd taken my life away like antipasto plates. Dropping my neck in public. Sweating out my spine when I hear some tracksuit-wearing motherfuckers a block away. *Yessuh. Nossuh. Fuck that.* Man can live a long life without a lot of shit. Arms. Legs. Some organs, probably. No way I was finna live without my plums. You don't ever get them back. A man without balls can't even kill himself. Just serve life like a bitch, swinging from pocket to pocket. The free man's prison. The tough man's hell.

"Row better," Juice interrupted my thoughts. I was distracted and we'd started to fishtail. "Get out of head."

"Just think about it," Lt. Perry smirked and slapped my knee, "it's not for everyone, but it gives your life purpose, direction… meaning and something to live for."

"How much more far?" Juice asked Perry, who was looking at the map.

"Not far," he squinted and pointed, "that little blip, right over there. Has to be that one."

We kept paddling, slicing the oars beneath the tranquil waves like a straight razor through underbelly.

"You boys don't look nervous. Just eager to finish this thing?"

We agreed without jawing.

Holy fuck, I was tired.

"Me too," Perry said. "I miss my bed. I'm looking forward to a roll with the wife. I'm remembering why I got out of the army full-time in the first place.

He leaned back and lit another dart.

"Bah, I always think like this. I leave fed up and come home missing the ding bat like crazy. Maybe I just need to get laid. Oh, speaking of which… Feb, how was the first time?"

"I don't remember shit. I woke up sticky and alone."

He threw his dome back and tossed his dart into the water. "Lucky boy, that's almost everyone's ideal sexual experience."

"We are closing down," Juice said, taking one of his arms off the oar and pointing.

"Ok. Light and easy strokes, boys." Perry turned and lowered himself into a tiger's prowl at the end of the boat. "I see our outboard. Paddles are in the water. Looks like they ran out of gas and had to get themselves here manually. Perfect. Those skinny rats should be tired. Curve around the right side. Yes, perfect. We'll dock there."

The boat slid up on the shore with the whisper of wet sand spreading to welcome our keel. We hopped off. I could barely hold my gun up. My branches swirled with pain from the wrists to the rotator cuffs like I was still paddling the motherfucker. That must be how birds feel after flying south for the winter.

Perry led the way in his ragged-ass tourist-wear, holding a rifle with one mitt and giving us hand signs with the other. Me and Juice followed him quietly with our biscuits raised. The pound in my mitts weighed a ton.

The island was small, circle-shaped, and thick with jungle. We split up and took our own zig zags that would lead into its heart.

I stepped carefully through the long vines, trying not to break sticks under my boots.

Then, I was hit with a vision.

It started off with me imagining what I'd do to D'Antonio if I ever got him alone. Murdering him. Fast and slow. With an ox, a strap, strangling him, pushing my thumbs into his eye sockets, tearing out his jugular, putting his head on a circular saw, cooking steaks over his bitch-ass... *Normal fantasy stuff.*

See... I wasn't plotting the ways that I *could* get at him, just *how* I'd put it to him. I was empty, angry, and in savage beast mode. It was easier to fantasize about the kill shot, the same way you fantasize about fucking, not the date or the foreplay or the ask-out.

I don't know if the next part was real or a daydream. When I say it out loud, it sounds made up. But it felt as real as you or me or Juice or Cancerface.

Then, they appeared out of nowhere. They might've always been there. Waiting for me.

Three island girls were dancing in a clearing beyond some hanging vines and tree arms. Naked as pagans dancing around a bonfire. Flowers laced into their long, black hair. They were much taller than the locals. I don't know how else to describe them: *They were perfect.* Their bodies looked like they'd been carved with scalpels. The fibres and sinews of taut muscle beneath their tanned leather skin were like beautiful tight bricks of shrink-wrapped coke. Fat bubbled out in all the right places. No sag, no drag. Showing out like Latin broads on the first hot day of the year.

I stood stupid like two dogs stuck. My mug, branches, stems, everything went slack… *almost everything.*

One took a step towards me, curling her finger. I followed through no power of my own.

"Ask us one question, James February," one of them said.

I paused, stunned or past-tired. Her English was better than mine. The situation felt real enough not to question.

"Ask us anything," another said.

"The meaning of life. The secret to happiness. The…" the third chimed in.

"How can I kill the man that killed my mom?"

They danced in a circle with their fingers laced. I got hard watching them. The blood flowing from my knot and filling up my pesh was making me big-dizzy. I should've asked for a line of powder, some Marvin Gaye, and a bearskin rug. But hindsight is twenty-twice, or something like that. The flowers in their hair started to lift and dance.

They were butterflies.

They started to glow in Easter colours, hovering from their wigs. They swirled around, above the broads who'd started to do a ring-around-the-rosy type dance, like a lilac-pinkish storm cloud. Suddenly, the butterflies broke out like a bomb-blast had sent them to some invisible limit. They stopped, returned, and then settled back onto the broads' domes in the shape of crowns.

The broads slowed and stopped spinning. Their eyes were closed. They had frank, serious looks on their mugs. The three of them broke the circle and faced me, still linked by their mitts. Their closed lids snapped open as they spoke.

The butterflies shimmered on one of the broad's melons. She spoke softly. "You must be patient, James February. You must not act with haste or you will surely perish. You must allow enough time to pass for him drop his guard. To forget. To allow your history to become ancient and buried. Focus on preparing yourself until time has ripened *you* and decayed *him*."

The butterflies glowed on the second broad's wig. She spoke in a raspy voice. "You must use the same tactics that were used against you, James February. Do not fear spilling the blood of the innocent in order to drown the lungs of your enemy."

There was a pause before the butterfly-knitted crown on the third broad's head glowed. Her eyes darted back beneath her lids and her knot rotated around her shoulders.

The butterflies issued a potent light. It made me squint. She spoke, serious-like. "There will be moments you may believe were designed for your revenge, James February. However, they will be created to mislead you. To challenge you. Your temper will only lead you down a darker path, should you act on it without forethought. I must tell you with utmost certainty that your vengeance, should you choose such a path, will require both patience and ruthlessness, as my sisters have said. But, heed my words. The moment when you will be able to exact your revenge will not be soon nor easy. There will be tests that will possibly lead to your demise and result in your mission being unfulfilled. This anger, your quest for revenge, and the hate you carry are all-consuming, which only serves to drain your energy and leave you incapable of rational contemplation. Only you control your existence. You must ask yourself: Would you rather live a life dedicated to revenge, or a life that you possess sovereign control over? As you manufacture your destiny, the steps that you negotiate will carry a ripple effect. Should you still choose to carry the cross, I can assure you that *he* will not be your ultimate test. A life of anger and hostility begets more of those outcomes, like moths to flames. There *will* be others. You must choose: *revenge* or *forgiveness*. It will be a long road ahead, and you will face many more challenges. How you handle them will act as the moon to the tides of your existence. Remember this, James February. Do not move with haste, do not half-commit, and… *fuck the shit out of us you scumbag-fuck.*"

"W-what?" I barely understood what that last broad had said until the end, which shook my tired-ass something fierce.

The three wise broads approached me. The butterflies started circling around my head too. The colours were so dazzling that my eyes could barely take it. I closed them tight, but I could still see like my eyes were open. My veins were pumping rainbows and my bones were lit up like an x-ray scan. Everything was making me woozy. I felt warm. Calm oozed into me like syrup on some pancakes. I stumbled. The three of them circled me, or triangled me, and held me up. I felt like I was floating. Two of them went low, while one stayed high. I remember, faintly, that I was trying to recall why I was there in the first place. They unhitched my pants. My pesh was full of blood, vibrating and glowing like an isotope. The head was blooming bigger and wider than I'd ever seen it, like a long-stemmed shiitake mushroom.

Snap.

A bullet missed my head and lanced the tree I'd been leaning on.

I shook my knot and locked eyes with a gunman: 20 feet away, orbs and grill quivering at me, full of fear and no lack of confusion. I had an erect pesh in my paws that was so hard I could have chiseled my name into a slab of granite without using my mitt or a mallet.

He fumbled with his stick. I shot. I hit him in the chest and watched him crumple like a Styrofoam cup in a campfire.

I was close to nutting. I pinched it off. The *flu game* of pinch offs.

I limped over to the cat, trying to tuck my pesh down my pantleg, and aimed the burner at his domepiece. I was about to end him, but stopped.

I booted him in the gut. It was one of those gorgeous kicks where the foot stops but the ankle and toes don't get fucked up. My foot drove a couple inches inside the cat's torso. His organs were like pillow stuffing. I broke at least one of his ribs and made one of his kidneys join the other one. Like I said: *Gorgeous.*

He rolled in agony. I'm not sure if the violence was keeping me hard, but whatever the case, my pesh wasn't shrinking. I stood over the writhing, bitch-made rebel and asked him where Preach was being kept.

He shook his head. He didn't know what the fuck I was saying but was rocking Perry's fatigues. I pressed my burner on his mug. He got the message and pointed *over there*. I dropped the biscuit on his eyebrow and dragged him with me for insurance.

My stiffness finally started to swoll-down. I grabbed the heater the rebel had tried to kill me with and jammed it into my waistband. Still hot, almost burnt my pubes. I kind of liked it. Felt like a fetish I probably shouldn't fuck with unless I wanted to scald my cock off. His head was bouncing off the uneven ground. The cat was going in and out of consciousness, moaning weakly at intervals. I bet the exit wound in the back of his shoulder blade stung something shitty.

I came to a clearing. A prime donut-hole in the middle of the island. I saw the remains of a fire and an emergency blanket rumpled on the ground like the foil of a TV supper that had gotten heated up and eaten in a hurry while standing over the sink. Perry and Juice had their guns drawn on a lone rebel who had Preacher by the throat from behind with a bammer pressed against his melon. *Quite the scene.*

"Tell him what I said, man," Perry lifted his head from his rifle sights to yell at Preacher.

"Ok!" Preacher tried to nod. He said something to the cat holding him hostage. They bantered brokenly for a moment. "He said he doesn't trust you," Preacher called back.

"Yeah," Perry smirked. "I wouldn't either." His eyes dropped back down to the scope.

Preacher's orbs were closed and he was thumbing the crucifix around his neck. His wet, scraggly hair was pressed against his mug. Sweat was dripping from his beard.

I wondered: *Why we gutting it out for this punk? Him? He looks like garbage-Jesus. Fuck him. Shoot them both. Robin Hood his bitch-ass and use one bullet to kill them all! Save us all some ammo and time.*

"Hey, Preach," I hollered, "tell him if he doesn't do what Perry says, I'll kill this bitch." I grabbed my rebel by the cabbage and twisted his head up to the height of my hips.

Preacher's eyes opened. He slowly moved his dome to peep me.

The rebel holding Preacher went pale when he saw his homie in pain, neck all twisted and bleeding from his gut. He loosened his grip on Preacher for a hot second, long enough for shitty-Jesus to duck after the lieutenant hollered *get down!* The second Preacher hit the dirt, Perry and Juice sent a bullet apiece through the rebel's skull. I mercied the cat I'd been dragging. *Sleep now, sweet prince.*

"Preacher!" Perry shouted while he walked towards him. The tops of the palms shook each time his boot smacked the earth. "Are there any others? Preacher! Talk to me, you son of a bitch!"

Preacher's mug was starched. He was on his knees, lost somewhere inside his knotty, greasy wig.

Perry snapped his fingers and shook Preacher by the collar of his grubby jacket. He fell to the ground, pulled his knees to his chest, and started sobbing. He let out high-pitched chirps like old brakes on a wet day.

Juice was still standing where he'd been the whole time, laying in the cut, kicking his boots and scraping the bottoms against a rock sticking out from the soil in silence. He cocked his brow and tilted his dome, making a strained mug like he smelled good cheese or bad kitty. He stared up at the sun through a clearing and scrunched his face even more.

"What?" I strolled over to stand beside the big guy.

"You hearing that?" His beak was pointed skyward.

"Nah," I shook my dome. "What is it? You're closer…"

"Shh," he spat milk-white saliva at my mug. He mentioned the noise to Perry, who was crouched down beside our spaced-out comrade, still trying to rouse his bitch-ass.

"Hmm?" Perry squinted and licked his top lip. "Oh fu…" The lieutenant's eyes opened wide.

The sound went from nothing to someone using an angle-grinder down the block to a head-rattling screech that popped my fucking eardrums. *All within seconds.*

It was hard to tell which came first: the sound of the low-flying jets ripping the air apart or the missiles.

Everyone knows what an explosion sounds like from the movies, but they don't realize what an explosion *feels* like. The deafening, ultra-ruckus that swallows you with static. At some point, you go deaf and stop hearing bombs being dropped, but you feel your insides jiggle every time one falls. Like a fly in a kickdrum, thick and cave-like, too powerful to be real. It *is* real though, because chunks of dirt and human sprinkle on you while you try to pull yourself together enough to flee your stunned-ass out of there.

Swirls of flame became towering tornadoes. Choking blasts surrounded us like we were drowning. Hot breaths of gas blew onto our cheeks from every direction. Dirt and grass spat up from the ground. The earth rippled and lifted like a sheet being fluffed and smoothed out by a hotel maid.

When the checkerboard of fallen trees and scattered crowns had finally settled, flattened, and unwrinkled, I tried to pick my blood-covered ass up off the ground with shaky legs. Like a newborn calf. Like Maria walking to the bathroom to avoid a UTI.

I couldn't get up.

My erection was completely gone.

I breathed in a mouthful of hot dirt and coughed a lungie onto the ground. I couldn't move. I was trapped. Squashed. I thought a tree had fallen on my back.

I stirred and heard a groan come from above me.

"You ok?" Perry, who had frog-splashed on top of me during the attack, asked.

"Think so," I said. "You're crushing me..."

"Built like an ape," he said, trying to wrench himself off me.

I wriggled out, crawled half a foot, and flipped onto my back, trying to get my air sacks past the near-dead wheeze they'd been playing while I'd been trapped under that stocky motherfucker.

I got to my knees. I wanted sleep. Curl up like a fox and tuck myself under the dirt. I looked around.

Juice had pulled a rebel over him like the covers on a too-early Monday morning after a weekend bender in Vegas. His blanket was blackened like Cajun-chicken skin. "Is gone?" he asked. We met eyes and my head bobbed *yes*. I didn't know, but I hoped I was right.

Preacher was balled up like a cum-rag, unscathed, with a single light descending from the battered jungle to illuminate him and only him. For a moment, I saw a halo around his head and the three wise broads walking towards him. Two of them were holding the shoulders of a white robe and the third was carrying a pair of Roman sandals.

I reached for a nearby burner and let off two shots that just missed him and made the broads disappear.

Juice stumbled over and knocked the gun from my hand. He backhanded me a good one. His attention was suddenly prickled by something else.

"You are ok?" he said from a crouched position beside me.

I lowered my mug and saw the lieutenant with a piece of shrapnel driven into his spine. His shirt was fully melted. His back looked like a blood-red tortoise shell, texture and all.

"Don't move," Juice said again.

"Come on, man!" Perry hollered like he was mad at himself. "It's just the skin, like a knee-scrape." He tried to lift himself up and ate shit.

"Can you bring the God-man?" Juice asked me.

I nodded. I finally pushed myself up and felt like I was trying to lift a whole leg of lamb with a cheap take-out spoon. My fatigues were wet with sweat, blood, and maybe piss. I got on my feet.

"Get up," I shoved my foot into Preacher's gut. "Let's get a fucking move on."

He kept lying there, quiet and unblinking.

"Can I leave him?" I hollered over.

Juice was carefully dead-lifting Perry over his shoulders. He got him up like a hunted stag. "No, bring," he said to me. He turned and hiked off.

"Fuck," I uttered under my breath.

"Let us help you get him up," the three wise broads said, appearing like vapour.

"Bend at the knees," said the first.

"Don't strain your back," said the next.

"I'll give him a boost," said the third.

Just like that, Preacher was over my shoulder. Luckily for me, he wasn't the portly bitch he'd started off as, or that he is now. The drugs had left him with little more than bones and rubbery skin. Otherwise, he'd have made a fine supper for the wild hogs or whatever other beasts lived on that island."

"Thanks, broads," I said.

"Bye, Scumbag," they said in unison.

Juice had loaded Perry into the boat. "Shit," he said as I approached with Preacher, "I forget petrol. Hold the minute." He scurried off towards the banana boat, shirtless with scrapes and cuts all over his chest and back.

I dropped Preacher on the shore and moved to Perry. He was hanging over the side of the boat with Juice's shirt laid over him. The hunk of metal sticking out of his back was giving off a tent-pole effect. I tried to lift the shirt to see the damage, but it was a no-go. It was like a grilled cheese had learned to feel pain and let out a harsh cry when I tried to pull it apart. The shit almost knocked Perry out. I left the shirt alone. Red was leaking darkly and dripping from his fingers into the water, leaving the topsoil of the ocean greasy and shiny like sunscreen.

"Feb," he said without looking at me. "Imma die."

"Nah…"

"Get gone, man," he grunted. "Imma die doing what I loved."

"In battle?" I asked.

"Fuck nah. Roasting in the sun like a raisin on some shitty little island," he laughed and spat some blood onto the floor of the boat. "God, I wish I had me some of that rum."

I checked the boat. There was nothing to use to dull his pain, which seemed big-searing.

"Look," he said. "You're young. You've got a long, well, longish life ahead of you. Hopefully. You know what?"

"What's that?"

"Be better, man. Do some good. Yeah, you ain't got nothing, but that's the best way to make something. Anything's better than shit-nothing. You got nowhere to go but up. I know that shit sounds cornball, but… *Listen man*. You got potential. I'm serious when I said that you should be a cop. The ones that go through the worst shit are the best ones for the service. You're not a villain, you're not a heel… you've just had a fucking shit go. I can see it. You got something, I dunno what it is, but you deserve to…" He squinted, licked his top lip, and took in a sharp gust.

"Save your energy, boss," I said.

"For what? So, I can live for five extra minutes?"

"We'll get you out."

Juice stomped over and filled the boat with gas. He tossed the jerry can onto the shore. We ripped the cord and fucked off that fucking island.

10

JUST A KABUKI AFTERPARTY

"Boys," Perry's breaths hissed and he jawed hurried-like. "Do me a favour."

We agreed, save for Preacher, who was sitting dumb and mute on the rear bench.

"Take these," he licked his finger, slid off his championship ring, and gave it to me. He took off his dog tags and gave them to Juice. "I want you both to have something to remember me by."

We said we wouldn't need them because he wasn't going to die. All three of us knew that that was a load of shit. It was a shocker he wasn't dead yet.

"One more thing," he croaked, trying to pivot. His shark-like fin and pain stopped him. "Tell my wife that I loved her. I loved her more than anything. She was the only girl I ever wanted, and

I was over the moon that I finally got her. Yeah I complained, yeah I made it sound like it was when it wasn't, but boys, I loved my wife. Please let her know that, let her know that I'm sorry… and that I wish I could've outlived her." He tried laughing but failed and slumped over the boat. He was too weak to spit. Blood dripped out of his grill and into the water.

Me and Juice clocked each other. We threw eyes at Preacher. We made an agreement. Nonverbal, but binding.

I slid the ring on. It was too big, even for my thumb. Juice wrapped the tags around his wrist and cinched the cable like a bracelet.

We slowed the boat and moved at Preacher. Juice grabbed his scraggly moss. I grabbed his sooty, shoeless dogs. We launched the punk overboard.

"And boys," Perry said, dazed and closer-still to death, "protect the minister. He *did* get us into this, but, some of it was fun. No? Fucking vacations. Have to end sometime…"

He gave up the ghost just like that.

Me and Juice eyeballed each other and groaned. We had no problem, clearly, letting that bitch-ass Preacher perish, but the goddamned lieutenant's dying goddamned wish was to get him home alive.

We hauled him out. He was huffing and chucking up brine. It made a frothy, bloody mixture with the spilt Lt. Perry swishing all over the floor of the boat.

"Woah, guys. Where are we?" Preacher said, soaking and con-fused. "What's going… is he ok?"

A gray vessel cleaved through the water from ahead. Me and Juice gripped-up, not caring. We were done and ready for death. By pirates, or whatever. If we were going out, we'd go out with the best brawl we could put up. Chuck the gats at the ship when we ran out of slugs.

A megaphone spat some jargon I couldn't make out. The ship got close. It was big. They spoke English.

It was a naval boat. It had come to *'rescue'* us. *Finally.*

Our tour had been done for a few weeks. No one had told us. They'd forgotten about their little unit in the South Pacific until Love had radioed for help. The bastard had actually fixed the motherfucker.

They told us that no one was left at the base. Not even Love. All the corpses were buried or burnt. They'd scavenged what they could from the tent, then written us off. Seeing the base and the bodies, they'd wanted get-back. *Not for us,* I assumed. *For ego.*

They'd attacked the island. Not just the one we'd been on, but all the islands near-around. Carpet bombing. Pre-emptive or revenge. Either way, it'd been a quick decision that had killed Perry.

"They questioned us back home. The army tried to say that it was Perry's fault. Said that he'd armed the militants and lacked awareness, or some shit. Treason was mentioned. I almost took a charge. Lost control of my tone like a runaway mine cart. I was saved by Juice holding me back from busting the general in his shit. We *still* covered for Preacher's bitch-ass. We said that he'd been abducted instead of going AWOL. Had PTSD instead of being zonked out on pysch-drugs. He played along without knowing it, he was fucked up… He's *still* fucked up, never came back from all that. Preacher ain't say shit they could make sense of. He rambled on about higher powers and cosmic bullshit 'til they told us all to step."

"What happened to the guy on the radio? Private Love?" Sofia asked.

"DeMarcus Love," I said, small-laughing out of my nose holes. "He found a cat lying toe up in his fatigues, broiled his ass, and went AWOL himself. Story goes that he changed his name and opened a chain of resorts in a few Filipino islands. Motherfucker's probably a millionaire, like he always said. A part of me wanted to ask them if the cat they reckoned was him was 5 feet tall or more of a giraffe than a man… I ain't no rat."

"What about you guys?" she asked.

"Well, this one," I pointed at Preacher, "was given a full discharge and…"

"I was on a spiritual mission from God from there on out." Preacher perked up like he hadn't just heard the story of him leading a bunch of cats to slaughter. "I set to inform the world of my epiphanies. To learn. To practice. To educate. Not only about Christianity, but all religions. To master all the ways in which faith and spiritual healing is…"

"He got home and went straight fiend. Look at him." Preacher had a vacant, *possessed-by-thoughts-outside-this-world* look in his eyes. "He's scrambled, Sof. He's perma-twisted."

"I merely opened my third eye. I don't need the two in my head when my spiritual gateway is in full service. I believe that Lt. Perry had you guys stick up for me because in all his sagacity, he knew that I'd go on to be a spiritual leader, a soothsayer who…"

"Spends his nights spitting crazy-ass theories at The Knowlton and his days in the soup kitchen," I finished.

"I volunteer, yes," Preacher said dryly.

"I meant you and Juice," Sofia clarified.

"Ah, well, that's a funny story…."

Funny… if you, like me, know that justice, right, good, and heroics only win caskets in this fucked up world.

After the war, Sarducci and O'Malley were given top honours in combat and heroism. Not February and Saliamonavicius. We got swept away quick-fast as to not blow up the spot. Those fuckers, the *real* Sarducci and O'Malley we were impersonating, took part in a parade, award ceremony, and even had a movie based on them. *Real fucking war heroes.*

D'Antonio gave me the *Don's Kiss* and said that nothing was personal. It was only business. If I ever needed anything, he'd see what he could do. At a price, of course.

I still had my blades out, but I needed to cool off. The taste for get-back makes venom puddle-up in your jaw like when you're about to eat fries soaked in vinegar. *Shit's deadly.* Better to let it harden. Cold dish, as they say. Turn to cement. Keep it at a distance.

Anyways, everything had a *we'll be seeing each other again* kind of feel. To me anyways. I never had any doubt he forgot about it. About me. Seeing him again was in my power. Whenever I felt suicidal enough, I knew where to go.

You see… The puddle of venom in my jaws wasn't even close to hard. Candlewax, at best. The second I heard his name, I got heated and it was all liquid again.

Me and Juice said fuck it. We didn't care, or at least we told ourselves we didn't. We got out. We did the damn thing and walked away. His sister was left to live and he was left to figure his shit out.

Me? I had more than enough figuring out to do.

We both went to Perry's funeral. The army had called his death, or murder as I saw it, *friendly fire* in the end. *No fire has ever been friendly to nothing or no one, if you ask me.*

We met Mrs. Perry, too. She was a former beauty queen, hard-nosed, elegant, and destroyed by her husband's death. I tried to give her the ring and Juice the dog tags, but she said no. We gave her the box of Perry's things which contained his wallet, complete with his badge, and a faded photo of them as youngers on the island.

What I didn't know was that that motherfucker had written to his wife every goddamn day. *He'd hidden it well.* As tough as he was, as much as he said he enjoyed *getting gone* from his woman, he'd always missed her. He wrote her at first light as part of his daily routine, before our morning runs, sending his letters out in the afternoon.

She was still getting fresh letters. The shit was spooky. Letters from a ghost. Acting like shit was tip-top. He big-liked me. He wrote that I was a hard-done-by, fatherless fuck just like him. You could clock his heart by reading his letters. He wrote about me *a lot*. He wanted to help. He told her that he was going to put me onto the force. Hook or crook type shit. He said that I was angry at the world and needed an outlet, like football had been for him.

"He wrote a letter for you, recommending you to the force," Mrs. Perry said at the reception, dressed all in black. *A little too sexy,* I thought, *but if you got it… you know how that shit goes.*

"He was… a good man." I didn't want to show any emotion. My guts were melting and the tide was rising behind my orbs, so I didn't say more.

"You're a lot like him," she said. "He wouldn't say boo when he was sad. Never wanted anyone to know. But he was a very passionate, emotional man. I loved him deeply."

I nodded.

"Here," she said, handing me the letter. "Take this to the precinct on 18th and ask for Captain Steele."

I said that I would. I wouldn't go that day. I wouldn't go tomorrow. Or possibly ever. It was something, though. Like a stock that I could cash in if I had to. I was only 17. At the time, it still hadn't hit me how fucked up that was. A boy. A motherfucking child. City kids grow up faster, sure, but…

She hugged me and I sunk into her little arms.

I left Juice at the chapel with a pound and a bearhug, half-cut from the booze at the reception, and went to the train station.

The letter said that I was a strong-willed cat who knew right from wrong and had enough experience to make decisions based on my own morals. It said that I was young, but old. I wasn't *there* yet, but shown the steps, I could make it. He wrote better than he spoke, and he spoke pretty damn nice.

Reading his letter brought a tear to my eye. I could blame it on the booze, but *nah.* Now that I was alone, I could afford a bit of face knuckling and fist biting. There's a hideous look that tough guys get when they *almost* cry. An ugly, violent twisting of the mug.

You want to cry like normal folk. You want to bawl like a bitch. But your tears turn to concrete, and those pebbles that want to worm their way out of your orbs and wet your cheeks just won't come out. Your mug looks like a Japanese mask for a hot second, then you break your mitts on a brick wall or push over a phone booth. Then, it gets added to the pile of fuck-shit that made you this way and leaves your heart a little colder than before. Blood doesn't have an easy time warming it up with the veins all frosted. What does all that tough guy shit get you? Dry eyes, busted paws, and a cardiac arrest at 40 like *all-out-the-blue.*

I put the letter and the ring in my locker at the train station. I peeled some cash off the bankroll from the heist and shoved it into my pocket. From a crouched position, I looked at the cold, dead gun lying there. Blood had dried on its handle like fish flakes. The train robbery was an ancient memory now. Felt like another life. *Poor Mario.*

His poor pa... Shit... My poor ma...

I thought for a long while about tucking it into my waistband, heading straight to find D'Antonio, and putting flames to him. *On some crash-dummy-with-a-banger shit.*

Words swirled around my knot. *It was only business*, said D'Antonio's voice. *Be better* and *get gone*, said Lieutenant Perry's. *Fuck the shit out of us you scumbag-fuck*, said the wise broads. I hated that that was all I remembered of their fine asses.

I stood up, closed the locker with the gun inside, and looked around me. No one seemed to be clocking me. No trenched-out goons were eyeing me above their newspapers. No tank-topped greaseballs were peering at me with their arms folded, gnawing on a toothpick and eyeing where to jab the ox between my ribs.

The dogs had been called off. The Gentle Don had kept his word.

I had nowhere to go. No place to be. Nothing to do. No one to call on.

A black coffee appeared in my mitts. I sat on a bench.

17 years old. No ma. No fam. The cats in my hood, if they weren't already locked up, would be too shook to take me on after all this fuck shit. One day-one, but he had his own shit to deal with. I could've asked him to come along, but some shit you gotta do on your own. I'd see him again. I knew it.

I had nothing. I'd lost and lost again. I was big-winning at big-losing. I didn't have an army or the Mafia breathing down my neck and telling me what to do anymore, but most didn't. They had teachers at school. A family. Parents. A mom and dad.

If I'd had a dad, he probably would've told me to tie up my boots and stomp out of there with my head up high. That I should be grateful to be alive and feel blessed to be young.

Shit. If I'd had an old man, he probably would've been a scumbag too. Asking me to slice him off some of my roll and hold his bottle of Thunderbird while he pissed in the alley, all while jawing that he needed *two hands for all that dick.*

So, I sat there. And sat. Don't know for how long. Stunned-stupid. Blank-mugged. In that state, you could tell a cat that his wife had split or his son had died and the most he'd do would be flex a stiff lower-lip, nod automatically, and say some shit like: *'Oh, well that's really unfortunate now, isn't it?*

Every thought I tried to form ended up in a solid gray clump. Like a fog, but thicker. There was no *other side.* A gun laser couldn't have sliced through it. A spiked bat wouldn't have made a dent.

I was alive. Poor and alone, but free. That freedom left me like a spaceman, rocket-shipwrecked and stranded, floating without aim or hope, in endless darkness. Numb. But there's a clarity that being numb gives you. When there's nothing left. No one remaining in your heart. No one to care about. No soul to fuel a single night's dream. No mind left to give for anything but survival.

My coffee went cold in my mitt and my dart burned out on its brown filter.

My mind was nearly blank… except for revenge.

It wouldn't leave. Ever.

It swelled and rang in my ears like a fire bell. I could shut it out with booze and drugs and shit, but it always came rushing back eventually. I told myself that it was a bad look. That it was impossible. That it was suicide.

It didn't matter, though. It never stopped.

Back then, I didn't know how long it'd torment me for. I assumed not long. I reckoned I'd get the chance, sooner than later.

It was like a chorus.

The get-back.

I knew that I was going to kill the Gentle Don one day.

"Oy, Dave," Winston tugged on my shirt. "Dave!"

I'd zoned out again. "What?" I moved my head towards the imp.

"That man, over there in the tan overcoat… that man's asking to see you, Dave. Said his name's Dave and he's looking for a man named Dave. A fixer? I think he said. Named Dave."

I doubted that his name was Dave as much as I doubted mine was.

I looked over. I saw Juice sizing up a short, bald, near-decrepit Italian-looking older at the door. Juice was greasing his mitts and finger-combing his beard. The older looked nervous and kept his head down. I didn't think he'd seen Juice grilling at him. All I could see was a push-broom mustache and round, wire-rimmed glasses puffing out from his horseshoe-haired dome.

"A fixer?"

"That's what he said, Dave. He did."

"Thanks, Winnie."

I let the fingernail of brown left in my glass slide over my tongue and down my gullet. I pushed myself away from the bar. I saw Sofia turn her attention to me from further down the wood. She was jawing with Marbles about her husband or some fuck-shit.

I went to meet the man whose name was most certainly not Dave.

***

I heard Juice pulling down chairs before The Knowlton opened as I came down the stairs. I hadn't clocked the hour or the fact that daylight had dissolved the darkness.

I'd been up all night. I'd barely slept since taking this fuck-shit job. I hadn't thought this much since the pen. It was alright. A dead-arm that'd come back to life. I was tired of talking to myself, pacing around my room, throwing darts at the wall with no bull's eye. I'd locked myself in like my flat was a prison cell. No celly to catch me gunning. *Small win.*

I stabbed a dart into the sea of cracked white paint, among the hundreds of other needle-holes in the plaster.

I hadn't lived in the joint big-long. I could've fixed it up if I'd wanted, made it a home, but I never would. It was barren. Shit, even the wall beside my bunk in jail had had more pictures. It didn't bother me, but a few pin-ups would've helped. I could always jerk-off from memory, but age sets in eventually. The imagination needs some new material. I was running out of buckets to take to the well and the well wasn't as full as it used to be.

"How goes it today, brother?" Juice didn't look up. I'd entered by the stairs, not through the front door. Couldn't have been anyone other than me or the few other elites that lived above The Knowlton.

"It's ok, big homie."

"Figured out your plan for the job?"

"Still working on it," I said. I took out a cigarette out and lit it. I started pulling the stools down on the opposite side of the bar, then sat on one and reached over the wood for an empty to use as an ashtray. You couldn't get away with smoking inside during business hours anymore. Sof was a sweet broad, so I followed her rules, mostly. Plus, Juice wouldn't say shit.

The big man hummed to himself and kept on with the stools at the high tables.

I had a list of places that D'Antonio owned. Just thinking about thinking about getting at him made that spot between my balls and ass feel like it was vomiting sweat. Wasn't much at that point in my life that got me hyped. Wasn't a whole lot that scared me either. It'd been a long time since I'd felt something that animals can't. It was nice to feel that shit again, like a reunion. I could almost understand what normal cats meant when they talked about how their feelings felt.

I never got nervous. Or excited. Or worried. Or giddy. I just did things. I never thought about the aftermath or any of that shit. Things had to get done. I'd only been anxious maybe a mitt-full of times in the last few bullets of my scumbag life.

This was one of those times.

I hadn't been tasked with killing or even hurting someone. No hit had been put on a motherfucker… not even divorcing a limb. The job was simple. The side job, the play I was trying to hustle… *not so much.*

I had my notes laid out in front of me. They contained all the spots I could get at the motherfucker. I'd hollered at some cats and shaken down others. I had ears in the streets. And eyes. And mouths. All it took was something for the nose: *llello or fist. They all spill.*

D'Antonio had built himself *some* dynasty. Even after the feds had made his bag lighter and he'd gone legal, or at least made it look that way. After the train fuckery, he'd taken the crown from the other families and turned into the most powerful mob boss in the city. *The new ruler of the old school.* A brand-new biscuit for the same old dirt.

The Blacks, Asians, Soviets, Mexicans, South Americans, and whoever else had all stepped into the arena. They'd pieced-up the city, snatched a hood or two, and done the same damn things.

When the gang wars kicked off, shit was like the Wild West.

All of them motherfuckers took turns assassinating the other the same way two crackers offer each other the last slice. *It just kept going.* There wasn't one king of the city, but there were enough mini-kingpins with XL-egos to think that they could HNIC the whole shit. The pigs just made things worse. *Believe me, I know.* Bribes went from envelopes to briefcases to car bombs. If you had the pigs, you had the sauce. If you had the sauce, you ate. If you were eating, you were clocking who wasn't.

Actually, ain't nothing changed other than the cats playing the corner.

D'Antonio made sure that his son went pure-legit. Law school, politics… even set him on the course to become a politician. I have no idea how the son of a mom-killing mobster could dream of doing that, but here we are, still being told to stand for the motherfucking anthem. The son cut his jab in city hall and was moving up to state-level. He had steam. His old man wanted him in the senate in the next few bullets.

His boy, D'Antonio's grandson… *Well, that's another-nother story.*

"Why bother with him? He old man now," Juice said, standing behind me and blowing at the spindly fumes corkscrewing from my dart. "It been so long. Why you need to? Have you no forgive…"

"Fuck nah," I said. "You think them Nazis got any less evil with gray hairs and hunchbacks? Nah. He needs to get his. I need to do it. I just need to figure out *how*. Big homie, this ain't no accidental… it ain't no fluke, you know? It's now. It's the time. It's…" I trailed off.

The laundromat, no. The restaurant, no. I needed to pick one of his businesses that'd bring him down from his fortress in the mountains. He'd knocked down Ferragamo's mansion and rebuilt his own. Salting the earth type-shit.

That's how I decided on the bank.

"A bank?" Juice said. "Why not just walk into police station waving glock saying, '*Hello, lock me up for rest of my life. Why not?*'"

"It's just a thought," I bit and squeezed the filter of my dart, "he's *still* a goon at heart… that'll always be how he thinks. I get goons. I know goons. How the mind works. The only thing they hate as much as rats are pigs. I bet the teller's panic button goes straight to some thugs in a pizzeria down the block. Any fishy shit goes down… *boom!* They'll send for the wig-splitters and stick-pullers before the sirens, brother. I need to get close to him…"

"Ok, so you get him out of his stronghold. Then what?"

Slowly, my plan was coming to me. It was all getting Filipino-ocean-water-like.

"Then, I throw everything in the pot, let it boil for a hot minute, and ladle out some get-back like red sauce on some noodles."

"Hmm… you make me hungry," Juice said. "Want to duck out and get bite?"

I spun my dart into the tray. "I could eat."

11

NEW RIVER, SAME FOOT

I took the shaky older to an oyster booth in the corner. I squeezed into the padding of the old, cracked leather settee and motioned for him to sit in the chair facing me. The joint wasn't near full, but this was a more private place to chop it up. A little, green-cased lamp hovered above us. Two cats were clacking pool balls to our left. The booth to our right was empty.

"Thank you for meeting me," the older stuttered in a thick accent.

I nodded and tapped my fingers from pinky to index against the tabletop. It was scrubbed clean of varnish and always sticky.

Sofia came by and asked us if we wanted a drink.

"Pellegrino for me," the man said. "And whatever for the man."

"Is club soda ok?" she asked. He responded by jerking his bald head up and down.

"Spill two fingers of Ballantine's. Add three rocks, a piece of lemon, and a splash of that soda, Sof," I added. She nodded and went to fetch the drinks, keeping an eye on us.

"What can I do for you mister…"

"Caligheri. Enzo Caligheri."

"Enzo, huh?" He bounced his melon. "What do you do for work, Enzo?"

"I'm a baker. I have a little…"

"Still on 83rd?"

"Y-yes! Have you been? Our cannoli are famous."

"No…" I said while letting what he was saying sink in. "But I've heard."

Sofia dropped off the drinks and stayed for a second. Enzo gave her a twenty-spot and told her to keep the change. We didn't jaw until she left.

"So, what can I do for you?" I asked as soon as I saw Sofia's fine ass swivel back to the bar.

"It's my grandson. I'm worried that he's coming under the wrong influence."

"I thought you greasy bastards dealt with everything on your own, in your own neighbourhood…"

"Yes, but that's the problem."

"Go on…"

"It is… *Gesù Cristo,* I hate to speak the name. *D'Antonio,*" he whispered so quietly that I had to read his shaking lips.

I hadn't been expecting to hear that name. *You* might've, considering how this story is going, but I sure as fuck hadn't. Not then. I paused with my scotch and soda pressed to my kisser. Not just with shock, but interest. The motherfucker had my attention on a string. I didn't blink. I lowered my glass back onto the wet ring on the table, slowly. "I thought the Gentle Don was straight now. Done with the fuck-shit. Retired to his castle."

"Yes, yes," Enzo said, dancing his knuckles on the table. His club soda hissed, but he didn't look at it. "He's retired, but he's not my concern. I pray to God that I'll never see him again for as long as I live." He crossed himself.

"Nah?"

Enzo pounded the table. "He killed my boy! I... I could never prove it. I could never breathe a word of it to the police, but... I know. My son, Mario, may he rest, was involved with the Mafia. One night, he says to me: *'Papa, I'm going to work. I won't be home too late.'* And you know what? *He never came back!* He always said that he was delivering pizzas, but no one ever got a pizza from my son. The Don said that he was sorry for my loss and would find the man or men responsible, but nothing. He said that he'd help... *but nothing!* He turned his back on me! They never found the body! Even now, his gang just comes to my bakery and eats... *for free!* Forever! Curse the Gentle Don." Enzo covered his mouth with both hands as soon as he said it.

"It's ok," I nodded. "Ain't no guinea fu... Ain't none of *them* in The Knowlton, Enzo."

I took a big gulp of my drink and ate the lemon, rind and all.

"Ok then, if not the Don, then..."

"It's his *grandson*, Joey D'Antonio."

"Who?"

"Eh, his son's son. *Joseph II.* You don't know him? He's always on the TV."

"Nah. Don't watch much of the box, old man."

"He's different," Enzo said with his face pointing down. He slid his glasses up. "He's a spoiled brat, like a Saudi prince. Wants to live the life of his grandfather. But he's not of the same… ehm… fabric. He's reckless and dangerous and foolish. He's a pest."

"Doesn't sound much like a *you* problem. Or a *me* problem, Enzo." I swirled the three shrinking cubes around in my glass. "Young fucks like that flame out pretty quick."

"But it is!" He waved his arms in a way-too-Italian way and nearly smacked the lamp overhead. "My grandson, my sweet little Claudio, looks to him and his gang like they're *the thing to be*. He wants to act like them. Have money like them. *Be in the gang like them."*

"If you're looking for some advice, I can give you that for free, fella. Tell the little idiot that it's a bad idea to be chopping it up with goon-fucks, real or fake."

"That's the problem. *He won't listen to me!* I'm only his grandfather and his parents have tried, but he won't listen! He's been brought home by the cops twice already. The next time, he could end up in jail. Or worse."

I always got bored with these kinds of conversations fast. Once Enzo moved away from D'Antonio the older, my eyes started dancing up at the ceiling.

"It's not something I fucks with, Enzo. I don't even know what you're asking me to do. Family shit, eh..." I swished my glass and took a sip. "The hell did you get my name anyway? You know who I am? You know what I do?"

"I don't know you. I don't know exactly what you do. I asked around, *very quietly*, if there was a man who'd do *anything*. Who didn't care and didn't have lines he wouldn't cross. You are known, sir. People know you and say that you have no rules. That you hate life and take money. That you do what it takes, that..."

"Stop," I waved my hand and picked some lemon veins out of my fronts. I guess enough years in the game will get your name thrown around. Enzo had needed, asked for, and found a dependable scumbag. That's what I was. That's how cats saw me. King Scum. Grime merchant. The Gulliest.

I had a choice. I could turn my back on this helpless little *pisano* and let his grandson taste the same fate his son had. *Or not.* I owed Mario something. I also owed Mario nothing. Both at the same time.

Fuck it.

"Fine."

"F-fine?" Enzo put his hands in a prayer position. "You will help?"

"Sure. You had me at money." I sat back. "Listen. I don't know what you think you know about me. What you've heard about me through the grapevine or whatever. I'm all of those things, but I'm trying not to be. *I'm trying to be better.* I'm not going to kill this kid..."

"No! Of course not. No one said kill..."

Enzo hadn't said it, but he wanted me to. I could tell.

"Like I said, I *ain't finna* kill this kid and I *ain't finna* do anything that'll get me locked up again. I'm making an effort not to be so… such… Well, I'm trying not to be such a scumbag."

"Yes, yes, whatever you say!"

Fucker. He'd agree with anything I said at this point.

"What's your offer?"

"What?"

"What does your grandson's life mean to you? And so help me sexy-Jesus, if you say a lifetime of cannoli I swear to…"

"$10,000."

Well, my sweet cock.

Enzo wanted a scared-straight deal for his grandson.

Claudio, aged 17. Enjoys soccer, cooling with his homies, and rap music. *Normal youngin'.*

I told Enzo that I could kidnap the kid and *pretend* to hold him hostage, dust him off a bit, tell him that I'd let him go if he'd quit being a punk, and *blah blah blah.* You know, the ol' fake an abduction, tie him to a chair, threaten his plums with rusty hedge clippers, and menace his family with the apocalypse-times-ten trick.

Nah. Too simple. I knew that once the fear wore off, he'd be right back on this Joey kid's dick. The geezer was paying me big-well, and I wasn't going to do the shit twice. Whatever I did, it had to stick like a fed charge.

Enzo bowed to me all the way out the door. I sat in the booth, alone, for another drink. Or bottle. The lights flickered for closing time, but I kept sitting and thinking. *It felt good*. I hadn't exercised that muscle in my skullet for a long-minute.

"Is everything alright, James?" Sofia asked me. She was doing her last rounds of tidying before heading back to her rest. To pamper her perfect pussy with fine French creams, I assumed.

"Of course, doll. I'm just planning."

"Planning? For what?"

"This and that."

She frowned. "It's hard to understand you when you say such cryptic things. Would you like to tell me about your plans?"

"Sure," I said smiling, the booze warming my cheeks. "Just a job. Night, Sof."

I slid out of the booth and counted her off a few bills.

"Rest well, James."

I kissed my teeth at the cats shooting pool, the kid Noel and Briscoe. They'd been hawking me the whole night. *Fuck those guys*. You know the feeling when you just want to duke it out with a motherfucker? Like there's no other way around it? That was me and Briscoe. The kid Noel was a bitch. But Briscoe, he had some smoke coming that'd leave his wig spinning. I was chill with them shooting all night so long as they left me alone. And everyone else.

Marbles grabbed my branch as I walked by and gave me bedroom eyes. I shook my knot and brushed her off. *Her and her man must be tussling.* That old record got a lot of play. She was big-faded. If she woke up in my bed, I'd have a whole new plate of caked-on grit to scrub off. I wasn't bent enough to say *yea*. Close, but nah.

On me, I'd always loved fucking that googly-orbed broad. It made me hate my pesh for always reminding me. There was something about her, about us. We were both psychos… *a good match*. When I think about the times we had back when… It got me twisted. I swear, she only got banged up on liquor to have an excuse when she did something stupid. Maybe I just needed to gun one out. I needed Juice's glare to sober me up and stop me from blowing her back out in my room upstairs.

I tried to breeze behind Preacher who spun around quickly and asked me: "…have you ever thought that when we dream, we're actually alive, and when we're awake, it's really a dream? That our actual world, the life we really live, is a lie? And that when we sleep, it's the only time we're able to see our non-programmed reality as God intended? That we might be forced to live in a false world because *they* know that our true reality and its consequences are too much to bear?"

"No," I said.

Preacher nodded. *"Huh, I do."* He spun back around.

"Night, Dave," Winston said to me.

"Night, tiny man."

I gave Juice a pound and a hug.

"You have good meeting?" he asked.

"Yeah."

"A job? You take job?"

"Yeah."

"Good man."

I paused. "Yeah," I said, convincing myself.

Joseph *'Joey Moolah'* D'Antonio was a 21-year-old dirtball. I wouldn't give him the honour of calling him a scumbag. He was a clown. A duck. But he had money.

It wasn't hard to verify the punk. His whole life was on some *caught-on-camera* shit. Once I saw him, I couldn't unsee him. He'd turn himself out if it meant getting his name in the dirt-sheets and in cats' mouths.

He was leaning heavily on his family name and fortune. I'd never heard of him, so I was bent to find out that he was kind of a celebrity. Off-brand, like two stripes on the sneaker, but still…

He spent his family loot lavish-like on status shit like cars and designer clothes. He had photos with rappers and actors. He was in the public eye and flexed his cream like the kids of slave owners who built hotels with their names on them. He was about *'that life.'* He was one of those upper class queefs who had never needed to dip his beak into any fuckery. He didn't even have to work, ever. Just sit back on a beach chair and listen to his green grow off interest.

But nah.

You see… there's a breed of greedy, spoiled dick-riders that clock the life of validated hustlers and *real* motherfuckers and want that shine. *Why?* Because they're stupid. Everything *still* isn't enough for some cats. They're selfish. Gassed-up. They think they *need* that glow, like it makes them official. They fool cats into respecting them for thinking that they came out of the cracks in the sidewalk, on some against-all-odds shit, just so they can say that they *made it out. Out of where, motherfucker? The country club?*

Respect. *Cats kill and die for that shit.*

Fronting-ass fucks always dig their own graves. They watch as the crew they built on the strength of their ducats chuck dirt at their confused, blinking eyes. You can put all the cream on all the cats' books that you want. But you can't pay for respect… only fake-ass loyalty. Cats like him should stay in their lane. I loved it when flunkies got their cards pulled in prison, and this felt like that. *Cowards. Hoes. Fake-fucks false-flaggin' and rocking fugazi back-stories.* Woofing a big game until they get tested. Then, the first time their card gets pulled, they roll it up and bang on the guard door screaming for *PC. Or end up using that Kool-Aid for lipstick.*

Stupid.

Don't fuck with hood shit if you're born rich. You already got what thugs are flexing on their gangster to get. *Sucker-asses. Why pretend?* Image and respect aren't the same. Respect keeps you alive, image gets you deaded.

One look and I knew *Joey Moolah's* type.

Soft.

The softest cats always work the hardest not to look it. Instead of doing dirt, they paint themselves in mud. This bitch had never been poor, hungry or homeless. Keeping it *all-the-way-real*, he insulted me just by existing. It was my duty as a hood-motherfucker to tighten-up this imposter. I'd try not to have too much fun.

This was bad news for him and hash oil in the blunt for me.

I got all that in one night of clocking the fucking chump.

The more I watched him, the more I wanted to hang him by his intestines on his momma's front door. *Nobody* ran up on this fucking punk. *Ever.* Apparently, the world had gone pussy. No one had told me. Fake-fucks were allowed to live with no fear. It didn't used to be like that. People used to get checked and served. There's no right in a world where fake-crooks and wannabe-gangsters get clout instead of curbed. Everybody was faking jacks nowadays. *Disgusting.*

I took note.

This kid was far gone from the careful and calculated way his grandfather used to step. He was wide open. He showed up to show out. He poured up all the time and got fucked up every night. Kid couldn't say no to anything. With all the loot in the world, he spent like he was trying to see the bottom.

Sloppy.

If I squinted, I could see why a kid like Enzo's grandson might be taken with that waste of cum. Joey Moolah had loot, designers, exotic whips, fly bitches, and jewels around his neck. *Symbols. Bang without the pow.* To a dumb teenager, that shit *looked* like power, respect, and success. *But nah.* That shit's like how cats confuse fucking with love and silence for stupidity.

His bodyguards weren't about it. All sheep, no lions. There should've been a thug playing each entrance and at least two more in the front and back of him. A good goon will always be on your back like a rucksack. If you're a big shot, they'll be on their *wolf-in-winter* steez: hungry as an undertow and ready to move at the slightest sound. *All-eye seeing and all-ear hearing. Down for whatever.* But not Joey Moolah's. Those clowns were making my job easy. They snapped and posed for pictures, ate food, drank booze, buddied around with the mark, and tried to get their moment in the spotlight. *Light work.*

I shouldn't have been able to get anywhere near his bitch-ass. A choked-out bouncer here, an ox pulled on a doorman there, and I was close enough to give the kid a facial. I was able to post up in the next booth at a bar and bump into his shoulder on the street. *Shit.* I even dressed up as a waiter at a fancy joint and poured his Cabernet. He slid me a fifty-spot for my troubles. I kept the cash but gave the uniform back to the banquet server I'd left tied up with the linens in the hotel's laundry room.

As bad as his security was, he was forever surrounded. His hang-arounds were like scabs on a fiend. Another thing, those pocket-holders were always filming him like his life was a movie. *That was the real test.* I had to lure him away from the hordes of camcorders so I didn't get knocked.

He had a penthouse where he threw parties on the regular. During the day, he drove his Lamborghini or Bentley around town with his icy wrist hanging out the window and a cat or two riding along. At night, he took limos or had one of his handlers chauffeur him home if he was too lit to drive. It took a lot of liquor for this fuck to drown all the *llello* he was sniffing.

He was as vulnerable as a newborn. All I needed was to get him alone.

12

FUCK 'EM ALL, FUCK 'EM GOOD

Selfish. That's the only word I could think of. Since it offended me, I knew that it was true. And salty. *I had reasons for both.*

My brain was scrambling for a way to roll the Gentle Don into this Claudio job. I knew there had to be a way to make it all work. It felt right. Like something from above. A message them religious fucks jaw about hearing. Sexy-Jesus's mug on a piece of toast or a highway sign. It was just *too convenient.*

My focus strayed away from Enzo. And Mario. And the ten-large. *It seemed big-perfect.* A sign. A chance for get-back. *What were the odds?* I couldn't pass up my shot to even up the score for my shitty, scummy life.

I could smell my chance for revenge. Taste it on my lips. It whetted my chops. I fought the fair one in my head about doing the right thing. But I didn't even know what the right thing was anymore. There was a good chance my *right* and most other cats' *right* were opposites. This was bigger than the old man and his grandson. It was something I'd sworn to do a long time ago. That I'd been trucking around my whole scumbag life. The reason *for* my scumbag life. Probably.

And this was just the beginning.

On the other hand, the fuck was the last time I'd done something good? Something not-bad, even? Something that'd thrown a little grease on the hinges of St. Pete's gate?

When was the last time I'd cared?

I was getting loot for straightening this kid out. *10 racks.* That was the job I'd been hired to do.

The godfather was the side bet. *Pro-bono as a motherfucker.* It might even silence the bones rattling in my closet and the screams coming out of the ground. Even just a little.

I wasn't about to let bygones be shit for shit. I had to drill it in, almost like a mantra. *I had a job.* I was a professional now, or at least trying my fuckest to be.

I got back to the bar with Juice after stopping at the little sandwich counter up the street. I had a turkey club and gave him the bacon. He got a smoked meat freakshow with sauerkraut and an extra pickle. I never got smoked meat. Why cats love it. Always dry. It *needs* mustard. Anything that *needs* some kind of sauce so bad doesn't have the legs to carry it. I didn't even know what kind of meat it was, pork or beef. I told Juice that. He told me that it was good and to shut the fuck up.

He flicked on the TV.

Yo, what up? It's ya boy Joey Moolah, here with Revolt TV and letting y'all know that in two weeks' time, imma be partying up at Mount Stafford, The Staff, for Revolt TV's High in the Hills party! You know I got that thang with me. The whole crew's gonna be there: Cheeks, DJ Kasset, the whole WBU Crew! Y'all peasants can enter to spend the weekend at Château Dumol… Dumil…. Du-Mo-Lin with us and party like rockstars. Y'all know I'll be driving up to the party in the Lambo with my main man C-Money. My partner in crime. My main homie…

I gazed at the screen. *Fuck, this kid was dumb.*

I felt Juice's eyes creak at me.

"Yup," I chewed. "That's the play."

I made the drive up to the mountain twice. I used two different cars that I'd hot-wired on separate occasions. The drive wasn't bad: a few sharp corners and one nasty switchback were all that could've left one of us taking the deep plunge. It was one of those upper-class retreats. A getaway that attracted the *three-forks-at-dinner* and *owned-sailing-clothes* crowd. Big-bougie.

I thought about my options.

I could vick a cop car and grab my old badge from the locker. Then, I'd post up like a pig and nab him on a speeding charge he'd probably do anyways. That plan meant keeping a stolen cruiser on-the-low until I got him, however. Also, getting back to the city without passing any real pigs that could jack me up. It was dicey, and something that'd put me back in the darkest corner of the pen. I'd have a little fame from the low-level crimeys, but nothing else.

I could fake like I was having car trouble and hope that the spoiled cunt had his first and possibly only moment of charity. I'd likely end up like all those poor slobs hanging from towels in their bathrooms trying to get that lethal nut by their lonesome. *Holding my breath with my dick in my hand, that is.*

I went with option three.

I needed a car with some balls and a trunk to goad the fuck into peeling away from the convoy he'd no doubt be rolling with.

I found the answer while I was posted up outside the bank reading the paper. I heard a throaty, angry rumble make its way down the street one afternoon while clocking Maria. I turned my head to see what kind of asshole was making the noise and, *bada-boom*. A Buick Grand National GNX.

I'd never been a gearhead, or even the type of cat to give a shit about cars, but this ride made the same noise as an alligator snarl when it idled. The driver parked it and got out across the street.

I walked over and waited for the cat to come back out. He looked to be in his mid-forties and had a gut beneath a sleeveless Metallica t-shirt with two pathetic branches poking out. A wire-brush Fu Manchu and greasy hair. *Nothing I couldn't dust if I had to.* Nevertheless, I'd start with a more-civilized, less-violent approach.

"Killer ride, man," I said with someone else's enthusiasm.

"Hey, thanks bro," the man replied.

"I ain't never seen this around town. You from here?"

"Oh, just outside the city. Knox area. I don't really take her out in the snow, or rain, or anything that'll fuck up the metal and paint. Nice for a cruise here and there… bring it through the city to turn some heads."

Knox area. He meant Knox Green. *Fuck.* I'd spent some time there. *What a shit hole.* I may live above a dive bar, but that place was fucking hopeless.

Fucking loser, I thought.

"Sick, bro," I said, imitating his aging rocker steez. "Can I borrow it?"

He laughed. *Worth a shot.* "No way, man. My wife isn't even allowed to *sit* in the driver's seat. This baby is a GNX, stock-car champion in mint condition. I'd rather sell my house and my kids than let anyone else get behind the wheel of Tessa here."

Cute. He stroked the hood. "Anyways bro," he said, unlocking the door, "I gotta be going. Take it easy." He threw up the hang loose sign and sped off.

I got the plate number.

Later that night, I called the pigs and asked for the drug unit. I told them about a drug deal that I'd seen, including the car description and plate number. They didn't like going out that way, so I told them that the guy might've had guns and Eastern European sex slaves and bombs and kill-bots. *Pigs hated going to KG*, but that did it.

I borrowed Crooked Mo's cab to tail the pigs to the guys' house and pulled over a block down. The owner of the whip flailed at the pigs on his stoop and finally agreed to open his garage. I was cooling across the street, away from the light of a lamppost with the cab parked around the way. I watched the shit, smoking a dart, big-smirking.

The fucking guy had a rundown house in the shitty area near the docks, outside the centre of KG. *The boons.* The lawn was patchy, a piece of cardboard covered the kitchen window, and the family in the doorway was ugly in a way that only poor folk can be. The wife was melon-shaped and hog-faced. The kids were buck-toothed and under-fed. One of them was a redhead. I hate those things. Pale. Feeble. There's something about sin-ugly redheads that makes my gut sicker than withdrawal. They always seem that much worse than any other kind of ugly white.

The cat unwrapped his car. He looked like he was going to have a heart attack after the pigs started messing with the insides. His voice went high pitched when he told them not to lean against the paint, to leave everything they took out on the workbench so that he could put it back in, and not to unscrew the glovebox because it was all original.

After half an hour of roasting, the pigs realized that they were jerking off a whiskey dick. They looked pissed as they piled back into their cruisers and set back to the city. They were probably *extra* pissed that they'd had to come all the way out to the waste-land.

I crept over to scope the house. The garage was molded into the house and the door was manual. The lock was rusted down to nothing. I wouldn't need a crowbar to get at the whip he'd probably spent his welfare cheque on to fill up with gas. For the fifteen-minute drive to get to where I'd spotted him. *Ha.*

I almost felt bad. He had nothing besides the car. *Almost.*

I heard him yelling at his broad through the busted window: *"This is fucking bullshit, Charlene. I work the night shift and I wasn't fucking planning on fucking being up yet. Stop fucking crying. I wouldn't sell drugs again. Why? Because I fucking promised you I wouldn't go back to prison. Why? Because who the fuck else will put food on our fucking table. Why? Because! You can't even leave the fucking house. Me? What the fuck do I do besides work? You're fucking cussing, too! Oh, the fucking kids know all the fucking swears already, goddammit."*

It continued on like that for a while.

There was a bombed-out Geo Metro in the driveway. So many weeds had pushed through the cracks that it looked like a lawn. There was a bike lying behind the hooptie, too shitty even for the local kids to bother to steal. The couple was still yelling at each other for another half hour before the guy finally came out and squealed off in his bucket.

I called the pigs two more times over the following days to make sure that anything heard from the house wouldn't be taken seriously. *Now, I just had to wait for my plan to work.*

The night came.

I was at Maria's crib and Joey Moolah was live on TV. He was hyping up his party at the chalet in the mountains. Claudio, or C-money, was in the background. Kid looked young. Kid looked like Mario a bit.

I left Maria. I told her I'd see her the next day at the bank, to be ready, and not to wear panties.

"Where are you going?" she asked. She was sprawled on the slick mattress, face down, arms and legs spread, voice muffled by the pillow.

"Business," I said.

"What's in that toolbox?" She shifted her head with one eye half-open.

"Pliers, a chisel, a slim Jim… the usual shit," I responded, not mentioning the biscuit.

I left in a hurry. I vicked Maria's handcuffs and polaroid camera. I tucked in my pesh and headed to a payphone.

I hollered at Crooked Mo. This time, his shiesty ass wanted a whole night's worth of fares *plus a rack* to let me borrow his taxi until the morning. And he'd *still* sell me out if I got pinched or brought the heat. *I didn't blame him.*

I rocked the cab to the outskirts of Knox Green and parked down the road from the cat's rest. I walked up and saw that the driveway was empty, just as I'd planned. I peeked through the window and saw the wife passed out on the couch. Her hand was in a bag of pork rinds and there was a bottle of Thunderbird lying empty on the carpet.

I popped the lock with the butt of my blaster and opened the garage door. It whined. I stayed still for a few seconds and waited for someone to put my non-violence streak to the test. *No one.* I turned and looked out onto the street. *Nothing.*

The car wasn't locked. I was just about to tear the column off the steering wheel when the little ginger kid came through the door, rubbing his eyes.

"Santa?"

I felt bad. This kid was ugly *and* dumb as fuck.

"No," I said. "I'm not Santa. I'm a friend of your daddy's."

"My daddy doesn't have any friends."

Shit. "He asked me to take his car to get cleaned," I scrambled. "Do you know where the keys are?"

"He hides them," the kid said. I cussed in my head. "But I know where they are."

"You wanna get them for me?"

He smirked. "What's in it for me?"

"What do you want?"

"What do you got?"

I rifled through my pockets. I had a rubber and a buck and change.

"I have a balloon and some monies," I said, showing him the condom and the loot.

"Woah, mister. You're rich!" the sad little fuck said. "Be right back!"

The kid was maybe nine and weighed fifty pounds, but the house was so shitty that I heard his little dogs scampering through that motherfucker. He came back with the keys looped around a leather Buick keychain.

We traded.

He smiled as he looked at the coins like diamonds. His poor little blue eyes glittered on his bleached white bread face.

I didn't waste time. I thanked him, hopped in the car, and jetted for the onramp to the highway. The car had big-power. I tried to not whip it, but the fucker was fun. I fishtailed a few corners and slammed on the gas down any stretch of backroad I could find. This was my kind of car. It was immaculate inside, not a hair out of place. Smelled alright too.

12

SIEGING

I got on the highway and drove to where I'd expected the plan hit its high note. I pulled off the road in a valuable location. There was a turn-around for truckers about a half-mile ahead. It was just before the climb to the mountains and there was farmland on either side. It was a flat and perfect area to hit top speeds. I took out a hammer and a chisel and made a bunch of potholes on the right side of the road. It was a two-way: narrow and well-paved. Well-paved roads, the ones with the new black tar that's as soft as the sentences rich crackers get, are easy to fuck up. I made the road look like it had eaten a chest of shotgun spray.

I circled back to the spot I'd chosen and pulled off the highway. I aimed myself towards the road, killed the lights, and sat there. I waited. I had a feeling that I'd know when the mark was coming.

The sky was just beginning to lighten when I saw it. Black SUV. Lamborghini. Black SUV.

It was time.

I tailed them for a while, waiting for the perfect spot to challenge the kid to a race. I had to get the timing *perfect*. He could probably blow this car out of the water. Sure, it had some kick, but the thing he was driving looked like a fucking spaceship.

It was early, or late, depending if you slept yet. We were the only cats on the road.

I made my move.

I swerved out from behind and opened the engine. It was fucking loud. I pulled up beside Moolah and clocked the kid. He looked still-fucked, half-drunk or not blowed enough. His head was tipping down only to shoot back up. Claudio was in the passenger seat. The little cat was more alert. He noticed me before the fucking driver did. His eyes moved between me and Joey. Looked like he was trying to say something. I rode beside at the same speed them until Joey's eyes met mine. My window was already down. I motioned for him to do the same.

I had my ski mask rolled up to look like a toque and my black Carhartt on like I was headed to the docks to load crates of crab into a van. I swerved towards him and back: "Hey faggot! Why don't you buy American? That little dego fuck-toy ain't shit." My voice was cartoonishly southern for some reason.

"Hey, fuck you! Do you know who the fuck I am?" he screamed back.

"I wasn't asking who you are, bitch. I was asking why you're driving that thing like an old bitch, bitch."

I sped ahead and felt the cool air punch its way through the car.

I imagined Claudio trying to talk him out of this, sensing that he was too fucked up to be driving at all. Or cutting up a line for him, to fill his balls with a little sauce.

His motor growled, angry-like. His horses were getting some spurs. I sped up and pressed on, fast as a motherfucker. I saw him snip out from between his guards and give me chase. *The plan was working.*

I kicked my foot down to the floor, the roar all around me. I couldn't look to either side. Shit was moving too fast. Colours were smearing outside my window like graffiti on a speeding train.

I was sure that he knew the roads as he'd driven them pretty often. Just up ahead was where things would level out before the twists and turns started getting big-snakelike.

He was coming up hot, flying towards me on the left side. The SUVs in the rearview were getting small, fast. I went to box him out. Barely turned the wheel and the slicks chirped beneath me. The whip shook and almost spun the fuck out. My plums bounced off the backs of my pearls. I was going too fast to make even subtle movements.

His side-to-side game was tight. Credit where it's due, the punk could out drive me. *Light work.* I had to keep him on the right. I boxed him again. He drop-shifted and went to cut around me on the left. We were close. I went back to the left and he veered a quick right.

He pulled up beside me: "Hey! You old bitch. See what money gets you? By the way, my name is Joey Moo…"

He hit the patch of Feb-made potholes and the last thing I saw before I stomped my brakes was his whole body flying up and smacking the roof.

The Grand National left fat skids on the street like dirty prison drawers. I turned and crept up on the other whip while pulling my mask down. I hopped out to find Joey Moolah upside down against the windshield. Claudio was in the passenger seat. He had his belt on and was rubbing his forehead and groaning.

"Boys," I said, smiling like a real villain at the window and taking the heater from the back of my waist, "good morning. Get out of the fucking car."

Claudio looked at me, terrified. Joey D'Antonio didn't and was visibly head-rocked.

"Wh-who are you?" Claudio asked.

"Name's Feb. From around the way. Now get out of the fucking car. I don't have no fucking time to play with some low-rent, two-bit mob wannabes."

"He's not a wannabe," Claudio snapped, "that's Joey Moolah. Of the D'Antonio family. The grandson of the godfather himself: *The Gentle Don.*"

"Jesus, kid. What are you, some kind of cheerleader for this piece of shit? You seem to have forgotten your skirt." I checked down the road for the SUVs, cocked the hammer of my biscuit. "Now... Get. Out. Of. The. Fucking. Car."

He put his mitts up and moved for the handle. I shook Joey's limp limbs and opened his door. He spilled out onto the street and laid there like the sexy-Jesus-piece around his neck.

Thank fuck the kid was a cokehead and had less meat on him

than Chinese drumsticks. I was tired and Maria still had all my testosterone in her pussy, teeth, and hair.

I dragged him to the Buick and popped the trunk.

"Wanna give me a hand, kid?" I said to Claudio as a half-joke.

I looked up. He had the gayest gun in the world pointed at me.

"Where'd you get that?" I asked.

"Glove box," he said casually. "It's Joey's personal nine." It was a cold front, but that shit can knock your power out.

I closed one orb and looked at it. "That's a six millimeter, you fucking dummy. You sure it didn't spill out of his purse?" I laughed. I holstered my heat to show him that I meant no harm.

"Look, Claudio," I said.

"How do you know my name?"

"Kiddo," I said, getting impatient. "You think this shit was an accident? Look around you. There are snipers everywhere."

That shook the kid. He trembled, squeezed both hands around the gun, and bit his lip. *The ol' snipers in the bushes trick.*

I slapped the biscuit out of Claudio's mitts and told him to go pick it up and bring it back to me.

I tossed the Guido Prince in the trunk and shut it. Claudio didn't try to plug me with my back turned. I was *mostly* sure he wouldn't. I was gonna be fine.

"Kid, Claudio. Get in the car." I opened the passenger door. "Now."

He obeyed. I could see the SUVs making their way up. I guess all this was normal behaviour, because they hadn't sped up at all.

I combed the Lambo. I found a duffle with some money and a brick of snow. There was powder caked all over everything and a small trace of blood on the bent steering wheel. I took the shit and fired the Grand National up.

"Who are you?" Claudio asked.

"I'm a friend of the family with unfinished business," I said before I puckered my shitter and sped in the opposite direction of the SUVs. "Gimme the fruity little pistol, kid."

He handed it over. The shit was encrusted with skittles: pink and piss-coloured diamonds. Even the clip was monogrammed. *At least it had bullets.*

I sniffed the gun. "Never been fired," I said, vrooming past the guards.

"I-it's got bodies on it," Claudio protested.

"Only the dead motherfuckers in Africa who mined the jewels. The kid's a phoney. A fake. A fraud. A punk-ass bitch in some scumbag's trunk."

I let that shit sink into poor Claudio's feeble skullet as I sped up. The sky was that weird kind of overcast where you can see fine, but no shadows pop up from the ground.

"If he's such a phoney… then, why does he do such hardcore shit?"

Ain't no getting through to this mook. "Kid. You ever seen him slang an ounce of wheat or a bird of white? Nah, I bet he just pays for it and hands it out. He ain't a boss, he's just got money. He plays a role like any actor could. Give him a little statue with a golden man on it, but not respect."

"Nuh uh. He doesn't... I don't... He's my brother. It's ride or..."

"Is he? You got a family, you little dumb motherfucker. Parents and shit. And home and shit. Worried and shit."

"But..."

I kissed my fronts: "This was too easy. You think that a random hood motherfucker like me would actually be able to get to his old grandad? *Hm?* This was light work. Look around, no one's running up on us. Go ahead, check the rearviews. Coast is clear as grain liquor, youngin'. No one's coming to save him. It's just me and you. And you... You gotta know that you *ain't* his brother. He might like you well enough... Maybe you got some memories... But a cat like that don't understand what a brother is."

He tried to get some words in. I told him to *shut up* and made like I'd backslap him. He turtled and kept quiet.

"You're probably just one of a hundred fall-guys that he has. Those cats, those are hang-arounds, shine-blockers, and other pathetic bitches are just out here waiting to be fed like some pigeons. Holding their books open, trying to catch motherfucking vapours to get a little stain and hood fame. You want to be one of them? One of those twats? Use and be used. Do you really wanna find out what happens if he gets raided? Pigs come and pigs ask him to tell. Sitting in that cold-ass room with some shirt-and-tie wearing pigs jawing that he could go upstate for 10 to 20. I ask you: *him* or *you*... You think he'd protect you?"

"I'm not! And… I know that some of the… Hmm… He wouldn't… Fuck this… Look man, you're only saying this because…"

"Because why?" I looked at him, slowing down to bend the offramp. "Because I got you next to me with both guns? You fucked up, worrying about his bitch-ass when you ain't even knowing what's gonna come of you."

"You gonna kill me?"

"Nah."

"You gonna kill Joey?"

"Nah. Well… *probably* not."

That was a good answer, if I do say so myself.

"His grandfather will find you."

"That's what I'm hoping for."

"You're insane."

"No," I said. "I'm what he pretends to be."

I almost turned on the radio, but didn't. The quiet was both of our punishment. We rode in silence for a bit. I hoped the kid was figuring his shit out. Like I said, I didn't wanna do this shit twice. This was the *soft* approach. I didn't even smack him.

"I got cats in the precinct," I lied. "Heard you'd been picked up already. Got paperwork on you." Claudio nodded without looking at me. "How many times your homie been pinched?"

"None," he said.

"How many of the crew doing bids? How many done had to take a charge to save his pussy ass?"

"Some."

"That's your future. Riding bitch with him," I said. "What your folks do… putting food in your gut and a roof over your knot, that's gangster. Not him. He ain't grown. He finna end up dead and forgotten. Then what?"

"To be honest," Claudio said, "other than drink and get fucked up, I guess Joey ain't do much bad guy shit."

"Nah, man. The kid's a ho. He'd be washing my boxers in the pen."

"That doesn't mean he deserves to die." There was something like desperation in his voice.

"You're a good kid, Claudio. You could have a future, but not with a fuckhead like this."

I felt like some kind of school counsellor. *Zip up your fly and do right by others.* Who the fuck was I to be spitting motivational poster quotes? I had a barely legal adult in the trunk. His gun, work, and loot would soon be sold off and spent. By me.

"Thanks," he said. "I just, I dunno… Before I hung out with him, girls ignored me. I never had enough cash for nothing. I had to work Saturdays like the stiffs and losers Joey always talks down about."

"And look where that got him," I remarked.

A mousey tap came from the trunk.

The sky was full of daylight when we got back to Knox Green.

Looked even worse without the darkness to hide some of its scars. I told the kid in the passenger seat and whoever might've been listening from the trunk that I had to make a stop to return the slab I vicked.

The shitty dude was on the front lawn screaming at his phone we me and Claudio pulled up.

"What the fuck do you mean *too many calls*? I never called y'all once! Y'all been the ones coming here and… and messing with me! I should… Shit! Listen! I see the *sonuvabitch* right here! He's driving my fucking car up on my grass! Get over here now! H-hello?!"

I hopped out and showed him my pistol. "Hey, man. I bet you're sore, but chill for a minute." I reached for the duffel and broke him off a few racks. "This should take care of any little ding on the car, put some food in your ugly kid's bellies, and buy some new drawers for the ol' ball and chain."

He didn't look too happy. He also wasn't in a good spot to jaw-shit. He took the money like I knew he would. I waved to the hideous ginger kid in the window as I led Claudio to the cab parked up the road. He waved back with the inflated rubber in his hand.

"Oh," I circled back to the Grand National, "I almost forgot."

The cat was counting the loot I gave him when I reached my arm through the window to pop the trunk. *What the…* the shitty dude said as a dyed-blond little goomba wearing a white leather jacket and dark wash jeans with holes on purpose flung out the joint and landed on the grass.

"Who the fuck do you think you are?" He went to take a swing at me.

"Shut up," I said. I turned his punch into an arm-bar behind his back like a balloon animal.

"Yo," I turned to the loser, "that's hush money. You talk, I come back." I stopped walking and quarter-turned my knot. "Thanks for letting me borrow Tessa, after all."

I threw Joey Moolah into the taxi trunk and told the younger Caligheri to hop in the back.

"Buckle up," I said.

"You're not Mohammed Al-Saladin," he said.

"So, what do you do then?" Claudio asked me on the ride back to the city.

"This and that," I said, unsure of what to say.

"Are you a hitman?"

"Nah."

"A taxman?"

I moved my head side-to-side and sucked some air through my teeth. "Nah."

"Then what?"

"I'm like a detective. A private detective. And for you, a guru or guardian angel or some shit."

"Detectives don't…"

"I said *like* a detective, kid."

"I see," he said. "Thanks, I guess, Mister…"

"Feb."

"Mister Feb?"

"Just Feb. Or, Mister February… Nah, just Feb."

"Thanks."

"Welcome."

He paused. "Where are you taking me?"

"Home. My job with you is done, isn't it?"

"What was your job?"

"Sort you out. Do I need to chain you to a chair in a gutter motel and torture you?"

"No… Yeah… I'm out, yeah. I don't want this kind of trouble again."

"Good boy." He seemed sincere. "Because I *really* don't wanna have to come back and do this shit again. I'm busy and that'll put me in a bad fucking mood."

"You won't. Hey… what about him? What about Joey? Is that a job, too?"

"Sort of."

"Is it personal?"

"Nah… Nothing personal. It's just business."

Claudio got out and headed into his grandpa's bakery. I nodded to him. As I went to leave, someone tried to hop into my cab.

"4th and Piper please," said a young man of great self-importance.

"No fares, bud."

"Your light's on, so drive, cabbie."

"Nah. Get your ass out."

"No," he said snidely. "4th and Piper."

"Let me out!" came as a muffled sound from the trunk.

"What's going on?" he asked, shook.

"Unless you wanna join him," I cocked my blaster at the cat, "fucking scram."

He did.

I dropped off the cab at Crooked Mo's and had him drive me back to The Knowlton. He started telling me that he'd had a nice night with a woman who wasn't his wife and I told him to turn up the radio.

This just in. Reality star and grandson of suspected godfather Joey 'Moolah' D'Antonio was abducted…

I told him to turn off the radio.

We got to the front of the bar and I shoved a fistful of loot at Mo.

He seemed pleased. I told him to pop the trunk and go blind for a second.

I pistol-whipped the kid's mug while he squirmed in the trunk. I don't know if it was possible for the kid's chin to be that weak or if it just was his spirit, but he instantly went limp and whimpered.

I told him to stay down and took a few polaroids, then took my coat off and covered his dome with it. I collared him and took him to my walk-up, telling him not to make a sound with my burner poked into his kidneys. The scumbags that lived there didn't need to be woken up so early.

I tied him to my only chair and stuffed a dirty sock in his mouth, duct-taping it tight. I slapped him and took another polaroid. I topped it off all by lighting a dart and lecturing him on all the shit I lectured you about earlier.

I wanted to take off on him but cooled on it.

I was tired. I needed to get to the bank. Maybe I'd stop by Enzo's bakery and try one of his famous cannoli on the way. I could sleep and shower after all the shit went down. For now, I needed to focus. I needed to be sharp. *Maybe some coffee? Or I could break off some of that brick in the duffel.* Shit. The Joey kid had a nice line's worth caked in his nostril alone. But the God said chill. One taste would have me standing over the stove or jacking cats in alleyways. Again.

The kid was fidgeting in his chair. I fooled on him for a bit, cupping my hand to my ear and smacking his mug a bit before tearing the tape off.

"What're you gonna do with me?" Joey Moolah cried while he watched his pathetic goatee choose the sticky side of the gray tape as its new home.

"To you? Not a whole lot," I shrugged. My mask was off by this point. I didn't care if he saw my mug.

I threw the used-up gray tape in the garbage can and grabbed a cup of coffee. I took a big slurp. I made that annoying sound that cats who big-hate to see trendy, younger bitches wearing their favourite band's t-shirt and don't know any songs make.

"So, you just stole me for fun?"

"You don't *steal* people. You kidnap them. And, nah, I kidnapped you for a reason."

"Why?"

"Loot."

"Yo, listen! I got money, man. I'm rich. Do you know who I am? You let me go, right now… I forget this shit ever happened. I forget your face, give you enough money to move out of this Section 8 shit, and just let everything slide."

"I'm sure you do. I don't need money, kid… at least not the way you do. I don't care about slabs or cut-up or respect. I'd rather earn that shit."

He looked around. "No offence yo, but you live in the ghetto. This place is…"

"I was born in the hood, punk motherfucker. I *am* what you're *trying* to be. Well, was. I'm a changed man now."

He scoffed.

"Changing," I corrected myself and made that Bobby DeNiro face. *You know the one.*

I looked out the window and thought about how this might not be the most professional office. I mean, I only had one chair and no desk. If I wanted to keep doing this *good* shit, I probably had to find a better place to conduct business. The Knowlton was fine, for now. It'd only attract the low-rent crowd. Too cheap for suit-and-tie hitters. Every villain needs a hero. Or a bigger villain. Or maybe there's no difference between any of them. No clue what that made me. The two dope dealers down on the corners weren't my concern. Nor the A-rab selling bootlegs at two-for-five. *Nah.* I could do good. I could do better. I could…

"Hey! Yo! Let's make a deal! Whatchu want? What the fuck, man? Who kidnaps someone for no reason? Did you even tell my peoples that you have me hostage? Yo! Get my nonno on the phone, he's got mad dough."

"Imma holler at him soon enough."

"Whatchu mean?"

"Don't worry about it. It's almost time."

He started hyperventilating and crying and shit.

"Come on man, what do you want? Anything, name it! I'm… I'm Joey Moolah. I can make dreams come true, man."

"Bring my ma back from the dead?"

He didn't say shit. Neither did I.

"I don't want shit from you. If there was one thing, it would be for you to stop fronting like you're some kind of thug. You ain't no G. You ain't a *jefe* and you ain't no hard motherfucker. My advice? Lay low. Leave the streets to the real hustlers and d-boys. Hand out turkeys on Thanksgiving or some shit."

"For sure, man. For sure," he said, nodding too fast and agreeing too easily, "I'll change my ways." He sniffed back some tears. "I'll quit being a star-fucker and partying and give to the poor, and… oh man, I think I just found God!"

"Shut up," I flicked his beak. It dripped clotty mucus onto his jeans. He winced and sniffled. It was nearly time.

"I'm serious, man. See this chain? This chain's iced out *heavy*. It's worth 20 bands. Take it, melt it down, and give the money to charity. The Lambo? It's yours. Sell it at an auction and send the money to Asia or where the fuck ever. Australia, I dunno. Where are the poor kids? I'm a new man, I'm…"

A booming knock rattled the doorframe and connecting walls. I grabbed a baseball bat and walked to the front door.

I opened it and gave Juice a big hug. He had a balaclava worn like a cap on and ducked under the doorway.

The kid squealed like a dog that had gotten its paw stepped on when he saw Juice. Guess he thought I'd brought in some big motherfucker to do a job I'd have *loved* to do myself. Either that, or he'd noticed the bat in my hand. Juice pulled his mask down and tore open a mouth hole. His beard was poking out around his lips. *I swear, a cat like him rocking one of them fuckers is what nightmares are made of.*

Juice asked if there was coffee. I pointed him to the still-fresh pot. He moved over in his matching three-stripe tracksuit and poured himself a cup. He took a sip, said it was too weak, lumped the filter brim-high, and turned it on again. I was surprised that the motherfucker didn't add baking soda.

"How long you will be?" he asked, taking a sip and heaving out a sasquatch wheeze.

"Could be a couple hours, could be forever. You cool with this?"

"Yeah." He nodded as he glanced up and down at the tied up, well, hostage. Technically. "I watch him and wait for you to come back to finish."

Joey Moolah cried.

"Word." I stretched out the gray tape and covered the kid's grill again.

"I'm not child," Juice said, offended-like. "I know how keep him quiet."

I had a good laugh. "Didn't mean to offend you. He might have pissed himself."

Juice sniffed. "Yeah, that's what I smell. Booze and coke piss."

I bounced the bat off Joey's melon twice for good measure and handed it to Juice, who was sitting on the edge of my bed.

I popped into the bathroom to put some water on my face and slick my hair all ready-like.

"You want anything while I'm out?"

"You make store run or get revenge?"

"Good point."

The kid was quiet as kept in the chair. The grey tape helped, but he didn't even move. Just sat there, shook and shaking, with his orbs trying to make a break form his skullet.

"Don't do anything stupid," Juice said. His head was turned to me and the bat was resting over his shoulder like he was at the plate.

"Sometimes you gotta do what you gotta do, man."

"Do not have to kill any innocents."

"Don't I?"

"I did not."

"You're better than me."

He just looked at me. "Go now. I got this."

I nodded and went to the door.

I turned and saw Juice just staring at the kid. He didn't make a peep and was looking at me. Piss was falling in single drops from the chair onto the shitty hardwood floor beneath him.

13

A GUN IN THE HAND IS WORTH TWO TO THE HEAD

Where was I?

Oh yeah. Battling off a motherfucking concussion, tied to a motherfucking chair in the back of a motherfucking mob bank. How could I forget.

The concussion, that's how.

D'Antonio did me the courtesy of stepping in front of my mug. My eyes were swollen, but I could still see him. He'd aged. His previously thick, black hair was thin and tarnished silver. He had that olive skin that Mediterranean olders get when their tans become soaked in all-year-round. Liver spots and shit. He wasn't dressed up in his pinstriped suit, but the white slacks and blowy shirt of an older who can't remember whether he'd yelled at the kids to stay off the fucking flowers. Except this older would have their kneecaps for doing it twice.

"Busboy…. I thought all of this ugliness was behind us. I thought being a cop, even going to prison, would've taught you a thing or two about respect. About forgiving and forgetting. I showed you leniency, after all."

I spat some blood. "Nah." I kissed my pearls. "Yea, you knifed me with leniency."

He cuffed me. "I let you live. I figured we were even."

"You murdered Ma. Sent me to war. Left me with nothing. We ain't squared up… Not even."

He said some shit in Italian and cuffed me again. He lined me up and swung like Bobby Bonilla. He had some big ass rings on. He rubbed his mitt. *Good, I'm glad that hurt.*

He opened my passport. "J-January? What a stupid alias…" *We agreed on that.* "I'm retired. I changed the family's direction. Licensed casinos. Hotels. Government contracts. Our criminal activities are in the past. For the most part, that is. *Hear no evil, see no evil…* As for me, I've transitioned into philanthropy and keep but a foot in the family affairs now. My begonias are more important to me than drugs and prostitution. My children inherited… not a criminal monopoly, but a legitimate enterprise. Joseph Sr. will be a senator soon. The legacy of the D'Antonio Familia."

"Model citizen, huh? Moving on like the past don't matter none. I'm an all-day-lick if you expect me to believe that you ain't still a boss man. Still a piece of shit."

"I must admit that I was greedy in my younger years. I wanted it all. It cost me a lot. There were many lives that probably didn't have to be taken, because of my need to stay on top, because of ambition and paranoia. That's in the past. Now, I'm trying to enjoy life. I leave the dirty things to others. I take tribute, instead of heads."

"Whatever, man. I don't care. You'll always be scum to me. You're a bitch. Your son's a bitch-puppet. Your grandson's a fucking *spoiled* bitch. You, at least, had balls. Where'd they go? Where's the ruthless cunt who used to kill mothers and children? I bet he's still in there somewhere."

"Oh, he's still there. Trust that. And now I ask: Do you think speaking like that will make your own death any less painful?"

"No. Just seeing if you've still got an edge. *Bitch.*"

"You think I've lost it?"

"I reckon you did-went soft when you gave up your turf. Scared of the Chinese. Russians. Whoever else. Chased from the city. Yeah, you got loot. But ain't no one scared of you, you old bitch."

His bottom lip and left eye twitched in unison. He breathed noisily out of his beak and nodded to himself.

"Bring the girl," he said to the big fuck. He turned to me. "I didn't want to do this. You're forcing my hand."

"No, no. Uncle, no!" Maria cried. The big fuck had her in a choke with a biscuit to her dome.

Is it bad I was small-jealous?

"You infiltrated my family and tried to steal from me. I'll show you how important my business is to me. Anything that's happened to you or those around you *was always business.*"

Yeah, the long dick of business.

"Wait, uncle?" I asked like the dumbest cat in the room.

"Yes," he said. "I assumed you knew that. And were working her to get to me."

"Huh?" I said.

"You didn't know that she was my sister's granddaughter?" he asked, seeming almost let down. "Jesus…"

"N… I mean, yes? Sure, I did."

It didn't matter.

The big fuck cocked his bammer. It was a funny feeling. I don't know if I loved the broad, but I had to bite my lip. I loved that pussy.

"You wouldn't," I said, kind of thinking that he might.

"Don't do it," he said to the goon. "Not with the gun. You want to go deaf? Use the knife."

The big fuck holstered the gun and took out an ox. He slid that blade over Maria's throat like it was nothing.

With her dying words, she said: "I love your…" She was near-perfect.

"Happy, mutt? That was your fault."

I shrugged.

"Heartless…" he shook his head. The room was filling with the iron-like smell of bullshit. Or blood. Or both. "This can't be how you expected this to go."

"Nah. But I'm exactly where I wanted to be."

"You're insane if you think you were ever going to successfully rob me."

I big-smiled. It hurt my punched-up mug, but it felt like a nut.

"What are you smiling at?"

"I ain't come to rob you. I came to use my safety deposit box."

"…what?" His mug wrinkled.

"The key's in my pocket. Hers is in that cluster around her waist. Number 0709."

He got the little fuck to sift through the blood puddle and unlatch her keys. He put his cute little mitt in my pocket and took mine out. It felt like a girl hand.

"Go ahead." I was smirking like a kid who's smarter than his second-grade teacher.

The little fuck unlocked the box. I couldn't wait to mash his face against the solid steel wall of bumpy metal. I was daydreaming about what I'd do to the big fuck. I thought about locking his head in the vault door.

He took the box out. D'Antonio walked to him.

"Move," he said to the little fuck.

He flipped open the box.

D'Antonio pulled out and looked at three polaroids of his grand-son, bloodied and scared-as-fuck in the trunk of a car and tied to a chair. Next, he pulled out a gay little 6mm handgun without the clip.

He snatched the rambo from the big fuck and spun at me with speed I'd never expect from a geezer.

"My grandson? What the fuck have you done?"

"Ah, yeah." I nodded, moving my whole body. "Right… I kidnapped your piece of shit grand-seed. I got him tied up in a room full of goons. They're green-lighted to ghost him if I don't come home. I know y'all are some close-knotted motherfuckers. Even if the knot ain't tight. Since you're too old to have a *madre,* I went for the next best thing. It was mega-easy."

He bashed my face with the back of the cutter. He took a handful of moss and pulled my wig back, pushing the tip of the ox into my throat.

"You kill me, and you'll never get him back."

"Tell me where he is," he said, like I knew he would.

"Nah. Can't do that," I said. "I'll show you. I'll take you, just me and you. He's safe… for now. You get me out of here and I promise he'll walk. Probably walk. Be carried away alive, at least."

He cracked me again. For the first time, I saw D'Antonio conflicted-like.

"What do you want?" he asked.

"Nothing major. A business proposition." I spat out a bloody-lungie. "After all, *it's just business.*"

"Tell me."

"Take me to wherever you buried my ma."

"We've buried so many barrels…" He pinched the bridge of his beak.

"Humour me. I bet they aren't too far apart. You cats are like dogs. You pick a hydrant and use it *forever-and-a-day*."

"I have an idea."

"Just something. Anything. I've been waiting for a long time. Take me. Just me and you."

His mug tightened like splashing vinegar on the cut-up.

"You don't have to, but my squad ain't going to wait big-long. Figure it out or he dies." I smiled. "Well, starts to die. Your goons better be as good at putting limbs back on as they are at chopping 'em off."

He said something to his cats in Italian. *Man, I should've learned that language. Regrets, I got a few.*

"Ok. I want to make sure that he's ok."

"You'll have to take me on my word, *Gentle Don*."

Activity in the bank was moving like there wasn't beatdown, murder, and hostage negotiation going on a few steps away.

We went into the bank manager's office. I reminded D'Antonio that if anyone hit a panic button, Joey would be as good as worm chow.

We got the manager to lock the Don's goons in the vault and say that the shit was off limits for the rest of the day. I saw him clock the creeping puddle from dead Maria's corpse, bleeding out like a calf in a halal butcher shop. It wasn't a hard sell.

The manager *had* been jerking off. We'd caught him when we walked in. Both the manager and D'Antonio were shook. Clearly, neither of them had ever been locked up.

D'Antonio's Mercedes stuck out like a sore dick. Big body. Shiny black. Chrome. Only missing some flags on the front fenders. "Give me the keys. I'm driving," I said. "Get in the front."

I backed out of the parking lot and bent the corner. D'Antonio was fuming. His grill was tight and twisted like warped metal.

"Cheer up," I patted his gam. *"It's only business."*

I crept slow. Drive-by slow. *Donnie-Brasco-slow.* The cats in the neighbourhood didn't honk. They stopped when they had the right of way: the car version of kissing the ring. They knew whose slab this was.

"Going to tell me where we're going?" I asked.

"It's outside town," he said, holding the safety deposit box.

"No shit."

He led me past the old Masonovich farm, abandoned now, and told me to take a right. We went down a dirt road, which led to a field. There was a gate. He told me that we had to go through it. I didn't want to leave him in the car or give him the chance to bolt. *Fuck that.* I floored the gas and punched through the motherfucker. He cursed. I said that he had the loot to fix the car and to shut the fuck up.

I rolled the whip over a trail towards the centre of a field. It was patchy. Some parts were grown over, some weren't. Some had freshly dug-up mounds with wet dirt caked up like the top of a Mexican concha.

"Somewhere here," he muttered, waving his mitt. "We've had a few of these over the years. Happy?"

"Get out," I said, grabbing the safety deposit box. He heaved himself out with the overhead bar.

I took out the pink-and-yellow-iced-gun, bent over, and pulled Joey Moolah's initialed clip from my boot. Never been fired. Could've been a toy. I tucked it, got out, and looked around.

"So, this is one of them, eh?" I said. "Don't know what I expected."

All pigs have heard tell about the Mafia graveyards. They're one of those little things we were paid to ignore. And it would take a lot of king's horses with a lot of shovels to find all the king's men buried in them.

"We own a lot of land. Some we sell or develop ourselves. Other lots, like this one, we never intend to do anything with. There are lots of mothers and sons and sisters and fathers here. Is it all you expected it to be? Do you feel better?" A sly grin spread diagonally over his mug. "Does this give you *closure?*"

I bent down and plucked a single blade of grass.

I took a deep breath.

I stood up and nodded.

I didn't feel shit.

I hate that word. *Closure.* What's the shit mean? Who's it for?

Does anyone who ever really wants it ever get it? If you gotta think about it, probably not. The dead don't care if you get it. Just like a salty ex doesn't care if you get it. It's a power that lives *outside* of you but keeps control *over* you. For the birds. For the birds and the worms and the fucking eels. Fuck *closure*.

I hadn't had a ma for more years than I'd had one. I had tats that were older than I was when she'd gotten murked. I couldn't bring up any big-good memories of Christmases or birthdays or trips to the zoo or crying on her shoulder or her spitting on her mitt to wipe the dirt off my cheek or telling me that my pops was out there and cared about me or taking me to her bed when I had a bad dream or baking cookies or singing songs or getting mad about my grades or skipping school to do hood-dirt or nothing.

I tried. I really combed through all the times I could remember to find something nice. None. I couldn't. I failed. It made me sad. I'd shared more time with fucking Preacher than I had with her.

Maybe my life was nothing and would always be nothing. Maybe this whole scheme had all been for nothing. The get-back and shit. *What the fuck was it good for?* Time had plugged up the holes and snuffed out a lot of my fire. *Had the thought of revenge been all I'd ever needed? Was the chase the only thing that kept my stems moving forward? Had the decades of built-up wrath always promised to let me down?*

Like the baddie of your dreams who can't suck or ride a dick for shit. Like a two-paper blunt full of dirt weed with seeds and stems.

Now what?

I bent down and pulled up some more grass. A fistful. With the roots. I let them catch flight in the weak breeze. I guessed I was done. The gun that'd been burning at my waist like I'd shoved it in there still hot from blasting was finally going cold.

I kicked the dirt.

"*Fool*," D'Antonio said.

I turned and saw him pointing a motherfucking *derringer* at me. I didn't know they were still around. That family had a thing for baby toys.

"You got enough bullets in that thing to break my skin?" I asked.

"There's more than enough to leave you here with your whore mother, wherever she is." D'Antonio walked a few steps towards me. "Here," he said, gesturing with the gun. "Or here," he mused, pointing beneath his loafers. "Or even over there…"

"Nah."

I grabbed and fired the Liberace gun. In a *smooth-as-freshly-waxed-and-baby-powdered-pussy-lips* motion, I put all eight bullets in that greasy fuck's face, neck, and chest.

The weather was cold enough to clock the steam rising out of his wounds like a half-put-out dart in a full ashtray.

I thought about putting my thumbs through his eyes and popping them like bubble wrap. Stomping his wig until his skull turned to powder. Gutting him like a lake fish. Nailing him to a cross and leaving it in the middle of Little Italy. The dreams that had kept me going all those years.

But he wouldn't feel any of that. He was already ghost. His soul was leaving with the steam from his bullet holes. It's like they say, I'd be painting something that's already gold with gold paint.

The wind blew D'Antonio's loosely buttoned shirt open. His medallion rolled off his chest. His unfocused eyes and fright-froze expression brought me no joy. I tried to smile. My lips curled up, but my brow stayed low and heavy.

It was just like the day I'd returned from the war and posted up on the bench outside Central Station. I didn't know what the fuck to think or what the fuck to feel. *Bittersweet numbness.*

I loaded him into the trunk of the Mercedes and started the whip. I knew what I was going to do. I had the shit planned out, but it didn't really need to be. Body disposal was down to common sense and routine.

I thought about the words *'happy'* and *'excited'* and *'relieved.'* I tried to squeeze meaning and feeling from 'em like juice from an orange. Nothing. Didn't feel anything.

All I knew was that there was more work ahead.

Sofia had explained *catharsis* to me. How it's a feeling of release. A big, emotional volcano busting out of your brain. I didn't feel that way at all.

I visualized letters that became words. Communist building-gray square blocks snapped together and made long-squares. The letters spelled *LET GO.*

I shook them off.

This was just the start.

Would some of the dark mists go away? Or would they get thicker? Was Sofia right? Were Juice and Perry right? Was the thought of get-back something I'd been using like gas to engine my identity? Or was it something that I had to finish now that I'd gotten a taste of it?

I needed a good sleep. I'd been up for two days and gone to big-trouble scheming, prepping, and running this play. Look at me, making plans and following through. I was almost proud. *Would Ma even have cared? Been proud? Was she looking down, or up, chucking roses?* Maybe she just liked pills and fucking more than she liked cooking me waffles and eggs.

Wouldn't be a sexy truth, but shit, the truth rarely is. Sometimes you need to look at it, right in its ugly ass mug, and peep it.

In the end, I think I'd done it all for myself. To prove that no matter who you are or how bulletproof you feel, you don't get-over on Feb.

The hood mentality. Never half-stepping. Never acting shook. Never losing face. Never taking an L. It never leaves. *It sticks like cheap toilet paper.*

I felt nothing watching the big-body Benz burn down to its frame. As I walked away from the smoldering slab, throwing D'Antonio's loose pearls over my right shoulder, I almost had a thought. It was like a question without meaning, without any words. It didn't know the answer, if one even existed. A solid that turned into a shadow when I tried to touch it. It was like the sayings '*I should quit*' and '*let it roll*' had fucked, and the sex juices that'd puddled on the mattress had become a message I had to decode.

Ain't a wonder why I have a hard time using my brain, I can barely explain the fuck-shit that goes on in there.

C-Money and Enzo… I'd helped those motherfuckers. I'd gotten one back for Mario. Or not. But something inside me, somewhere close to where I made things turn into piss and shit, inside that deep, dark place with gears and pistons… it felt warm in there. *Somewhere.*

"What'd he say?" Juice asked me while the flakes from Enzo's cannoli got trapped in his beard like dolphins in a tuna net.

"He said thanks. Free cannoli and whatever else for life."

"You take the money?"

"Take the money…" I shook my head, "Of course I took the fucking loot! I tossed the roll and the diamond gun into my locker. I'm done with banks, brother."

Juice nodded.

"What'd you do with the kid?" he asked.

"After you left, I bopped him on the head, hauled him down the street by myself with no help from your bitch-ass, and left him in a dumpster a few blocks away. The crib needed a good wash. He pissed a lot. The puddle was like a pond. Shit his pants, too."

He nodded, looked at me, and cleared his throat.

"I know what you're going to ask. Yeah, there was death. But only one by my hand, and he deserved it."

"How feel?" Juice asked.

"You know… not how I thought it would. Figured it'd be like having a weight lifted off of me… but I kind of felt the same after. If anything, heavier."

"How so?"

"I did it. Not for nothing, but for good. I guess that's nice. I felt better about helping Enzo than I did killing D'Antonio."

"You see? It's nice to helping people."

"I guess. Maybe I'll make a habit out of it. *James February: shitty guy who sometimes does good shit.*"

"How about, *James February: guy who does good shit when others are too scared to do it?*"

I liked the sound of that. It made me feel like less of a scumbag.

"Just *Feb*, though. Otherwise, it's too…"

"How about, *James February: on the verge of being a fiend again who thinks he's better than everyone else but is really no different and no better than any other scumbag fuck. A crazy piece of shit and a drunk loser without any hope in the world?*" suggested Cancerface. She'd slithered in behind us to listen.

"You're just mad because I locked you up when I was a pig."

"You've done a lot more to me than that, you piece of fucking shit."

"You deserved everything you got."

"Me? How the fuck dare you fucking say that shit you fucking piece of shit? If you never came… If it wasn't for you… I can't wait for you to crash and burn. For people to see who and what you really are. Fucking scumbag."

262

Sofia came in. She was early for her shift; must've had extra prep to do for the night. Her smell had that Chernobyl radius: *I got weaker the closer I was to the centre.* To be in the eye of that lavender hurricane was the closest thing I had to paradise.

I waved Cancerface off and smiled at Sofia.

"James, hello," she said, smiling and placing a soft hand on my shoulder. "You look tired. Did you sleep well? At all?"

"Bah… Early day, long night. You know how it goes."

She smiled. It was a different smile. One that was both pleasant and trying to figure something out.

"Sounds interesting." She slid behind the bar and started counting the bottles of beer in the little fridge. "What did you do?"

Juice gave me a side-glance.

"Maybe I'll tell you one day. After a couple drinks. For now, let's just say that I'm open for business. *James February: if no one else, then me.* Or, just *Feb.*"

I pulled out a list of names I'd written down the last time I was locked up. *Four cats.* I crossed one out. *Three cats.*

I had Sofia pour me a cup of overly sweet, disgusting dark rum and said *salud* to Juice. To him, to Lieutenant Perry, and to that skinny bitch Maria whose memory I'd always jerk off to.